ADRIFT 2

SUNDOWN

K.R. GRIFFITHS

ALSO BY K.R. GRIFFITHS

The Adrift Series:

Adrift 2: Sundown

Adrift 3: Rising

Wildfire Chronicles series:

Panic

Shock

Psychosis

Mutation

Trauma

Reaction

Other Novels:

Last Resort

Survivor: A Horror Thriller

Join my mailing list to be the first to discover new releases, launch-day discounts, and free annual subscriber bonus content.

SUNDOWN

PART ONE

PROLOGUE

Frank Mather straightened, massaging his aching back with one hand and mopping at his brow with the other. He'd been on plenty of digs in Kentucky over the past few years and, one way or another, had always found some reason to curse the weather, which veered crazily between boiling and freezing on his every visit. This time, northern Kentucky had been baking for two weeks at over a hundred degrees. It was the kind of heat that made you feel like you'd pass out if you got off your chair, but the searing temperature hadn't slowed Frank and his team all day.

Not since they first uncovered it.

Since that moment, when the site of what was supposed to be just another Native American burial mound had spat up something extraordinary, they had worked feverishly; tirelessly, until Frank's muscles protested loudly and his head began to pound from dehydration.

He climbed from the hole and made his way to the shade of the trees, where the team had stowed its gear, took a plastic bottle from his pack and drained a pint of warm, clear water without pausing. It was the last of his stock, and he was *supposed* to be rationing it out. Nobody had expected to remain at the site this long, and they hadn't brought adequate supplies for a dig that had already stretched into the early evening.

He shrugged to himself. They'd be back in the nearby town of Ashland in a couple of hours, once they lost the last of the light. He'd just have to go thirsty until then.

"You slacking there, Professor?"

He looked up and smiled when he saw Nicole walking toward him, wiping her own brow and leaving a trail of dirt across her forehead which somehow managed to make her even more beautiful. Not for the first time, Frank thought that she was far too attractive to pursue a career in archaeology, of all things.

He tried not to stare, and Nicole tried not to smile flirtatiously when she noticed.

Neither quite succeeded.

Nicole crouched and rifled through her pack, retrieving her own bottle of water. Instinctively, Frank lifted his bottle to his lips once more, momentarily forgetting that it was empty.

He already felt parched.

Damn Kentucky.

"Any thoughts yet?" Nicole asked, taking a deliberately dainty sip and looking at his dry bottle with teasing eyes. He dropped it on the ground next to his pack.

It was the same question they had all been asking all day, one way or another.

What is it?

He shook his head. "I've got no idea. I called Princeton, and *they've* got no idea. In fact, I'm pretty sure they think I'm trying to stage something here."

"They're idiots." She rolled her eyes.

Frank scratched at his chin. "They're worried. I can understand why. The work we're doing has the potential to prove that we have been teaching our own history wrong. It might not sound like much, but it would ruffle some feathers."

Nicole snorted.

"Feathers get *ruffled* in the faculty if someone orders a new brand of coffee."

Frank ignored her depressingly accurate jibe.

"And then," he continued, "on top of that, I call them with *this*? Hell, there's even a part of *me* that thinks this has to be a hoax. Or I'm dreaming, or something."

Nicole cast a quick glance around to make sure the others could not see them, stepped forward, and kissed him lightly. It was the first time she had done any more than flirt with him, and the unexpected contact left him dizzy.

"Does it *feel* like you're dreaming?"

"Right *now*? Yeah, kinda," he grinned.

She laughed and pulled away from him.

"So, what did you *actually* tell them? Princeton?"

Frank's grin faded.

"The truth. A Native American burial mound erected in the middle of a copse of white oaks which were deliberately planted to mirror a European-style Neolithic henge. They pretty much started laughing right there. Then, I told them the mound contains two bodies: one human and one...uh...*not.* I described the anatomy of our unidentified friend, and it felt kinda like I was handing in my resignation."

Nicole snickered.

"Did they ask for an estimate?"

"Yeah. I told them circa one-thousand B.C., based on the racial features of the human skeleton. Most likely one of the Adena people."

"And the...*other* skeleton?"

"I haven't got the faintest idea what to tell them. I'd say it looks older. A *lot* older, but that would be impossible. As far as I know, there's nothing like it on record."

"What do you *think* it is? You must have a theory? *Something*. Don't hold out on me."

Frank frowned, willing his mind to come up with a response. Nicole, incredibly, was a young, beautiful woman who actually seemed to be interested in his theories about pre-Columbus America being settled by Europeans who had subsequently disappeared. He was not supposed to engage in *inappropriate behaviour* with students, of course, but their little flirtations were harmless—at least until that kiss—and by God he *did* get a thrill out of impressing her.

He wished he could conjure up some exotic theory that might blow Nicole's mind, but his own thoughts were muddled and scattershot. As things stood, *Bigfoot* was as plausible an explanation for the thing buried in the mound as any other he could dream up.

He shook his head and walked back to the edge of the dig site. He still had two students down there, working diligently at the remains with soft brushes; easing away the earth by inches.

The more of the bones they revealed, the more mystified Frank felt.

He could see all but the thing's left arm and leg now: it had been a huge creature, bipedal, but with multijointed arms and legs of a type that he had never seen before. Upright, Frank figured it would have been well north of seven feet in height. A densely packed ribcage: each rib almost fusing to the next to form a protective carapace, like a beetle. Its hands were long and thin, three many-knuckled fingers topped with talons that made Frank think of birds of prey. Yet it had opposable thumbs, a trait found only in humans and certain primates.

And its skull...

Those teeth...

"Well, it's not human. It can't be. Not even some genetic anomaly. These bones aren't the product of some sickness or mutation. Whatever it was, I think it was *supposed* to look like this. But as far as I know, nothing even remotely like it has ever been recorded before."

"You're thinking *alien*, right?"

Nicole's eyes sparkled, and Frank chuckled. It wasn't the first time that day that she had brought up *ET* as a potential explanation for the bizarre remains, and he doubted it would be the last.

"I'm sure it's not an alien, Nicole. As much as I know you want it to be, it's not."

Nicole mock-pouted as another voice joined the conversation, floating up from the base of the dig.

"He's right, Nic. But I can tell you one thing about it."

Frank looked down at the woman who'd spoken. Bella was the polar opposite of Nicole: all work and no play, but she was damn good at her job. While Frank, Nicole and Dirk—the final member of the team—had focused on the bizarre skeleton, unable to tear themselves away from it, Bella had worked alone; concentrating only on unearthing the human remains.

"What?"

"Whatever it is," Bella said, "it was murdered," she pointed at the smaller, human skeleton, "by this guy."

Frank frowned.

"I think our human friend here was buried holding a hatchet of some sort," Bella continued. "Handle's gone—rotted, most likely—but this was the blade." She waved a hand at a flat, smooth piece of stone a foot or so away from the human skeleton's right hand. "Can't be sure without tests, of course, but I'm willing to bet that this hatchet matches the wound on the side of *El Diablo* over there's skull."

Frank peered at the stone and nodded.

El Diablo. In a way, that seemed to fit.

They had already surmised that the unidentified creature had died as a result of head trauma, and now they had both murderer and murder weapon, but still the facts did not present a clear picture in Frank's mind. Some ancient people had buried a man right next to something that he had killed; the two skeletons arranged ceremoniously next to each other, almost like a couple sleeping peacefully. But why?

His gaze was drawn back to the huge skeleton once more, as if the bones and teeth and talons exerted some magnetic pull. So many questions, all of them orbiting around a single, vast conundrum.

What the hell were you?

———

THE TEAM CONTINUED TO CAREFULLY BRUSH DIRT away from bone for another hour, until the gathering dusk began to thwart their efforts. It wouldn't do to stumble around blindly in the dark, perhaps missing or destroying something vital, and so Frank told the others to wrap it up and head back to their hotel in one of the team's two cars. Frank would sleep in the other vehicle overnight. No way he was going to leave the site unattended; not yet.

With weary smiles and groans, Nicole, Bella and Dirk began to gather their things.

And all froze as one, rooted to the spot by the sudden noise that split the late evening air.

At first Frank thought it was the sound of distant thunder, the stifling weather breaking at last, perhaps, but as the noise drew closer, he realised what it was. Engines. More than one, approaching fast.

The team squinted up into the gloomy sky as one, and Frank gaped in astonishment when he saw three fat, dark helicopters roar overhead, flying so low that their metal bellies barely cleared the trees. For a moment, bright spotlights bleached the colour from the dig site, and he shaded his eyes until the light was pulled away abruptly.

The choppers disappeared from sight, but the noise of their engines remained ear-splittingly loud. They were circling nearby, Frank realised, searching for a place to land.

A voice on a loudspeaker boomed through the trees, shattering the tension and making Frank flinch.

"This is a restricted area. Remain where you are."

He glanced at the rest of the team. Nicole, Dirk and Bella were all looking at him with wide eyes, their expressions almost comically baffled. Nicole arched a quizzical eyebrow.

Frank held his hands up.

"I've got no more clue about this than you do."

"Princeton?" Nicole looked like she knew the answer even as she asked the question.

He shook his head, his expression dubious.

"They're the only ones I called. But *this*? This isn't Princeton. This is something else."

"Police, then?"

"Must be."

Nicole opened her mouth to reply.

Snapped it shut again, and turned to face the murky forest.

In the distance, Frank heard raised voices and heavy footsteps trampling toward them through the trees. Beyond that, the roaring of the engines was slowly fading. He felt a surge of anxiety, and told himself to stay calm. They had done nothing wrong. If the police were looking for somebody, it clearly wasn't them, and they were digging with a permit. It had to be a mistake.

Still, some part of him wanted to turn and flee into the woods.

"Frank?"

Dirk's voice. He sounded as nervous as Frank felt.

"It's okay, Dirk. Let me deal with this. It has to be some misunderstan—"

The words died in Frank's throat as he saw the first of them charging through the trees, and knew that the picture was wrong immediately.

Not police.

More than a dozen heavily armed men burst into the clearing, none wearing anything which identified them as law enforcement. They were all dressed in plain black paramilitary uniforms; all wore balaclavas; all had the same unsettlingly cold edge to their gaze.

More questions erupted in Frank's mind, these ones even more troubling: *the government? Men in black? Is Nicole right?*

Aliens?

The notion was surely ridiculous.

Frank began to lift his hands in surrender as the men surrounded the dig team and hefted assault rifles, aiming them directly at him.

"Th-there must be a mistake," he stammered, flushing, before adding a feeble "we have a permit."

"Not for *this*, Professor Mather." A woman's voice. "Step aside, please."

The woman, who spoke in a smooth southern drawl, wasn't dressed like the others. She emerged from the trees behind the armed men, wearing a plain suit and a gun holster that immediately made Frank think *CIA*. When he moved aside, the woman walked past him and made straight for the dig site. She was young, he realised; mid-twenties at most. Surely too young to be a government agent.

For several seconds, she stood at the edge of the dig, looking down silently.

Frank divided his time between staring at the back of the woman's head and glancing fearfully at the barrel of the nearest rifle. The tension in the air was intolerable; the air of menace the woman and her people carried like a naked blade. He had to speak.

Had to say *something*.

"Uh...are you with the government? Because—"

She laughed.

"My name is Jennifer Craven." She turned to face Frank with genuine mirth in her eyes. "Don't worry; you haven't heard of me. I hadn't heard of you, either; not until a couple of hours ago. Maybe it's fate that we meet. You believe in fate, Professor?"

Frank searched for words.

Found none.

"You've discovered something which my family has been searching for for a very long time, Professor. So long, in fact, that we didn't really believe it could even exist. When you're dealing with myths, after all, it's hard to know which ones to believe."

Frank's brow creased.

"I don't understand."

"Of course not. That one, that one and...that one." Jennifer Craven pointed at Dirk, Bella and Nicole, and before Frank could process what was happening, the air in the clearing erupted with rifle fire. He watched in horror as his young team dropped in a storm of blood. They were all dead before they hit the ground. Before the cry of shock could even gather in Frank's throat.

He stared fearfully at Craven, and at the ruined bodies on the dry soil, and tears stung his eyes. He shook his head and let out a low moan.

Craven motioned at her men to lower their weapons.

"Now, Professor, you have a choice. You can die *right now*..."

She pointed at the bodies leaking on the floor and nodded encouragingly at Frank.

"O-Or?" Frank breathed, staring with terrible fascination at the ragged holes in Nicole's long, graceful neck.

So much blood.

"Or: you can give me the honest truth about that hole you've been digging over there. And maybe, just *maybe*... you won't have to die at all."

Frank shook his head.

"I don't under—"

He bit down on the word as Craven took her pistol from its holster and stared at him evenly. She gripped the gun casually, not aiming it at him. There was no need. Frank couldn't take his eyes off it.

"We got here this morning," he said, the words tumbling from his mouth chaotically. "We've been digging, and—"

He snapped his mouth shut abruptly, aware that he was babbling and it was likely to get him killed.

Taking a deep breath, he started over.

"What do you want to know?"

Craven's eyes narrowed.

"Who have you told about your work here?"

Frank swallowed painfully, and thought about lying.

"Princeton," he said weakly. "I called a colleague at Princeton."

She'll kill me now.

Craven nodded curtly, almost as though somehow she had expected to hear that.

"Who else?"

Frank's eyes widened.

"Nobody, I swear to you. Nobody at all. I don't even know what I'd say. We don't even know what it is—"

"It's a vampire, Professor Mather. More pertinently, it's a *dead* vampire, and that makes it *very* interesting indeed. Tell me, Professor," Craven said, grabbing Frank's elbow in surprisingly strong fingers and guiding him to the edge of the hole, "the way these skeletons are positioned...do you think it was deliberate?"

Frank stared down at the bones.

"Yes," he said nervously. "That was our assumption."

"And would you say that the position of the bodies indicates that the human killed the vampire?"

Frank's brow furrowed.

Vampires? Is she actually serious?

The woman was clearly a lunatic, but Frank thought better of telling her as much.

"Bella thinks..." He felt a lump forming in his throat, and coughed. "Bella thought so. She was working on the human remains. She thought the human was buried holding some sort of hatchet."

He pointed at the sharp stone near the bones.

"Thank you, Professor. Very helpful."

She raised the pistol, aiming it at him, and Frank stared down the barrel of the weapon in horror.

"B-but...you said if I helped you, I wouldn't have to die!"

Jennifer Craven grinned, and he saw the detached cruelty in her eyes clearly then, and knew exactly what it meant for him.

"Everything dies, Professor Mather."

CHAPTER ONE

D*rip. Drip. Drip.*

DAN BELLAMY SHUT HIS EYES, SEARCHING FOR SOME sort of calm, but memories lurked in the darkness, waiting for him like a starving predator.

Stalking him like wounded prey.

"ARE YOU *SURE* THAT YOU WANT TO GO THROUGH with this? You don't have to, you know; not for me. I'd be happy to spend our honeymoon right here, as long as we're together."

Elaine smiled, and he was struck by her beauty for the thousandth time; the way her eyes lit up when she looked at him. She was telling the truth, he knew. She *would* be happy with that, and she wouldn't resent him for letting his illness taint what was supposed to be the best vacation of their lives.

"I'm sure. You deserve it, and I need to give it to you. A proper honeymoon, I mean." He rolled his eyes and chuckled when Elaine arched a salacious eyebrow. "Defuse those eyebrows immediately," he said in a mock-stern tone, and they both laughed.

"I'm serious," he said earnestly, leaning forward and taking his fiancé's hand. "I know it's scary, and I know it's a big step—"

"A 'big step' for an agoraphobic is picking up milk from the nearest store," Elaine said, and the smile faded from her lips, just a little. "You're talking about taking a cruise! Three weeks trapped in a giant floating box with thousands of other people, and no way for you to escape from it; no way to get home. That's far more of a *giant leap* than a *big step*, and you know it."

He nodded.

"You're right. But I have to do this, El. Not just for you; for me, too. I have to beat this. Normal people go on honeymoons; they take cruises without a second thought. All I want is to be normal again."

"We've talked about the N word," Elaine said sternly, and gave him a playful punch on the shoulder.

"Okay, okay," he said, mock-flinching away from her. "Not *normal*, then. *Healthy*. Better?"

Elaine surprised him by darting forward again, this time planting a kiss on his lips.

"Much better," she said. "I have my doubts about you doing this, but—"

"So does my therapist," he interrupted with a grin.

Elaine ignored him.

"—*but*, if you're determined, then I believe you can get through it. You know I do."

She left a little extra emphasis on those last two words, her eyes sparkling with excitement, and he felt his heart swell with happiness.

Elaine had protested when he first raised the idea, reeling off all of the perfectly rational reasons why a man with his condition absolutely should *not* book a cruise, but he knew as he looked into her eyes that, deep down, she wanted to say 'yes,' and that she was just being cautious; protecting him. That was the way it had been, ever since the attack: every decision, no matter how small, had to take *how Dan might react* under consideration. His illness had done that to her—to them both—but he could see the excitement in her eyes now; the flicker of *hope*. Of *course* she wanted to take a cruise.

And, as much as the prospect of actually going through with it unnerved him, he found to his surprise that on some level, he wanted to as well. The more he thought about it, the more right it felt. Scary, sure, but in a good way. Different to the terror that had crushed him for too long; this was a fear that felt healthy and positive and, yes, even conquerable.

He'd endured over a year of therapy, and had sampled more medications than he could count. *Klonopin* and *Zopiclone* and *Mirtazapine* and *Fluoxetine* and others whose names he couldn't even recall. One by one, the doctors took him through the drugs, searching for the elusive combination that would quiet the shrieking in his mind. The process of trial and error, they informed him, was regrettable but necessary. It was, after all, impossible to predict how any one individual brain might react to treatment.

As a result of the search, his mood had oscillated wildly between despairing numbness and a hyper-alert state of anxiety. The only constant amid the chemical chaos had been the fear; insidious and resilient, the cockroach of the emotions. For two years, it was as though his fight or flight response had been permanently engaged, constantly yelling at him to pay attention to the fact that he was *unsafe*. Eventually, submerged by a tsunami of modern and alternative medicine, even the iron grip of that clammy dread had started to weaken.

Progress. Real and tangible.

It had been more than six months since his last seizure, and on more than one occasion in recent weeks he had left the house all by himself, venturing out into the world for a few giddy moments.

Above all he *was* feeling a little better. Maybe enough that he was ready to take that giant leap forward. Ready to finally overcome the crippling condition that had shaped his life ever since a street thug buried a knife into his skull. All that was left was for him to actually *do it*. Take action; get back out into the world and *live* again.

"Earth to Dan. Come in, Dan. Over."

Elaine waved at him and grinned. He had been lost in his thoughts for several seconds. He blinked, and returned her smile.

"I *am* determined," he said. "This won't set me back, I promise you. This will help fix me. Besides, have you seen the brochure? The ship is massive. I'm sure that if I get too freaked out, there will be plenty of places for me to hide away from the normal folks."

He smiled as Elaine pursed her lips. The N *word* again.

"I'll be like the *hunchback of the Oceanus*," he said

with a laugh. "Lurking in the shadows, scaring the *normal* passengers."

He pulled a face, and Elaine giggled despite herself. She always admonished him for making jokes at his own expense, but in the end, she always giggled.

"Come on, El," he said brightly. "Let's book the tickets. It's just a cruise, right? I mean, how scary could it possibly be?"

She threw her arms around him and hugged so fiercely that he feared for his ribs, and he knew then that the debate was over. Cost be damned, fear be damned. It would be the honeymoon of a lifetime. The one this wonderful woman deserved.

And it would *fix* him.

He hugged her tightly, burying his face in her hair and breathing in her scent.

No.

Not her scent.

Blood.

He pulled away from her, and saw Elaine's once-beautiful, sparkling eyes fixed and glassy. Her mouth hanging open in a silent, terrified scream.

And the creature hulking behind her, its hideous talons hooked underneath her jawbone, beginning to *pull*, and—

———

DRIP.

Drip.

Drip.

His eyes flared open, his mind retreating from the once-joyous memory as it became toxic.

Back to the nightmare of reality.

Somewhere, the shipping container had sprung a leak. Just a little one, by the sound of it, but it would be enough. The air in the dark space was finite, and each drop of water that forced its way through the battered steel walls merely accelerated the end.

For Dan, it couldn't come soon enough.

He wished over and over that he had died on the ship; that he had been torn apart in a single, merciful instant when the Oceanus finally exploded. Because when it came down to it, a choice between a moment of pain and a lifetime of it wasn't much of a choice at all.

And pain was all that Dan had left.

His body was wracked by it: in addition to the bright chasms of fire that a taloned hand had ripped across his chest, his body felt like it was covered in bruises. When the container had been thrown clear of the blast, Dan had tumbled around inside like a ragdoll, crashing into the metal walls and colliding solidly with the man who shared the dark, sinking prison with him.

Herbert Rennick.

Herb was a talker, and apparently hadn't considered the fact that every word he uttered used up more of the container's dwindling oxygen. Or maybe he didn't care either. He sounded young—certainly younger than Dan's twenty-nine—and terribly afraid. Maybe that was why he kept talking. Maybe to Herb, the silence was the scariest thing of all.

Dan didn't want to talk.

Didn't want to listen.

The darkness in the container was absolute, like being buried alive, and when he tried to tune out Herb's incessant chatter, he found that the only thing his eyes had to look at was the past. Yet, no matter which happy memory he tried to conjure up for his mind to retreat to for these final minutes of his life, what he saw was Elaine's face as it had been in her own final moments; her absolute terror when she realised that she was about to die, alone, at the hands of a creature whose very existence was an impossibility.

I could have saved her.

You were busy crying and falling apart; busy being Pathetic Dan. You should *have saved her.*

He grimaced.

Didn't want to *think,* either.

All he wanted was to wait for the end in peace.

He tried to clear his head. According to his therapist, it was possible for a person to remove themselves from their thoughts and feelings, to become no more than an impartial observer in their own mind, and, through that detachment, to find some respite from emotions that might otherwise overwhelm or paralyse. The trick was simply to focus only on the physical world, on physical sensation: the texture of a coin in your hand, perhaps, or the taste of a breath mint. To concentrate on anything that *wasn't* torturous introspection.

In a therapeutic setting, the technique—*mindfulness*—had yielded some modest rewards for Dan. In the container, things worked out differently.

That was, perhaps, due to the smell. It was difficult to focus on clearing his mind when every breath he took delivered the sickly-sweet odour of charred meat.

Herb's arm.

Shortly after Herb had first started to talk, he had explained to Dan that his arm had caught fire back on the Oceanus, and that he couldn't even feel it.

"No pain. I think that means the nerves are all burned away, right? Second- or third-degree burns, must be," Herb had proclaimed. He had almost sounded proud of it. "Guess I'll need a skin graft. Do me a favour and call me an ambulance, mate?"

Herb had laughed at that, before descending into a violent coughing fit. The fire—and the smoke—had apparently damaged more than just Herb's skin.

Dan didn't respond.

The minutes wore on.

He remained impassive as Herb ranted about his father and about what he called *The Great Lie*. How his *dear old Dad* was responsible for the deaths of thousands. Charles Rennick, Herb said, was a *servant of darkness*.

The entire Rennick family was a part of a global cult which Herb referred to as the *Order*. A network of families which had existed for thousands of years, keeping the existence of vampires secret; feeding them when they awoke from 'hibernation' and covering up the catastrophic results. His father's next move, Herb said confidently, would be to throw himself at the mercy of the rest of the vampires, to beg forgiveness for the sacrifice that had gone so disastrously wrong. More souls might have to be offered—perhaps a lot more—and the Order would find some way to bury it. They always had.

It can't be allowed, Herb had snarled. *We have to stop it*, he said, over and over. *The world has to know. We can fight them.*

Dan said nothing.

None of it mattered. What mattered was gone, and dwelling on the reasons for the loss—or even dreaming up implausible ways to avenge it—was a raw, scraping sort of pain. When he allowed himself to think about *her*—about that beautiful, terrified face in the darkness—it felt like a part of his mind was being taken from him; peeling away like the burnt flesh on Herb's injured arm.

Better to focus on nothing.

He counted his breaths, trying to tune out Herb's incessant muttering.

In, out. In, out.

He wondered how many more he had left to take.

In, out.

In.

Out.

Finally, even Herb fell silent, and Dan knew the reason why: the air in the container felt like it was getting thicker. His breaths were becoming shallower, he realised. More rapid, like each inhalation couldn't quite deliver the required amount of oxygen to his bloodstream.

Not long now.

He shut his eyes in the darkness and did his best to think of nothing, letting his final minutes slip away.

And then the damn doors opened, and scraps of fading moonlight illuminated the interior of the container as a chill wind blasted fresh oxygen into Dan's lungs. Cold, grey rain fell outside—the tail end of the storm that had ripped the sky apart for several hours—and even before he stepped wearily from the container, Dan recognised the rolling steel of the Atlantic Ocean in the distance.

He was on another ship.

Still alive.

And there would be no peace.

HERB WAS ALREADY OUTSIDE THE CONTAINER, snarling at somebody that Dan could not see. He followed the bigger man out in a daze, stepping onto the deck of a boat that was much smaller than the one he had left hours earlier.

He shivered at the cold; the rain soaked through his clothes in an instant. He was still wearing shorts and a faded T-shirt; what he had jokingly called his *honeymoon outfit* less than twenty four hours earlier, when there had been somebody to laugh at his lame gags. When he had been capable of making them.

Now, his honeymoon outfit was bloodstained; the thin fabric reeked of death and did nothing to keep the biting wind at bay.

Yet, despite the searing cold, Dan felt his internal temperature rising inexorably; the emotions that he had tried so hard to suppress spiralling beyond his control in an instant.

Herb pointed a gun at a broad-shouldered man who looked to be in his early sixties. The older man knelt on the deck, his head bowed.

"I'm not going to kill you, Dad," Herb said. "I couldn't. You're family. *Blood.* To some of us, that actually means something. I wish I could kill you, but I can't." He turned and tossed the pistol toward Dan, who caught it instinctively. It felt remarkably heavy in his hands.

"That guy can, though."

For a moment, Dan just stood there, stupefied. He was dimly aware that there were several people clustered somewhere behind him on the deck. Their hostility when he caught the weapon was an invisible hand that pressed into his back, but he could not focus on them; only on the man kneeling on the deck before him, his piercing grey eyes wide and trained on the gun that Dan clutched in uncertain fingers.

This, then, was the *servant of darkness* that Herb had ranted about in the container. *Dear old Dad.* Charles Rennick, the man who had sentenced the three thousand souls aboard the Oceanus to death.

The one who was responsible for—

Dan saw her face in his mind again, twisted by animal panic; dying alone.

He dropped his gaze to the weapon, watching it tremble in his grip.

His first instinct was to use the gun on himself; to grant himself the oblivion that had been so cruelly snatched from him at the last. Once, he had thought he could go through with killing himself; had believed that suicide was the only way to stop the terrible pain that buzzed in his head incessantly. But he had made a promise that he would never go through with it.

A *promise*.

Tears filled his eyes; blurred his vision.

He lifted the gun unsteadily.

Kill him.

For her.

He choked back a sob as grief and despair over-whelmed him, and aimed the gun at the old man's face.

Kill them all.

The thought erupted into his shattered mind so easily; so *naturally*. *Kill them all.* Just like that. He pictured himself pulling the trigger again and again, could almost *see* the perforated bodies dropping around him. The blood. His mind pitched alarmingly; a feeling like a rollercoaster cresting a huge drop and plummeting toward the ground. A wave of dizziness and nausea washed through him.

Dan's hands shook wildly, and the air around him congealed. Suddenly, his chest felt like it was being crushed in a vice, and each attempt to draw in a breath lodged white-hot razors in his throat.

Familiar sensation.

Crawling up my neck.

Unsafe. Get away.

Must get away.

Adrift on the terrible black river, surging and boiling; carrying me toward something awful. Something unstoppable, and—

His head felt like it was cracking open; as though the contents were seeping out, expelled like toxic waste.

She's dead...

Dan blinked, and suddenly he wasn't seeing an old man kneeling in front of him anymore; wasn't seeing the ship and the falling rain. He wasn't even seeing the face of his dead wife. All were gone, torn away like a band-aid; reality submerged beneath a terrifying vision of cascading dark water.

The black river roared, and the dam that he had sought to build with medication and therapy finally crumbled.

Dan's mind began to flood.

Somewhere through the tears and the blackness that ringed his vision, spreading like a cancer, he vaguely understood that Charles Rennick was rising to his feet, grasping for the gun frantically.

Dan squeezed the trigger, and the back of Rennick's head exploded. He died instantly, but when his body collapsed to the deck in the blood and the rain, Dan stood over the corpse and fired again.

Again.

Again.

And with each bullet fired, the corpse at his feet twitched, and the darkness in Dan's mind intensified.

After the fourth shot—which took out most of Charles Rennick's jaw—Dan felt the gun slipping from numb fingers that no longer seemed to belong to him, clattering to a deck which he could no longer see.

The world tumbled and spun as the boiling black tide swept away his thoughts.

Foul water in my mouth—

Can't breathe—

Dan bent double and retched as a flare went up in his mind; white-hot pain that lanced across the back of his skull. His jaw clenched involuntarily and he bit deeply into the soft flesh of his cheek as his neck began to spasm.

Tasted blood.

And the river took him.

The last thought that went through his mind before the seizure snatched away his consciousness and he collapsed to the deck was that there was, at least, a fair chance that he might never wake up.

CHAPTER TWO

A stunned silence fell on the deck of the trawler, and for a moment even the ocean seemed to hold its breath.

Herb watched in open-mouthed astonishment as Dan Bellamy collapsed.

The guy hadn't spoken a word in hours, and Herb might even have assumed that he had lapsed into unconsciousness in the container, if it weren't for the occasional low moan of despair or soft grunt of pain. In that heavy darkness, Herb got the distinct impression that he was sharing the space with a broken, tortured man.

Herb's oldest brother had given his life so that Dan would live, because Dan was the only man in recorded history who had killed a vampire. That made him important, but as earnest and certain as Edgar had been that Dan might hold the key to resisting the vampires, Herb had a hard time believing it, especially now that he could actually see the guy properly for the first time.

Dan was slim—almost scrawny—and of average height, with dark eyes almost buried under a mop of hair that made him look younger than he probably was. He didn't look like a fighter. What he looked was either scared out of his wits, or crazy. Perhaps both.

The fit—seizure; whatever it was—only served to rein-force the notion that events on the Oceanus must have fractured the poor guy's mind. Herb wouldn't have thought it were possible for a man's muscles to spasm so violently, but when Dan hit the deck, his limbs jerked hard enough that Herb expected to hear the snapping of bone at any moment. Dan's collapse was, in a way, even more violent and shocking than his father's execution.

Every member of the trawler's small crew watched in amazement, unable to tear their gaze away until Dan finally stopped thrashing and lost consciousness.

And the ocean finally exhaled.

Herb turned his attention to his father's ruined corpse.

Furious, trembling hours spent in the container, dreaming up the harsh truths he was going to deliver to Charles Rennick, but as soon as he saw the old bastard's face, the rage had just been too much. He had no idea what would happen when he tossed the gun to Dan, but Herb had spent his entire life listening to his father preach about fate *this* and destiny *that.*

So Herb let fate decide, figuring that maybe for his father, fate—if such a thing even existed—might look exactly like Dan Bellamy.

So it proved.

And it felt infuriatingly like Charles Rennick got off easy.

Herb took a couple of steps forward, stooping to retrieve the pistol which Dan had dropped. Four more paces, and he was staring down directly on the punctured, leaking remains of his father. He knelt and retrieved a second gun from the dead man's waistband. That had been the only gun permitted on the trawler: even with his followers comprehensively brainwashed, Charles would not allow anyone else to carry a firearm. *Too much potential for trouble*, he had said.

Herb grimaced. The old bastard had been right about that, at least. He stood and tucked both guns into his belt, turning to face the rest of the crew.

They regarded him with fear, but also with reverence and loyalty that made his nerves quiver. His father's words came back to him, laced with contempt.

You're going to kill me? Then who'll be the head of the Rennick family? You?

According to custom, Herb *was* the head of the family now, though he was the last actual Rennick left. The rest of Charles Rennick's people weren't blood, but families who had attached themselves to the Rennicks over the generations; people for whom the vampires had become gods to worship. Herb's duty now was to take his father's position as the leader of those people, to represent the Order and—above all else—to keep the oath; protect the ancient truce.

To feed the vampires.

Custom.

Duty.

Tradition.

Destiny.

Herb drew in a deep, shuddering breath.

I'm in charge now.

The crew looked at him like machines awaiting the input of their next command, and the corpse on the deck stared at him reproachfully, making his emotions tumble.

With a grunt, Herb grabbed a fistful of his dead father's coat, and dragged the steaming corpse to the low rail that ran around the deck.

When he tossed the body overboard, Herb stared down at it for several moments as it refused to sink; bobbing stubbornly on the dark water. What was left of his father's eyes seemed to point accusingly at him, no matter which way the waves rolled.

Herb turned away.

"Turn this boat around," he said in a flat tone to nobody in particular. "We're going home."

———

THE *SEA SHANTY* HAD BEEN A FACTORY FISHING trawler in a previous life. At a little over one hundred and twenty feet, it would have looked like a toy alongside the cruise ship its black-market weaponry had sunk hours earlier, but in its heyday the Shanty had been just about the largest dragger money could buy.

Two huge freezer holds—once piled floor-to-ceiling with squirming life plucked from the Atlantic— devoured the majority of the space on the boat. The engine room took up most of the rest. What was left over was all about compromise: humans were afforded very little space to live and work in, no more than skinny corridors connecting a few anaemic rooms which were barely big enough for the average man to stand up straight in.

The deck area, when the Shanty had been a working vessel, had been a complicated network of potential death traps which tested the awareness of the boat's crew continually, underlining that people and their comfort were strictly a secondary concern. After all, it was the fish in the Shanty's belly that truly mattered.

The larger of the two holds was reliving its glory days; once more it carried precious cargo.

Herb had two of the crew place Dan inside, atop a pile of rags and filthy blankets. All of Herb's attempts to wake the man—up to and including delivering a slap that made his palm sing—had failed. Whatever was wrong with the guy was far beyond the medical knowledge of anyone on the trawler. If he had a role to play in *destiny*, Herb thought sourly, Dan Bellamy would have to come through whatever was ailing him of his own accord.

He padlocked the hold, slipping the key into his pocket, and made his way back out onto the deck, his head bowed against the wind and rain until he reached the wheelhouse. Three of the crew were in there, watching him nervously, but Herb moved right past them, stepping into a smaller room to the rear which his father had turned into a sort of private office.

Inside, there was a small desk and a couple of chairs and not much else, other than a half-empty bottle of brandy which was rolling slowly from one side of the room to the other with each wave that buffeted the hull. Herb snatched up the liquor and slumped into one of the chairs, and for a while he focused on nothing other than the pleasant burning sensation in his throat as he took large gulps.

Through the gathering fog which the alcohol lowered across his thoughts, the question came, as he knew it would.

What am I doing?

Herb knew what he *ought* to be doing, and that was running; pointing the Shanty at some remote island somewhere and never looking back. He had always wanted to run, to just pick a direction and get as far away from the fanaticism of the compound on which he had been raised as he possibly could. In the end, he told himself that he stayed for his brothers, but would have readily conceded that it was more likely a simple matter of cowardice. Even if he had managed to flee, his father would have come after him. Rennick blood, after all, came with a sacred obligation.

Even if Charles Rennick had let his youngest son go, some other part of the Order would have hunted him relentlessly, until they were certain that he was dead—along with everything he knew.

He had failed.

Failed to run.

Failed to persuade his brothers that mass murder would cost them all their souls if not their lives, that they were far from the *good guys with a noble burden* that their father had always maintained.

And, even while Herb was aboard the Oceanus, surrounded by death and madness, he had tried to save a man—just *one* man; to do *one thing* that was good amongst all the horror...

...and that man was dead.

Corrosive memories flooded back to Herb, crystal clear and debilitating: the wall of fire and the hideous monster that strolled through it nonchalantly, laughing as it prepared to devour him; the security officer blowing his own head off rather than face the abomination on the other side of a barricaded door. Edgar, pushing Herb inside the shipping container and locking the doors, turning to face the monster that he knew was behind him.

And screaming right outside those doors as the last of

the Three tore him to pieces. *That* had been an armour-piercing sound, and hearing it had cast a sickly pall of grief and anger over Herb's thoughts which he doubted would ever truly lift.

He shook his head thickly, and a groan escaped his lips. He had to occupy his mind with something. Reliving the nightmare would drive him mad.

He took another large swallow of the brandy and began to rifle through the desk drawers, finally finding what he was looking for in the lowest of them: a first-aid tin which looked like it hadn't been opened in decades. He pried off the lid and surveyed the predictably disappointing contents. A single half-empty bottle of antiseptic; a box of painkillers that had to be years out of date; a faded yellow bandage.

He set the open tin on the desk in front of him.

Took another drink.

Gritted his teeth as he peeled off his jacket and removed what felt like most of his left arm along with it.

Wincing more out of revulsion than pain, Herb dropped his gaze to the burned limb. His pale flesh had been painted a livid red and was covered with weeping blisters. Along the forearm, where the fire had really taken hold, Herb saw that his skin was pockmarked by wide, shallow craters: layers of meat and fat that had melted away to leave revolting indentations. The arm smelled sweet and cloying and sickly, like a plate of pork and apple sauce that had been left to rot in the sun.

Herb choked back the urge to retch and dumped his jacket on the floor before prising the crusty cap off the ancient bottle of antiseptic. When he poured the clear liquid across his wounds, he was grateful that he still felt no pain, but the sight of his own dead flesh being sluiced away was its own kind of torment.

Once the small bottle was empty, he wrapped the arm tightly in the old bandage, uncertain whether a burn should be covered or left to breathe, and ultimately deciding not to risk leaving his skin exposed.

When he was done, he took another long drink.

Set the brandy down on the desk.

And dropped his head into his hands as the tears came at last.

CHAPTER THREE

Herb was still staring at his feet, sniffling softly and trying to sift through the chaos in his mind, when the door opened and footsteps made their way toward him. He knew there was only one man on the Shanty who would dare to follow him into the cabin and, in the end, he was surprised it had taken that man so long.

"Hi, Jeremy," Herb said without lifting his gaze. "Thought you'd come sooner."

"Had to weigh up the odds of you shooting me. There's a lot of dying going on, after all."

Herb snorted.

"Crew's a little nervous, Herb. I don't mind admitting that includes me."

He glanced up and saw genuine concern etched on Jeremy Pruitt's face. Pruitt was the older man of the two by far, getting ready to wave a sour goodbye to his late-fifties and sporting a balding pate that made him look like he belonged in a monastery somewhere; an impression that was undone somewhat by his hulking physique.

Jeremy had been a part of the family since before

Herb was born, filling an ill-defined but necessary role at Charles Rennick's side as adviser, bodyguard and, Herb had long suspected, occasional assassin. There had been times through the years when the Rennick family secret had come close to being revealed. On those occasions, it was Jeremy who ensured silence, one way or another.

Despite his murky, violent past, the big man was one of the few at the compound that didn't treat Herb like a live grenade, and he considered Jeremy the closest thing he had to a friend. They had even talked openly at times about the oath, and about Herb's unswerving belief that the creatures his family was sworn to protect—and the whole secret history of the world that went along with that duty—could not possibly exist. Jeremy disagreed of course, but while he was certainly a believer, he was no fanatic.

Unlike the rest of them.

When Herb had been preoccupied with the fantasy of running away, it was Jeremy that had dominated his thoughts. The older man would, in all probability, help Herb with the practicalities of fleeing the compound, and then immediately be tasked with hunting him down, and perhaps even killing him. Knowing Jeremy, if Charles Rennick had given such an order, he would have carried it out, friendship or no friendship. What Jeremy would do *now*—now that the man who had been his personal dictator for decades was dead, Herb had no idea.

But he was glad that he was the one with the guns.

Jeremy slumped heavily into the chair opposite Herb's.

"Do I have a mutiny on my hands?" Herb smiled thinly and offered the older man the brandy. Jeremy waved the bottle away.

"*Please*," he said. "Loyalty isn't a problem; you know that. At least, not for *those* people."

He gave a knowing stare, and Herb felt his mood darken.

"He deserved to die."

Herb infused those four words with venom; poisonous enough that Jeremy couldn't possibly miss the fact that his father's death was not up for debate.

Jeremy held his calloused hands up in an apologetic gesture.

"Just saying. These people have been a part of your family for generations. They don't serve the Order. They serve the Rennicks. You *are* the Order."

Herb grunted, but said nothing.

After a moment's pause, Jeremy cleared his throat a little awkwardly.

"I'm sorry, about your brothers."

Herb's eyes clouded, and he pointed them at the floor.

"I tried to stop it, right from the start. They wouldn't listen. Nobody *ever* listened. Maybe my father had the right idea. Perhaps the only way to make sure your point gets noticed is to underline it with blood."

"Yeah, that sounds like something he would have said. Never thought I'd hear it from you, though."

Herb shook his head angrily, and for a few moments a dark silence settled on the small room. He wanted desperately to change the subject, but it appeared that all subjects were currently soaked in violence, one way or another.

"When was the last time you were in contact with the compound?"

Jeremy's expression hardened.

"Not since the Oceanus was sunk. Your father was

unwilling to accept his failure, not until he saw it for himself. He wanted to find the container before he called home."

"We need to warn them," Herb replied, "tell them that the rest of the nest may rise."

Jeremy shook his head.

"Impossible."

Herb's eyes narrowed.

"Why?"

Jeremy sighed.

"Your father had the satellite phone in his pocket. I wish you'd checked before you decided to throw him overboard."

Herb squeezed his eyes shut and clenched his jaw, and silence fell once more. It was Jeremy that broke it.

"The guy who pulled the trigger, what's his story?"

"According to Edgar, he killed two of the Three with a cleaver."

Jeremy arched an eyebrow.

"*That* guy?"

Herb snorted a laugh.

"I know, right? But Edgar was very definite. He thought Dan Bellamy was important. I imagine, at the end, my father thought so, too."

He grimaced.

"Dan Bellamy," Jeremy repeated softly, as though the name might mean something to him. Apparently not. "Did he talk, in the container?"

"He called out for somebody, once. His wife, I think. Don't think he knew exactly where he was. Once he realised, though? No; not a word. I guess he's in shock."

Jeremy looked dubious.

"Never seen shock do *that* to a person before."

Herb had no response to that.

"Did Edgar say anything else?"

"Just that he had told Dad about the vampires dying, and that Dad's response was to fucking kill us all."

"He hoped to cast this as an accident, I think. Maybe even claim that it was the vampires who caused the explosion and hope that the rest of the nest wouldn't retaliate. Losing his own sons added a certain...authenticity to his story."

Jeremy delivered the words without emotion. Herb tried to receive them in a similar fashion. Failed by a wide margin.

"'Authenticity,'" he spat bitterly, and snatched up the almost-empty brandy bottle. He took a mouthful. "That sounds about right. Lies piled on top of lies; that's the Rennick way. Tell me, Jeremy, did he know, before all this? Did he ever give you any indication that there might be people out there who the vampires *can't* control?"

"No. There's nothing in the texts, Herb, nothing that—"

"The *texts*," Herb snarled. "More lies."

Jeremy blinked at the ferocity in Herb's tone. "Even if that's true, nobody has found any evidence to contradict them. Think about it, Herb. Your own family has searched for information on the vampires for centuries, and what have you found? Nothing. The Order exists in more than thirty countries; families just like yours, all of them searching for exactly the same thing. Christ, the entire Order has devoted itself to uncovering the truth, and all they have discovered is evidence that these things *can't* be resisted."

He sighed.

"So maybe your friend Dan Bellamy is one of a kind.

Good for him. But what use is that to anybody? The vampires have nests across the entire planet, probably including many that we don't even know about. We'd need an army of Dan Bellamys to fight them."

Herb felt his irritation rising. It was exactly the same sort of argument that he had heard countless times back at the compound. Devout belief in a bunch of ancient arte-facts which claimed that the vampires were gods and that servitude was the only option. Nobody would listen to Herb when he tried to tell them that something being written a long time ago didn't necessarily make it true, and that recent history was full of lies concocted by the Order, which made it likely that ancient history was as well. It seemed that only he was able to countenance the idea that the ancient clay and stone tablets which formed the bulk of the Order's knowledge might be inscribed with lies.

"And what if he's *not* one of a kind? What if there are thousands like him? Millions? What if it's something to do with his genes, or his upbringing, or the fact he eats *Tasty Wheat* for breakfast? Dan was one of three thousand on the ship. What if those are the odds? If one in every three thousand people can resist them, *there's* an army. I mean, how many of these things can there possibly be out there? Why all this trouble just to feed *three*? Doesn't that suggest that there are a lot less vampires out there than the texts claim?"

Jeremy shook his head firmly.

"If anyone had found evidence—any evidence at all—that there were *ever* any other Dan Bellamys out there, we would know."

"Would we really? You think my father would have shared that information with the rest of the Order?"

Jeremy said nothing.

The more Herb thought about it, the more certain he felt. His father would have killed Dan Bellamy at best, or handed him over to the vampires at worst. Anything to preserve the status quo.

"Do you know that virtually all historians agree that the Great Fire of London only killed five people?" he asked.

Jeremy stared at him, puzzled. He did know plenty about the Great Fire of 1666, of course. It was an event that was branded onto the mind of everybody who lived at the Rennick compound, the exact date celebrated annually like a twisted Christmas.

"It's amazing, isn't it," Herb continued, "how the truth can get twisted until it no longer exists? By 1667 my family was wealthy beyond all measure, fattened by meat plucked from the bones of a burning city. It's the same story all over the world, everywhere the Order exists. *They* get fed, we get rich. We become people of influence and wealth. *We* get to shape history. I wonder, if a Dan Bellamy had been walking around London in 1666, whether my ancestors would have viewed his existence as a good thing? For all we know, other families have stumbled across people just like Dan, and have buried that particular truth along with all the others."

He focused on the horizon.

They were travelling east at full speed, heading toward the sun that had not yet risen.

"I wonder what else is a lie," Herb continued softly. "According to the texts, the vampires were super-predators, and they killed us so relentlessly that we were at the point of extinction. That's why they chose to stay underground, because the alternative was to feed themselves out of existence right along with us. They sleep in order to give their *crops* time to grow."

"And?"

Herb flinched, so lost in his thoughts and the dark, rolling waves that for a moment he had forgotten that Jeremy was standing next to him.

"And there were only *three* to feed. During the Great Fire, it was just *two*. It makes you wonder, doesn't it?"

He glanced at Jeremy. The older man's expression was pitched somewhere between confusion and concern.

"Wonder what?"

"Whether they buried themselves out of our reach because they were killing too many of us...or because we were killing too many of *them*."

For a long time, Jeremy said nothing, and the two men stared out at the dark horizon in silence. Herb thought he knew what the older man was thinking: exactly the same question that burned in his own mind.

The texts—every scrap of information uncovered by the Order, right across the planet—all agreed on one thing: that the vampires would rise to punish a failed sacrifice. Entire civilizations had supposedly been wiped out as a result of their failure to satisfy the creatures' demand for blood. What if that, too, was a lie? For all Herb knew, there *were* no other vampires in England. Maybe the entirety of the English nest had already been killed in the mid-Atlantic.

"They're going to come for you, you know."

Herb blinked, and switched his gaze to Jeremy.

"The vampires? Yeah, I've heard all the prophesies of doom. *Bloodlines that fail them are erased from history—*"

"Not just the vampires. The rest of the Order. We were supposed to sail north and broadcast a fake distress signal, remember? The Oceanus will be discovered sooner rather than later, and that means that this boat is full of loose threads, Herb. You should know enough about what happens to loose threads in situations like this."

Herb shrugged.

"We're in the age of information now, Jeremy. It's time the world knew everything."

"And a lot of people will die as a result."

"A lot of people have *already* died, and all because we believed these things were gods. But they're not immortal. We can fight them, whether Dan Bellamy is a one-off or not. While they have been sleeping, the human race has spent centuries perfecting the art of killing. We have weapons these things can only dream of."

Jeremy's shoulders slumped.

"Guns and bombs and tanks. I doubt you are the first to consider such a course of action. But what good are those weapons if we have no idea where to point them? What effect can a man holding a gun have, when they can take his mind before he can pull the trigger?"

Herb returned his gaze to the horizon.

"I guess we'll find out, one way or another. Assuming that there *are* any other vampires out there."

"And if you're wrong about all of this?"

"Then I'll be wrong. It won't be the first time."

"And you're willing to gamble your life?"

Herb shrugged.

"I'm meant to be dead already, remember?"

Jeremy sighed wearily, and began to make his way back toward the wheelhouse. After a few paces, he paused.

"You know," he said, "your father always said you were reckless. Never one to think things through."

"And now he's dead," Herb growled in a low, dangerous tone.

Jeremy nodded.

"For my part, I always thought you were both more alike than either of you ever realised."

Jeremy left the deck, leaving Herb alone with his racing thoughts.

He checked his watch. Almost five in the morning. It was late in the year, and dawn wouldn't break over England for a couple of hours yet. Sunrise had been their final deadline for returning the Three to the earth, where more of their kind were supposedly hibernating. If that were true, by the time light washed across the land, the rest of the nest would surely realise that their kin were not coming back.

Herb was sure that they would not attack the surface in daylight. The texts weren't lying about *that* part: the vampires had demanded total darkness aboard the Oceanus, and had been sealed in the shipping container to avoid all light during their transportation. The notion that sunlight might actually *kill* them was fanciful; just another part of the false mythology that had been allowed to spring up around the vampires over the centuries, but they avoided light nonetheless.

If there *were* more vampires out there, ready to rise and avenge the death of their kind, he figured he had around twelve hours of daylight to figure out how to deal with them; twelve hours to unwrap the riddle of Dan Bellamy.

Twelve hours.

CHAPTER FOUR

C lick.

Barry Reid shut the front door to the farm-house softly behind him, and his face twisted into a sour grimace.

Rain again.

He stepped out into the still-dark morning with a sinking heart, and felt the downpour plaster his prematurely greying hair to his forehead in seconds. The weather forecasts had been right: a storm had blown in from the Atlantic overnight. Just like every other damn night.

The year was shaping up to be the wettest on record; a hard-won accolade in the UK. Winter lurked around the corner, and the sun had barely shown all summer. Instead, there was the endless rain. In some low-lying coastal areas, that had meant flooding, and vaguely hysterical responses from a government that did all but declare it was going to be *tough on weather and tough on the causes of weather*.

Barry's farm, a few miles inland from the coastal town

of Brighton, had not flooded, but the inclement weather had a profound effect nonetheless. Most people probably assumed that drought was a farmer's worst enemy, and they weren't exactly wrong, but wet day after wet day could be just as troublesome.

Amazing how something as simple as an extended period of rain—as damn *arbitrary*—could put a man's livelihood at risk. The silage crop had suffered a near-fatal blow from the lack of anything like a summer. Without silage stocks, Barry was forced to resort to buying in animal feed to get the cows through the winter, and the price of the stuff just kept on going up. Meanwhile, the supermarkets continued to drive the price of milk down, and Barry found himself caught in the middle, slowly having the life squeezed out of his business.

Getting up at four every morning was starting to feel a lot like drowning, and every hour spent tending to the farm as it haemorrhaged a little more money had become a dreadful burden that squatted heavily on Barry's soul. He could almost *see* the pennies draining away in front of his eyes, minute by minute. Now, each morning when Barry left the farmhouse and headed for the tractor to begin his first circuit of the land, he carried a vague sense of dread with him which lasted all day.

And he got soaked, of course. There was always that.

Barry broke into a trot as a fork of lightning gave the darkness an early taste of the daylight to come. For a moment, his land lit up around him, bright and bleached of colour, but he paid it no attention. His surroundings were as familiar to him as oxygen; he could have navigated the farm wearing a blindfold.

The house behind him, garage to his right. Outbuildings to the left—mostly containing tools and supplies, along with a few chickens. A small barn directly ahead that was a prelude to the much larger version further down the dirt track that led to the heart of his two hundred acres. He usually parked the tractor in the larger barn, but had been so tired the previous evening that he hadn't bothered, instead leaving it close to the house. He was glad of that now; less distance to run in the storm.

He reached the tractor and yanked open the door, and had hauled himself into the seat with a grunt before his mind processed the image his eyes had seen properly, the odd detail that had lurked in his peripheral vision as he ran from the house.

He froze, his hand still on the open door, his arm getting soaked, but all of a sudden, he didn't notice the rain at all.

What the hell was that?

Just for a moment there, during that monochrome snapshot taken by the storm, he could have sworn he saw something moving beyond the main barn a few hundred feet ahead of him. Something big. He might have dismissed it as an animal, maybe even one of his own, but for the fact that in that brief instant, Barry was certain that whatever he had seen was walking upright.

Like a man.

Righteous anger sparked deep in his gut. It wasn't just the rain and the silage that had ruined his year; it was the sickness in the animals: a relentless tide of poor health that no vet seemed able to stem nor adequately explain, and which slowly ate away at the cows and sheep. Way more deaths among the sheep, particularly, than at any other time that Barry could recall. And all in the same year that he received several offers for his land from the wealthy bastards who owned the land adjacent to his own.

Strange folks, the Rennicks, no doubt about that. When a sheep had once broken through the fence and ended up on Rennick land, Barry caught a glimpse of the house, which seemed almost deliberately hidden by trees, and could have sworn he saw people dressed in robes, like monks. Local rumour had it that the Rennicks ran some sort of commune out there in the woods. When the locals had taken a few drinks, those rumours darkened: the Rennick family was involved in *strange rituals*, they said. *Occult practices*, they said. *Satanism*.

There were a lot of them, Barry was sure of that. Maybe they wanted his land to expand their...whatever the hell it was.

Too bad for them.

The Reid family farm had been handed down through the generations, and it didn't matter if the Rennicks added a couple of zeroes to their offer. What mattered was that Barry's father had charged him with maintaining the farm and passing it on to his own son someday, and there was no way he could sell it. It simply was not possible. When an agent representing the Rennicks turned up at Barry's doorstep with an offer, he told them exactly that.

And then the animals started to get sick.

Barry was no fool; it was impossible for him not to put that particular two-plus-two together, but he had never had any concrete evidence.

So far.

Someone had been poisoning his livestock for months, Barry was sure of it, slowly tightening the financial noose around his neck. And now he had seen the bastard, right there on his property; had caught him red handed as he skulked around in the pre-dawn.

Barry squinted into the darkness, searching for movement and seeing none, and thought about the old shotgun he kept back at the farmhouse, and which he had never found a use for beyond firing a blast in the general direction of foxes.

Bad idea, Barry. You might just get angry enough to fire that weapon.

He felt adrenaline coursing through him like rocket fuel, and gritted his teeth.

Besides, you don't need no gun for this.

He climbed down from the tractor cab with a grunt, balling up his fists, and headed purposefully toward the distant barn. By the time he reached it, Barry was almost sprinting, working himself up into a thrumming mess of fury. He burst into the dark building, drawing in a breath to holler a wordless roar of attack as he charged at the intruder like some marauding Viking, and stopped abruptly, surprised.

It looked empty.

Barry frowned, and unclenched his fists. Flicking on the overhead fluorescents, he bathed the barn in a cold, white light, and blinked as his eyes adjusted and the shadows evaporated.

Nothing.

The barn looked empty, because it *was* empty. Of people, at any rate. Yet there was one significant addition to the old building's interior, and Barry's eyes fell upon it immediately.

Right in the centre of the barn, somebody had dug a large hole. A good three feet in diameter, at least.

What the hell?

Barry stepped forward slowly, and his jaw slackened. Even from several yards away, it was impossible to miss the truth: the hole hadn't been dug at all. Tell-tale furrows were cut into the dirt floor, as if the hole had been created by fingers or paws, not by a shovel. It looked more like something had tunnelled its way *out* of the earth.

Like a mole the size of a damn horse, Barry thought, and let out a nervous snort.

He fished his keys from his pocket. His keyring held a penlight, and he flicked it on and leaned into the hole slowly, half-afraid that something would leap out at him. He held his breath as the light played over a passage that appeared endless, swallowed entirely by the blackness beyond the feeble illumination provided by the tiny bulb.

For several long seconds, Barry's mind played devious tricks on him, and he felt a crawling certainty that something *was* lurking there, just beyond the cone of light, watching him hungrily; something that would at any moment streak toward him on all fours, snarling and—

There was nothing.

No movement in the strange tunnel beyond the shivering shadows cast by the light Barry held in fingers which had begun to tremble, as if they possessed some knowledge of the situation that his slow-moving mind did not.

Barry grimaced, and told his raging nerves sternly to calm the hell down.

Whatever the tunnel had been created by, it was clearly empty now.

Because it's already out there, you idiot. It tunnelled out of the ground, and now it's out there in the darkness, watching you; getting closer…

Barry's brow knitted as his thoughts began to race forward, taking on a lurching life of their own.

It?

That was a troubling development: Barry was not a man given to flights of fancy. When his mind suddenly conjured up images of bizarre creatures rising from the ground like zombies; like some bad horror movie had been made real in the ground beneath his property, he felt a nervous laugh building. The notion was ridiculous, of course.

Yet he *had* caught a glimpse of something out there in the rain, just for a moment. Something that walked upright, like a man.

He suddenly felt terribly exposed in the middle of the barn, and he spun to face the open door, tensing his muscles in readiness, certain that whatever he had seen out there would be charging toward him; some horror that had crawled out of the earth...

Beyond the gaping barn door, all he saw was darkness and rain.

He stepped outside warily, leaving the lights in the barn blazing, and swept his penlight in a wide arc. The farm buildings looked still, but the light wasn't powerful enough to be certain. Barry forced himself to focus, concentrating on listening, trying to sift through the ceaseless sound of the rain falling and the incessant whine of the wind. For a moment, he thought he heard footsteps coming toward him, and he sighed in relief when he realised it was the sound of his own pulse, hammering in his ears.

In the distant darkness, he heard a faint thud.

The front door?

Did I lock it?

Barry's muscles called a time out, and he stood there for several moments, frozen. He tried to tell himself that he was alone; just him and the rain. His tired mind was playing tricks on him, that was all. It was nothing.

But it *wasn't* nothing. Barry knew that on a fundamental level, like some long-forgotten animal instinct had suddenly awoken and screamed for his attention. The darkness felt wrong. Dangerous.

He took a couple of steps toward the distant farmhouse, set on fetching the shotgun and a powerful flashlight, and his breath caught in his throat.

He heard it.

Above the rain.

A sound that Barry abruptly realised had been ongoing for several seconds before he became conscious of it. A noise that twisted around the howl of the wind, as though trying to conceal itself.

Screaming.

At the house.

Sara normally woke an hour after him, the kids around seven, depending on how hungry they were. But someone was awake early, and they were screaming; pouring everything they had into bellowing out a noise that made Barry's soul wither.

He ran for the house without thinking, sprinting blindly through the storm, careering across a nightmare that made his mind and muscles feel oddly sluggish. Another scream cleaved the dark morning air, worse even than the first.

A different voice, Barry's mind tried to think, scrabbling for clarity. *A male voice. My boy...*

With each passing yard, his sense of dislocation from reality increased.

Time stretching taut; threatening to snap.

It took him mere seconds to return to the farmhouse; each one felt like a lifetime. When he burst through the front door, the screaming became a deafening symphony that drowned out the storm outside. The noise echoed off the walls, making the air itself vibrate. It sounded like the screaming was coming from everywhere all at once, but for Barry, there was no mistaking the source of the awful noise.

Upstairs.

The bedrooms.

Acting on autopilot, he yanked open the cupboard next to the front door, and pulled out his shotgun: an old, double-barrelled affair that would persuade any intruders that they needed to rethink their life choices. He took the stairs three at a time, inserting shells as he went, his thoughts a shapeless roar. When he reached the top of the stairs, he had a direct line of sight to the bedroom his two youngest daughters shared.

He stopped.

Tried to process it.

Couldn't.

Sara was in the bedroom with the twins. He recognised the shape of his wife immediately, even in the dark; the lines his eyes had traced lovingly for more than twenty years.

And he recognised another shape: one that was spread across the floor in ruins. Barry's teenage son. Josh had been ripped apart like wet paper; human form reduced to a slick pile of steaming meat.

Sara didn't seem to see Barry; she cowered back toward a wall, attempting to position her body as a shield in front of her young twin daughters. Trying to protect them from...

...from...

Barry had no word for it.

The creature in the room with his family was tall and impossible, a sneering, seething mass of teeth and claws. Something that Barry's mind tried to assimilate and couldn't. As he watched in stunned horror, paralysed by the sight of the thing, the creature drove its right arm forward, plunging it into Sara's chest with a sickeningly moist *snap*.

When it withdrew its hand from her ribcage, it clutched Sara's heart.

Popped the glistening muscle into its hideous mouth like a piece of candy.

And Barry was screaming along with his daughters.

Lifting the shotgun.

Aiming it at the hateful demon that had crawled from the earth to take his family.

Squeezing the trigger, and—

It looked right at him.

Right *into* him.

Eyes like claws.

Reaching into his thoughts, sinking into the surface of his mind like meathooks.

Twisting and tearing.

The shotgun blast that was supposed to tear the abomination in two never came, as if somehow the finger that cradled the trigger no longer belonged to Barry at all.

Somewhere, buried deep in the basement of Barry's mind, there existed a part of him that clung to sanity, but it finally began to collapse when his arms moved of their own volition, aiming the shotgun at his young daughters as they huddled together in abject terror.

Screaming.

Staring at him with fear and confusion that made his soul whimper.

No—

The creature allowed Barry to imbibe the last of his family's fear for a dreadful, eternal moment, before the finger that was no longer his squeezed the trigger at last.

And he saw it all through eyes that he was powerless to shut.

A liquid explosion.

Painting the wall.

Chunks of grey flesh impacting against stone with a barely audible thud as the echoing blast of the shotgun faded.

Small, precious bodies falling together; a twisted, unrecognisable mass of shredded flesh.

And the creature *chuckled*. A mirthless, rasping noise like metal grinding on metal. The soundtrack to a maniac's fevered nightmares.

The abyss of insanity finally swallowed Barry whole.

He dropped the gun.

Fell to his knees in the blood.

And the entire world was teeth.

CHAPTER FIVE

D*arkness.*
 Pain.
He broke the surface.

Gulped down a lungful of air that scorched like napalm.

Screamed.

And the black river pulled him back under, thrashing him in its jaws like a predator. Shaking his senses apart; breaking and remaking him over and over.

Carrying him toward something terrible.

And below the boiling black surface, down in the stinking undercurrent where light barely existed, he realised with horror that he was not alone.

There are hands down there; oh dear Christ, arms in the darkness. Reaching for me.

Grasping.

Pulling me down and—

CHAPTER SIX

D an awoke with a scream that emptied out of his throat like acid, and for a moment his vision swam dangerously, as if the noxious sleep was trying to take him back, like it was outraged that he had escaped its clutches, its

—hands in the darkness—

He shuddered at the blank space filling his mind. He was unable to recall anything beyond fear and shadows that seemed to cling to him, draped across him like a veil. Even his own name escaped him for several aching seconds.

When his vision cleared, he found that he was lying on his back, staring up at a ceiling of featureless metal, and all around him there was a roaring thunder. The entire world seemed to be lurching, rocking crazily, and for a moment Dan was back in the nightmare which had felt endless; back in the raging torrent. No longer sure whether he was awake or dreaming.

He sat upright, squeezing his eyes shut and gasping for air as the corrosive memories returned to him.

"Thank fuck for that," a voice said.

Dan flinched. He wasn't alone in the large, gloomy room. He didn't recognise the man's face, but he knew the voice perfectly well. He had heard it plenty.

"You've been screaming for the past ten minutes. Figured maybe that meant you were coming round. Or dying."

Herb leaned casually against the wall to Dan's right, his arms folded across his chest. He grinned broadly as Dan met his gaze.

"It's Herb, from the container. You remember the container?"

Dan began to nod, and it felt like something in his skull was loose, rolling around queasily, driving a spear of pain into the back of his head. He pressed his palms to his temples, breathing deeply and evenly, and waited for it to pass.

As he had guessed in the pitch black container, Herb was young—he would have said the guy was early-twenties, no more—and a good few inches taller than Dan himself. He was stocky, with a severe haircut that made him look like he'd just joined the military. Overall, it was a look that Dan thought he should have found intrinsically threatening, but Herb's easy grin belied his forbidding appearance.

"Yeah, I remember. How long have I been unconscious?"

"About eight hours, give or take. It'll be midday soon. Thought you were never gonna speak again," Herb said.

Dan swallowed. His throat felt dry and raw.

"I killed a man."

It wasn't an appropriate response—far from it—but it was what Dan's mind threw up. He *had* killed a man, right before the seizure had swept him away. And not just killed him; he had *executed* him on his knees.

The world tilted suddenly, lurching like a drunk, and his gut cramped. If he'd had anything left in his belly after a night spent witnessing horrors that would have turned even the strongest of stomachs, he was sure he would have puked.

The psychotic break he had always feared had finally happened. A dark corner of his mind had been reserved for the certainty that he would someday wake to find that he had done something terrible while in the grip of his illness, and here it was at last. A fragmented image of the event surfaced in his thoughts; the memory of the body of Charles Rennick twitching like a marionette as he poured bullets into it.

His therapist had warned him that he might not be ready for something as *tense* as a cruise. She hadn't known the half of it.

I'm a murderer.

The world bucked beneath him once more, and this time he did retch, and a thin string of painfully acidic bile trickled from his lips.

For a moment, all he could do was cough and gasp for air as Herb stared at him quizzically.

When the nausea passed, Dan wiped at his mouth with his wrist and scanned the room properly. It looked like he had been placed in a large steel box; he could almost have believed it was another—even larger—shipping container, but for the light spilling through a single narrow window near the ceiling.

"Where am I?"

"We're still on the trawler." Herb's brow furrowed in apparent concern. "What's wrong with you?"

Dan spat and shook his head, and suddenly, incredibly, a bitter laugh spilled from his mouth. It was the exact question he had always feared, the very reason that he had spent two years locked in his London apartment. The overwhelming certainty that strangers would be able to see straight through him, right to his broken core. To the *wrongness*. Once, being confronted by that question would have filled him with a paralysing anxiety—maybe even severe enough to induce a full-blown panic attack.

"I'm not *normal*," Dan said through gritted teeth, biting down on the hysteria that wanted to burst from him. "That's what's wrong with me. What the fuck's wrong with *you*? Daddy issues?"

Herb's expression hardened, and Dan's eyes widened in shock.

Did I really just say that?

"Not anymore," Herb said sourly. He threw a bundle of material at Dan. "Some fresh clothes. We are leaving soon, so get ready."

We? Dan thought ominously as he examined the clothes. A heavy sweater and jeans. He looked up at Herb.

"Leave to go where?"

"I live on a...compound of sorts. Thanks to my father's obsession, it's probably the safest place we can go until we figure out our next step."

There it was again. *We.*

Our.

"Safest?"

"Steel shutters, thick walls. UV lights in the grounds. When the place is on lockdown, it's practically a fortress. And if there is *any* information in the texts about people who are able to resist vampires, that's where we'll find it.

In my father's library. Best thing we can do is get there fast, and seal ourselves in before we run out of daylight. Hope you're not afraid of flying."

"Flying?"

Dan's mouth asked that last one on autopilot, and he rebuked himself bitterly. He sounded pathetic, timidly batting Herb's words back as feeble questions. He began to shake his head firmly. The conversation was heading down a path that could only lead to a very bad place. He had to get a grip on it, fast.

"Yeah," Herb said. "Trawler's too slow. As soon as we're close enough, we'll take the chopper—"

"There is no *we*," Dan interrupted, surprising himself with the authority in his tone. "I'm going home, and then probably to prison, unless you people plan to kill me. Whatever it is you want to do, I want no part of it."

Herb looked surprised, as though he hadn't even considered what Dan might *want*.

"Yeah," Dan continued, "I was listening in the container. Vampires rising, ancient oaths, Hell on earth and human sacrifice. Insane; every last bit of it. I don't know who or what you think I am, but I assure you, I'm not it. I just want to go *home*."

Herb blinked.

"You can't go home," he said softly. "Don't you get it? You're special. Important. You killed two vampires. You don't just do that and go *home*. Home no longer exists for you. How could it?"

Dan clenched his fists in frustration.

"I got lucky, don't *you* get it? Those things weren't expecting me to attack them and they hesitated. That's all there was to it."

"Except that they *don't* hesitate," Herb snapped, "and

in records stretching back thousands of years, nobody has *ever* got lucky; not once. So what's special about you, huh?"

"The only thing that was special about me had her fucking head torn off right in front of my face. If I'm *special*, how come I couldn't stop that?"

Herb shook his head.

"It doesn't matter. Whatever your life was before—it's over now. The others will come for you, and one way or another, they'll find you. You're too important."

"Others?"

Another pathetic question.

Dammit!

Herb stared at him thoughtfully for a moment before responding.

"This is a lot bigger than my family. There are nests across the world, families just like mine. Our ancestors realised the value of cooperation a long time ago. The Order is the product of that realisation. They—we—have people everywhere. Resources you can't begin to understand, and when they find out about the Oceanus, they'll be coming. Going home and pretending this isn't happening is not an option."

Dan stared at him dubiously. "So it's a global conspiracy, then? A vast secret which *hundreds* of people are keeping? Or is it *thousands*?"

He made no effort to conceal the disbelief in his tone. Dan had spent two years locked in his apartment, and that equalled plenty of time spent on the internet. The web was full of conspiracy theories; it was almost impossible to avoid them. He didn't necessarily disbelieve them all, but still, he had serious doubts that a secret such as the one Herb described could be kept for so long, by so many people. It just wasn't possible. Maybe it had been centuries earlier, but now, when information was so freely available?

Herb caught the sarcasm. "You think being tasked with killing thousands of people doesn't offer opportunities? Families like mine have been around for centuries, benefitting from their relationship with the vampires. People keep secrets for two reasons. One: keeping the secret is advantageous to them personally. Two: they fear the consequences if their silence is not maintained. If *both* of those statements are true, who *wouldn't* hold their tongue?"

Herb shrugged, as if there was nothing more to say on the matter.

Dan shook his head. "What possible *benefit* could there be to what you people do?"

"Money. Power. You know how many politicians were given complementary tickets for the Oceanus? How many heads of corporations? Celebrities? Even a member of the royal family. If you want to murder someone important, what better way than to put them at the scene of some tragic disaster? Then they are just another poor victim of circumstance."

Dan rubbed at his forehead.

"I'm not following."

"This is how things have always been done," Herb said with an impatient sigh. "You know all those wacko theories about the people lurking in the shadows, controlling the world?"

"Sure," Dan said wryly. "The Illuminati."

Herb snorted. "Call it whatever you want. Whatever label you come up with will be about as accurate as the word *vampire*. We refer to ourselves as the Order precisely because the word is meaningless. Virtually every family within the Order has accrued wealth and influence you can't imagine. *Old* money. Power handed down for generations. When the vampires rise, the families under their control rise right along with them. My father called it a truce; our family's tragic *duty*. I call it an alliance, and I want no fucking part of it."

Herb took a deep breath and paused, apparently aware that he was beginning to rant.

"But we haven't got time for this, not now. I have to get you somewhere safe before it gets dark."

Dan spread his arms wide and gestured at the hull of the trawler.

"Seems like I'm *safe* right here, if what you say is true."

"Here's fine," Herb said with a grin, "though you might not think so when you start to get hungry. Besides, search and rescue will be headed in our direction soon enough, along with just about every news outlet on the planet, and I doubt even the Order has enough influence to cover up what they're gonna find. The Oceanus was probably declared missing hours ago. We were supposed to draw the authorities in the wrong direction once it was done," he shrugged, "but the days of the Rennick family keeping secrets are over."

Dan shook his head wearily. Herb had sounded crazy in the container, but now that he was out and apparently running the show, he sounded even crazier.

He thought about replying that he needed his medication; that he had a *condition,* dammit; that he had to go home and seal himself up in the only place he felt safe before he hurt himself or anybody else, but he clamped his lips shut. There was nothing to gain from going through it now, when he was trapped at sea.

Play along, he thought. *Just until you get your feet on dry land.*

And then, run.

"Follow me," Herb said, and he turned, striding away from the freezer hold, leaving the door open.

Dan watched him go, and slipped on the sweater and a one-size-too-big pair of jeans, Herb's words running through his mind like a fever.

Afraid of flying, he thought, and his face twisted into a rueful grimace. He was supposed to be afraid of just about *everything*, but now the fear that had been a constant in his life ever since the knife attack felt...unstable somehow, like the fury that had descended on him aboard the Oceanus had unbalanced it. He still felt a flicker of the old anxiety: apprehension at being trapped on the boat with a group of strangers who were apparently insane, but there was something else, too, right down there in that broken core. Something new.

It felt terrifyingly like anticipation; a thread of something like *eagerness* that ran through his nerves.

He knew then what the loose sensation in his head was. Something had changed, and he had woken up *different* in some way he couldn't yet fathom; altered irrevocably.

As he started after Herb, he couldn't help but wonder if *different* meant *better*.

Or worse.

———

JEREMY WATCHED DAN BELLAMY FOLLOW HERB UP

onto the deck, and when both men were out of sight, he stepped into the freezer hold, easing the sliding door shut and wincing as the rusting metal runners squealed softly.

He'd always felt a connection with Herb. His father had never forgiven the kid for killing his mother as he entered the world, and the wrong side of Charles Rennick was a bad place to be for anybody, let alone a young child. Herb grew to be an isolated character at the compound, tolerated by his brothers and despised by his father; unable to form any sort of friendship with the initiates of the Order who worshipped his blood like it ran through a king's veins.

But the boy *was* reckless. Charles had been right about that, though even he might have been surprised to learn just *how* right. Charles' primary concern had been that Herb would *run*; that without him the EMP device would not get built and the operation would be a failure before the Oceanus even entered international waters. *That* was supposed to be the worst-case scenario, not that Herb would return to the Sea Shanty with no vampires and a bullet with his father's name etched on it.

The operation had been a complete disaster, and now Herb seemed intent on making the situation worse.

Jeremy had hated lying to him.

He crossed the hold, kneeling at a low ventilation grate, and prised it open.

Reaching inside, he pulled out the satellite phone that he had hidden immediately following Charles' execution. Thanks to Herb's insistence on placing Bellamy in the hold and locking the door, Jeremy hadn't been able to retrieve the phone for several frustrating hours.

So much time already wasted.

He paused for a moment, listening carefully to make

sure there were no footsteps headed in his direction. After a few seconds, he switched the phone on and punched a number into the keypad.

The compound needed to be warned, but not just about the possibility that the nest in southern England might rise in a matter of hours. They also needed to be warned that Herb had taken charge; that he needed to be controlled before he threw a light on the Order for the whole world to see.

The phone rang.

And rang.

Jeremy frowned.

Hung up.

Dialled again.

Still no answer.

It could mean only one thing. There was no way a ringing phone at the compound would go unanswered, not on this of all days. Not unless they *couldn't* answer.

The vampires had risen already. Jeremy knew it was the truth as soon as the thought occurred; felt it squirming in his gut like a tapeworm.

How could that be possible? How could the vampires know that their kin had died? The creatures had psychic abilities far beyond Jeremy's understanding, but could they really communicate with each other over such vast distances?

Jeremy terminated the call again, and for a few moments, he just stood there, staring at the wall and seeing a dark future written in the dull, dented metal.

There was nothing else for it. Herb wanted to rally humanity to fight the monsters, but there was no way his story would be believed. Not until the vampires rose and splattered the truth across the TV news. By then, it would be too late.

He gritted his teeth. It was daylight back in the UK now. If the vampires had surfaced in the night, they would surely have retreated underground until nightfall. Just a matter of hours. Everything was moving too fast, and Herb was dangerously volatile. Matters had to be taken out of his hands.

He dropped his gaze to the keypad once more, punching in a different number. This time, the phone rang just once before a voice answered in a rich American accent.

"Yes?"

Sorry, Herb.

"I need to speak to Jennifer Craven," Jeremy said.

CHAPTER SEVEN

———————————

J ennifer Craven terminated the unexpected call and felt a thrill coursing through her body like nothing she had experienced in sixteen long years; not since she first peered into a hole in the ground in northern Kentucky and saw the truth staring back at her.

The British man on the other end of the line had sounded scared, as well he might, but more importantly, what he had told her confirmed as fact something that she had long suspected: none of the other families that the Order comprised really *did* have any idea that the vampires could be killed, or that there might once have existed humans who were able to resist their will.

Jeremy Pruitt had sounded shocked and uncertain as he informed her that the Rennick nest in England had demanded sacrifice, and that the sacrifice had failed in the most spectacular way possible. The discovery that the buried gods were mortal had come as a monumental surprise to the English; that much was clear from the man's tone.

Jennifer had fabricated a little surprise of her own for his benefit.

Unlike the Rennicks, the Craven family had nurtured suspicions about the vampires that stretched back centuries, ever since one of Jennifer's distant ancestors had discovered a clay tablet buried in northern Africa. That tablet, which appeared to depict a human striking down a vampire beneath a word which translated roughly into English as *hermetic*, was assumed for a long time by her forebears to be simply a product of hope; just some poor barely-evolved bastard doodling a daydream before the monsters took him. Yet, when Jennifer's own father had the tablet carbon dated back in the eighties, the scientist he had *persuaded* to carry out the test reported that the clay had definitely been buried at around 5,000 B.C.

Such a discovery would have made the scientific community at large take a keen interest in the tablet, had the scientist who collected the data been permitted to live long enough to share it. The earliest known etchings on clay were dated at around 3,000 B.C., and current academic thinking on the first human civilizations would have been turned on its head in an instant by the discovery that recorded history was at least two thousand years wide of the mark.

More importantly, as far as the Craven family was concerned, that carbon dating test had confirmed that the tablet was the earliest known written record of the vampires by a distance. No part of the Order claimed to possess any artefact more than five thousand years old, though of course they would keep such a discovery to themselves. After all, there was a slim chance that any object which was that old might even contain something close to the *truth*.

The word *hermetic* didn't appear anywhere else in the known texts, and its meaning remained shrouded in mystery. No matter how thoroughly the Craven family searched for *anything* that might corroborate the story the clay tablet wanted to tell, nothing had ever been discovered.

Until a Princeton professor made an ill-advised phonecall from Kentucky, and Jennifer Craven herself saw the bones.

It was all the confirmation that she required.

Vampires *could* be struck down by humans, just as that ancient tablet had suggested, and for some reason, some ancient civilization had buried a man who actually did just that right alongside his monstrous victim. Perhaps the man had died of injuries sustained in the battle with the vampire, and the burial had been a celebration; perhaps that ancient people had wanted to warn future generations of something, who knew.

Who *cared?*

For a man to kill a vampire with a *hatchet* could only mean one thing: the vampires had not been able to control him in the way they did everyone else. *He* was the Hermetic. The word literally meant 'sealed off,' and that's exactly what the ancient vampire slayer must have been: his mind sealed away from the vampires' grasp; untouchable.

The trouble was that there had been no record of any such person having existed in the past seven thousand years. Maybe the hatchet-man was part of a race that had long since died out, his genes containing some treasure that extinction had buried, never to be found again.

Finding out whether that was true or not would have been all but impossible, given that the only way to know whether a person could resist the psychic assault of a vampire was to put them in front of one.

Jennifer had long ago filed away her curiosity about the possibility that Hermetics might actually have existed, because there was another, more pressing problem.

She was barren. The sole remaining Craven. A long time ago, she had attempted to conceive with several of the men at the ranch, but her efforts were for nothing. Finally, a doctor revealed the terrible truth: she would never have children. Her name would die with her, and some other bloodline would take control of the Order in America.

Unable to further her line, Jennifer's thoughts turned to her legacy. The legacy of the entire Craven family; a crushing burden on her shoulders. Despite being only thirty-eight, she thought about her remaining years constantly; how to imprint her name onto the Order so that it would *never* fade from history.

The rest of the Order was so focused on the past that it rarely thought to look to its future. But Jennifer did, and she saw trouble on the horizon, approaching like twister season.

As far as she was aware, there hadn't been a vampire rising anywhere in the world for more than a century, and in that time, the world had changed greatly.

Way back in 1999, Jennifer's father had seen the future, and he predicted that it was a cellphone in every pocket and a camera on every street corner. He hadn't lived to see just how right he had been. By 2015, there was a *camera* in every pocket, and the world had become obsessed with filming itself and sharing the result indiscriminately.

The days of keeping the existence of vampires a

secret were coming to an end, one way or another. Unless the next rising took place in some extremely remote part of the world, the chances of any one family successfully covering it up were very slim.

The last recorded rising had taken place in rural Russia, consuming an entire village; leaving a ghost town. If something like that happened in the modern era of *always on* and *rolling news*, the truth would travel around the world like wildfire. If it happened in a densely-populated area like northern Europe or parts of Asia, the next rising would probably be streaming live on *Youtube* within minutes.

What if the next rising occurred in her own homeland? What if—God forbid—the Great Nest rumoured to be buried deep beneath Yellowstone was next? North America hadn't seen an awakening for more than five hundred years; as far as Jennifer was concerned, that meant the country was overdue, in the same way scientists claimed that Earth was overdue a massive asteroid strike. Not a matter of *if*, but *when.*

It was just a matter of time, and the possibility that Hermetics might once have existed was not important. The only thing that mattered was accepting that the true —global—vampire rising was as inevitable as the onset of winter, and figuring out how to twist that fact to her advantage.

Hermetics or not, vampires *could* die.

What she needed was an army. The Order remained as small as possible in other countries, trying to conceal its importance, but if Jennifer was right, and the next vampire awakening was the equivalent of The Big One, secrecy would no longer matter. Strength would.

Shortly after the turn of the millennium and the

passing of her father, Jennifer began to build the American arm of the Order into the world's largest underground religion. The huge Colorado ranch which served as her base of operations had been expanded several times, and was now home to almost fifteen-hundred people. New initiates were young, of course, and subjected to anything up to a year of psychological and physical abuse, coupled with enormous quantities of LSD, before their loyalty was tested to determine their readiness to learn the truth and ascend to the position of cleric.

The test itself was simple and, so far, infallible. Two initiates, one knife. It was an equation that always equalled one devout believer. The only way to join the Order was to walk through a storm of blood, and nothing guaranteed a person's obedience quite like making them kill.

Jennifer's army grew slowly, and she waited.

For sixteen long years.

Until her phone rang, and an anxious-sounding British man introduced himself as Jeremy Pruitt, and said he needed her help.

JENNIFER STARED AT THE NOW-SILENT PHONE FOR A long time, running through Pruitt's words in her head over and over, until their ramifications began to solidify in her thoughts. She already knew that vampires could be killed, of course, but now they actually *had been*. She hadn't truly expected to witness such an event within her lifetime, and certainly not to discover that when it happened, it wasn't even the headline news.

A *living* Hermetic had been discovered, and had survived the encounter with the vampires. Even better, the English Order already had its hands on him.

The potential ramifications of *that* refused to settle properly; they sloshed around her skull, full of messy possibility, lighting her up with anticipation.

Judging by what Pruitt had told her, the Order was finished in the UK: now led by an emotional boy who sounded like he suffered from some sort of hero complex —or simply wanted to die. Charles Rennick and his immediate successors were dead, and Herbert Rennick had no idea what he might be transporting, how important this man Dan Bellamy could be. Rennick was heading back to England, apparently following some ill-considered notion of blowing the whistle and letting the world know that vampires existed. He was, Pruitt said, determined to rally the world to *fight* them.

The boy was a fool. Killing vampires had already ensured that—at a minimum—the remainder of the English nest would rise to retaliate. England was one of the most heavily-surveilled countries on the planet. The secret was out, all right. The world just hadn't noticed it yet. But it would, and there *would* be fighting. For survival.

It was only a matter of time.

According to Pruitt, the remaining vampires in England had expected their kin to be returned to them before dawn; the deadline had long since passed. The vampires would not act in daylight, of course, which meant that Jennifer had around seven or eight hours to play with—and it would take at least six of those to actually get a team across the Atlantic. There was every chance that—even with a Gulfstream jet to make the journey—she would not be able to get a team to the UK before darkness began to fall.

She had to act fast.

She nodded to herself and picked up the phone, dialling a four-digit internal number.

Her call was answered immediately.

"Get a team together, Mr Mancini," Jennifer said. "The best we have."

"Elimination or extraction?"

"A little of each, I think."

Mancini grunted.

"Where are we going?"

"*You* are going to the UK. To England."

"You're not coming with us?"

He sounded surprised. Jennifer had always enjoyed what Mancini sardonically labelled *field trips* before.

"Not this time. The world is about to catch fire, Mr Mancini. I'll be putting the ranch into lockdown as soon as you leave."

Another grunt. He sounded pissed off at her insistence on addressing him so formally. Given their history, that wasn't so surprising. Pissing him off was, after all, the reason that she did it in the first place.

"How long?" he snapped.

Jennifer checked her watch.

"I want your wheels up in thirty minutes, tops, and, Mr Mancini?"

He sighed heavily.

"Yeah?"

"I want you to understand this up front: there's a very good chance you'll be...uh, *going in hot*, okay?"

Mancini paused just long enough for Jennifer to hear the vague concern that lurked behind his silence. She knew full well that Mancini wasn't a true believer in the existence of vampires, and it hadn't ever mattered before: he was a hired gun who had no problem following orders which might lead to morally dubious outcomes, and he knew how to keep his mouth shut. That was more than enough to help with keeping the clerics and initiates at the ranch in line.

Yet this was different; belief *mattered* now. She trusted in Mancini and his combat expertise implicitly, but she knew that no amount of battlefield experience could have prepared either him or his men for what they might be faced with if they were still on English soil when night fell.

Bravado and training wouldn't save him, not then. Belief might—if it helped Mancini to understand that there were some situations in which fleeing wasn't just the best option; it was the *only* option.

"Going in hot," Mancini repeated, sounding dubious.

"There is a very strong possibility that England will suffer a full-scale vampire rising in around seven hours. I need you to find and extract a man before that happens, and I don't expect it will be easy. I know what you believe, but you need to believe this: if you engage the vampires, you *will* die. Trust me. Stay in the light."

Mancini coughed.

"Yeah, all right. Understood. Who's the target?"

CHAPTER EIGHT

B ad things happened to homeless people all the time.
Sam Thompson understood that depressingly obvious fact only too well, but even from a distance, when he looked at the bridge, some dark instinct tugged at him and he felt a twinge of alarm.

The place looked completely deserted.

The bridge, crossed by the rail line that led toward central London to the north, was a regular meeting spot for Morden's fast-growing homeless population, and Sam would have expected to see *someone* there at midday. At the very least, there should have been *one* person under the bridge: the one Sam was supposed to be meeting.

He saw nobody, and checked his watch. The face was cracked, but it still kept time. When he'd checked it five minutes earlier, it had informed him that he was late. It still said the same thing.

So where the hell is he?

The bridge was wide, spanning a patch of wasteland and a couple of derelict buildings. The space beneath was wreathed in shadows, but it was immediately obvious that there was no one at all waiting for him.

Dammit.

Sam frowned and slowed his steps a little as his thoughts raced ahead.

He travelled to the bridge a couple of times a week, usually to pick up heroin. The guy who he had been buying off recently—a white-haired ex-rocker for whom the seventies had never really ended—called his product *Brain Damage*, but Sam was under no illusions. It wasn't high-grade stuff: anyone who bought beneath the bridge knew that going in. What Sam got from the bridge was always the same. Not mind-blowing; not poison. When you had a habit to maintain, the *not-poison* part quickly became important. Far more than any desire for quality, at any rate. Quality drugs were for those people who still had jobs.

Sam had a job, of sorts.

Well, he had a way to earn money.

And now that he had some to spend, Brain Damage-guy was nowhere to be seen.

Fucking drug dealers. Untrustworthy bastards, every last one of—

Sam's heart fluttered. If there was nobody under the bridge to sell to him, he only had one other option. A man by the name of Trev, who never went anywhere near the bridge, and who had promised a few months back that if he ever set eyes on him again, Sam would regret it *big time.*

Sam had believed him. Trev wasn't a guy for making jokes.

Shit.

He quickened his pace, moving across a strip of

patchy grass behind a supermarket car park. It was lunchtime, and the store was busy. Several shoppers glared at him as they loaded groceries into their cars. His clothes were a dead giveaway: filthy and tattered, hanging off a frame that had nudged the needle from *slim* up to *unhealthy* in recent months. They probably thought he was planning to steal a car or mug them.

His cheeks burned, and he looked away, forcing himself not to acknowledge their stares.

Moved quicker still.

By the time he reached the bridge, he was running unsteadily, panting heavily. He hadn't exercised in a long time, but it wasn't his lack of fitness that made him gasp for air. It was the growing need in his body; the anxiety which spiked at the thought that there was nobody to buy from.

Sam hadn't taken a hit in a couple of days, and the churning in his gut was quickly becoming intolerable. If he had to wait too much longer, the growing tension in his nerves threatened to blossom, becoming an insufferable agony. He jogged into the shadows beneath the bridge, and when his eyes adjusted to the sudden change in light, he saw that it wasn't deserted at all, and his train of thought derailed.

He hit the brakes so hard that he fell on his arse, jarring the breath from his lungs.

Yeah, bad things happened to homeless people.

But not like *this*.

The area beneath the bridge, next to a skeletal building, looked like a slaughterhouse. There had been several people taking shelter from the rain there by the look of it.

And something had ripped them apart.

It was a massacre.

Sam figured there had to be at least seven or eight bodies on the ground, each and every one missing significant pieces, as though they had been set upon by some pack of wild animals.

I'm the first on the scene, Sam thought dumbly and, for a moment, he was so struck by the ridiculousness of the situation that he was sure he was hallucinating. Withdrawal symptoms beginning to kick in.

That had to be it.

He squeezed his eyes shut and took a deep breath.

When he reopened them, the bodies were still there. It was like a scene from a damn zombie movie. Sam couldn't even begin to understand what had torn the homeless people apart, but he didn't need to. This was *not* a place to hang around asking questions.

He glanced around, feeling his skin prickle. His eyes hadn't deceived him: he was definitely alone. The building in front of him was no more than a shell; he could clearly see that it was empty.

He struggled to his feet, choking back the urge to retch again when he saw a severed head staring right at him, the skin flayed away to reveal the muscle and tendon beneath, and he recognised the wispy white hair, now matted and darkened by streaks of gore.

It looked like Brain Damage-guy was smiling at him, his ruined face split in a horrific grin, but the worst part was the eyes, *oh dear, sweet Jesus, his eyes...*

Sam had never seen eyes so wide, so marked by naked terror. Brain Damage-guy had been so scared when he died that it looked like his face hadn't even been capable of registering the pain.

Sam turned to run for the distant supermarket.

And suddenly his legs just...refused to move.

You can still get what you came for.

The voice of his addiction, unspooling in his mind. Crooning a siren's song that he was powerless to resist.

He turned back to face the atrocity, gritting his teeth and biting back the urge to retch again.

Brain Damage-guy's head is there. *So where are his legs? Where are his pockets?*

Sam saw a *lot* of legs tangled on the ground, and the prospect of rifling through clothes caked in human offal made his stomach twist. Some distant alarm began to sound in his head, like his soul was shrieking at him not to allow himself to sink to this new low. That it would lead only to darkness.

I could just check a couple *of bodies.*

He scanned the hideous mess.

Maybe the ones to the right, which looked almost intact. Even if none of those limbs belonged to Brain Damage-guy, there was still a chance he'd find something. Perhaps some meth. Hell, even some fucking weed would take the jagged edge off the sickness he felt growing inside him.

No one will know. Just check their pockets and get the hell out of here. Two minutes, tops.

For a moment, he felt like he couldn't move, torn between the almost overwhelming desire to run from the horror under the bridge and the surging narcotic need lighting him up like a cigarette; burning through him steadily.

If there *was* a bag of Brain Damage just...*sitting there*, it would be a criminal waste to leave it. It's not like the poor bastards torn apart in the shadows needed it, and when the police discovered the carnage, they would destroy any drugs they found without a second thought. Or 'confiscate' them as 'evidence.'

Sam shot another glance at the distant supermarket.

If you're going to do it, do it now, you idiot. Don't just stand here gawping. Waiting to get caught.

He took an uncertain step toward the nearest body.

Tried to visualise himself actually rooting around in the wet remains. What kind of person could fumble around the exposed innards of other human beings? How low could a person possibly sink in their need for a fix?

He tried to picture himself doing what he knew he should do; running as fast as he could. Never looking back.

Pictured a fat bag of powder instead.

And suddenly he was walking forward quickly on autopilot, the decision taken. The addiction won. It always did.

The bridge was high, the underside laced by struts. The walls offered a series of alcoves - prime real estate for the homeless people who sheltered there overnight. Those were always the first spots to be taken. Sam studied them cautiously as he moved, imagining that some demented killer was lurking there in the shadows, impossible for him to see.

Watching him approach.

There was no movement, of course. He was alone beneath the bridge.

Do this quickly, he thought, and he ran to the nearest body, patting down a pair of trousers which were soaked through and sticky to the touch. Empty. He moved on quickly to the next body, kneeling on something slippery and soft, gagging as he tried not to think about what it might have been.

Again he searched through pockets and again, he found them empty.

His pulse raced almost painfully. Every second he spent among the bodies felt like he was taking a bigger and bigger risk; each body searched, another round in a game of Russian roulette.

This is crazy, Sam. Get the fuck out of here. Do you know what will happen if the cops turn up and find you here?

He patted the next couple of bodies down quickly—too quickly, almost, to be certain their pockets were empty—and shot another glance at the distant supermarket.

And a bomb detonated in his central nervous system.

Movement in his peripheral vision.

Close.

He looked up into the shadows, certain that he had seen something moving toward him. Moving *above* him.

What the fu—

Sam's eyes widened even as his left hand closed around a promising lump in a sickeningly moist pocket; a small bag of something that had been so important only moments earlier.

There *was* something up there, clinging to the struts beneath the bridge, hanging in the shadows like a bat.

Something *big*.

Watching him intently.

Sam squinted.

Saw it clearly.

Should have run, he thought, and his sanity began to dissolve, melted by the heat of terrible eyes which glowed a furious crimson in the gloom, puncturing his soul like scalding needles.

Taking him.

Sam's body walked away from the bridge at a casual pace. By the time his feet reached the entrance of the busy supermarket and his left hand pulled out the small flick-knife he always carried for emergencies, Sam was long gone; broken and banished to a shrieking cell in the deepest recess of his mind.

Still, his body carried on, piloted by another; muscles moved by something dark and terrible and unfathomable.

It wanted to play.

PART TWO

CHAPTER NINE

O*ne day, you will remember how to enjoy new experiences.*

The words of Dan's therapist came back to him as Herb led the way onto the deck of the trawler. Twenty-four hours after his first cruise began, and around seven hours after he had committed his first murder, Dan was about to experience yet another first: a helicopter ride, in the company of disciples of an insane cult which genuinely believed that the world was about to end at the hands of vampires, and which had, to all intents and purposes, kidnapped him.

Maybe that counted as two *firsts*. Even three.

Either way, his therapist had been dead wrong.

He stepped out onto the deck, blinking at the grey sunlight filtering through the clouds, and did his best to remain invisible. It didn't work; he felt the eyes of every man on the boat boring into him. The crew—most of whom looked bizarrely young; some even younger than Herb himself—regarded him with open hostility and more than a little fear.

Herb led him past the battered container to the helicopter which took up the remainder of the foredeck. He waved half-hearted introductory gestures at the crew as he passed by them, reeling off names, but Dan didn't try to commit them to memory. There was a Jay, a Stephen, a Christian, a Lawrence, but he couldn't have put a face to any of those names if asked. He didn't want to.

"And that's Jeremy," Herb said finally, pointing at a man standing at the bow, who was by a distance the oldest person on the trawler. Jeremy didn't speak or acknowledge Herb's gesture. He stared at Dan across the deck, studying him as a surgeon might study a patient's wounds, as though trying somehow to *solve* him.

Dan stared back for a moment, but it was he who blinked first. Jeremy looked twice his age, but he was large and appeared physically fit, with stern eyes under a heavy brow. Staring down a man like that...well, it just wasn't in his repertoire.

He turned away, taking a deep breath, and gazed out across the ocean. For a moment, watching the hypnotic rolling grey waves of the Atlantic, he almost became convinced that he was hallucinating, and he rubbed at the wounds on his chest, trying to wake himself up; suddenly certain that he was actually lying in a hospital bed back in London, and that Elaine was at his bedside, waiting anxiously for him to wake from his latest seizure-induced coma.

Almost.

He shook his head, trying to clear it. Herb was somewhere behind him and was still talking, of course, but Dan had lost the thread of whatever he was saying. He glanced around the crew again, counting, before returning his gaze to the ocean.

He frowned.

There were a dozen men on the boat in total, including himself. A further four of the strange extended Rennick family had already perished, either at the hands of the vampires, or Dan himself. Judging by what Herb said, there were even more waiting for his return back at 'the compound.' How was it possible that all of these people shared the same delusion?

He tried to get a handle on the bizarre relationship that the crew had with Herb, but could not fathom it. The people he saw on the trawler were young—with that one exception—and looked uniformly nervous. Yet it was almost as if they subverted their fear in deference to Herb. They looked at him as Dan imagined a peasant might have looked upon royalty back in the Middle Ages. When Herb approached them, Dan saw the men that he referred to as 'clerics' straighten their slumped shoulders, trying vainly to conceal their obvious fear.

Dan could hardly bring himself to believe that it was actually happening. The creatures that had attacked the Oceanus had been bad enough, but the idea that the extraordinary tale of a secret history which first Edgar and then Herb had told him was actually *true*? Vampires that had been feeding on humans in secret for thousands of years, aided by a global network of cultists?

It was just too much. It couldn't be real.

Couldn't.

Yet the look on the faces of Herb's clerics left him in no doubt that *they* believed it. And hadn't Dan seen them with his own eyes? Felt the thick blood washing over his hands as he decapitated one? What else could the monsters be? Did it even matter what Herb called them?

This, Dan decided, was what insanity really was.

Torn equally between two competing beliefs; unable to trust fully in either. Logic told him that he was back in London in that hospital bed with doctors frantically trying to wake him, but his senses told a different story. Logic—no matter how compelling—mattered little when he could taste the sea air and feel the pain of the slashes across his chest. When he could vividly remember the snarling teeth and the talons and the ship of blood—

He shook the memories that threatened to overwhelm him away. He had been staring at the ocean for a long time. He turned back to face the deck, taking a deep breath.

Herb was still talking to the crew, apparently declaring that they were within range, and Dan tuned in to what he was saying. They would take the chopper the rest of the way, and plant charges to sink the trawler behind them. Speed was of the essence now, Herb said. Getting the Sea Shanty back to the UK was taking too long. Already it was gone midday, and soon enough the light would be fading. *If* the vampires were going to rise, Herb continued, it would happen soon.

"That's the only thing we know for certain," Herb said. "We have time, but not enough. So get moving."

Dan watched without emotion as the crew began to filter onto the helicopter, obeying without question or hesitation.

What the hell is wrong with these people?

Herb gestured at him to board the chopper with a friendly smile that set his teeth on edge. *He's almost acting like I have a choice*, Dan thought, and his temperature rose, just a little.

He took a calming breath through gritted teeth and nodded, making his way toward the chopper as a kid who looked barely old enough to drive swung himself into the pilot's seat.

My first helicopter ride.

As the vehicle lifted off, leaving a ship primed with C4 behind it, beginning the two-hour-plus trip to the Rennick compound, Dan wondered what his next new experience might be.

And how much damage it would cause.

CHAPTER TEN

When Herb had said that he lived on a 'compound,' Dan had pictured something militaristic: featureless buildings surrounded by an electrified fence, maybe; perhaps even some underground complex, the sort of place a villain in a *James Bond* movie might call home.

What he saw, when the chopper finally flew over what Herb called *our land*, was nothing like that. The Rennick compound was huge, buried deep in a thick forest that Herb said was protected green-belt land: no developer had been permitted to build on it for centuries; nor ever would. Dan hadn't thought it was possible to find such a wilderness hidden in the crowded south of England.

The buildings themselves were even more of a surprise: Dan did see several modern-looking pre-fabricated structures, but they were all clustered around a spectacular mansion that had to be three hundred years old at least. As the helicopter swung around it, he thought the house looked more like a castle, or some vast museum:

a huge, imposing stone structure liberally sprinkled with Gothic trimmings. Buttresses and delicate arches and sneering gargoyles that had been carved into the walls; they looked like they were leaping from the house, desperately trying to escape the clutches of the stone that birthed them.

Dan's heart sank when he saw the place, not because of how oppressive and intimidating it appeared, but because, even from the air, he could tell immediately that it would be very difficult to escape from.

Once they were travelling over England, the familiarity of the landscape had allowed him to feel a spark of hope; of normality, and he had started to daydream about fleeing the moment the chopper set down. But even if he *could* somehow slip away from the watchful gaze of Herb and his followers, the compound looked *so* isolated. There had to be a road leading from the place somewhere but he couldn't see it through the chopper's narrow windows. All he could see was trees. If he was going to make a run for it, he would have to do so blindly; fleeing through unfamiliar countryside as night began to fall.

He didn't know whether to believe Herb's tale of a nest of vampires rising to avenge their dead at sunset or not, but the notion of finding some way to escape, only to end up stumbling around the forest, lost and alone in the gathering dark, made a shudder course through him.

Like it or not, with daylight fading quickly, the only way forward was to go into the house, but he had no intention of staying a minute longer than he had to. He told himself that at the first opportunity, he would slip away—presuming that neither Herb nor his strange band of followers decided to physically restrain him—and find a way to get home. It was all that mattered now: retreating to the apartment, taking his pills, praying that the medicine would somehow knit together the yawning chasms forming in his head before he lost his sanity entirely.

"Circle it again," Jeremy barked suddenly. It was the first time the older man had spoken. During the helicopter ride, Dan thought Jeremy had looked increasingly agitated, and he had tried to avoid meeting his gaze as much as possible.

"What? Why?" Herb lifted his voice from the co-pilot's seat.

"We need to know that it's clear, Herb. We have more than enough time for that. It won't be dark for at least an hour."

Herb looked like he wanted to argue the point, but decided against it.

"Fine," he said, staring at Jeremy quizzically. "Go around again, and then take us down."

THE CHOPPER TOUCHED DOWN ON A SMALL HELIPAD set alongside a long, flat building which looked like an enormous garage, a hundred yards or so away from the main house. As the engine began to wind down, a pensive silence settled over the men gathered inside.

The Rennick compound looked deserted.

Dan watched as Herb dropped his eyes to his wrist.

"Almost three-thirty," he said without emotion. "We have around seventy minutes until sundown. Maybe less."

He squinted up at the gloomy sky.

Seventy minutes, Dan thought bleakly. It was like there was a timer in everybody's head, counting down toward the moment when darkness would arrive and bring the monsters. Yet despite that terrible ticking, nobody moved a muscle.

They all just sat in the helicopter, staring at the distant house.

Dan followed their gaze.

"What's wrong?"

Herb scratched at his jaw, his expression thoughtful.

"What's wrong is that there are around forty people in that house, and all of them should be pretty frantic about not hearing from us."

"And?"

"And a helicopter just landed on their front lawn," Herb said, "but I don't see a single person at the windows."

Dan studied the enormous main house. Herb was right: it was eerily quiet. The tension in the chopper became a bloated, terrible presence, and it suddenly struck him that the vehicle carried an exclusively male crew. Based on what Herb had told him about the make-up of the people who lived at the compound, at that very moment the others were all thinking about their wives and sisters and daughters and mothers.

All wondering.

And in the distance, through the rain and below the darkening afternoon sky, the mansion waited.

CHAPTER ELEVEN

I t was the smell which hit Herb first, the unmistakable odour that washed across him immediately as he pushed on the front door of the mansion, and it swung open easily.

Metallic, thick; hanging on the air like a threat.

The stink of blood.

Herb could almost taste it.

The rest of the group paused behind him. The smell was an invisible boundary: it worked on a genetic level, like the stench of so much human blood conveyed a simple biological message which triggered an automatic muscular response.

Stop.

The mansion's main reception area was huge, a cavernous space stretching back more than sixty feet to meet twin staircases at the back of the room which wound their way up to the east and west wings of the mansion.

At ground level, the walls of the reception room were lined with bookcases and display cabinets that stood below huge canvases in ornate frames. Several plush leather couches were dotted around the centre of the space, beneath a vast chandelier that caught the grey light diffusing through the windows and sparkled like a diamond.

The fragmented light it reflected illuminated a nightmare.

There was blood everywhere.

And in the centre of the room, directly beneath the chandelier, was a sight that made Herb's blood run cold.

Bodies.

Tangled and torn, stacked chaotically in a gruesome pile; a dripping pyramid of death.

Somewhere behind him, Herb heard someone gasping in horror.

Someone else collapsing to the floor and emitting a low moan of despair.

And all he could do was stare at it.

It wasn't a massacre; it was a *message*. It had to be. These people didn't even look like they had been fed upon—just killed to erect the gruesome monument in the middle of the mansion.

This must be for me, he thought. *For anyone who came back from the Oceanus.*

Behind Herb, someone vomited loudly, and he snapped out of the daze that threatened to overwhelm him.

"They've been here," he said softly, his voice laced with wonder, "they're on the surface already. How is that possible? How could they have known about the Oceanus before dawn?"

"They could *still* be here," a gravelly voice hissed, and Herb turned to see Jeremy, hanging several yards back from the doorway and taking slow steps backwards toward the distant chopper. He was the only one among them—aside from Dan—who couldn't fly the helicopter, but judging by the look on his face, he wanted to learn *fast*.

Herb shook his head and pointed at a large panel on the wall just inside the doorway. Inside it, a range of switches controlled the mansion's steel shutters, and UV floodlights which covered the grounds entirely for several hundred yards.

"The shutters aren't down. If they were in here, why wouldn't they block out the light?"

"Uh, gee, I don't know. Maybe because they're monsters who don't understand your damn alarm system?" Dan said.

Herb glanced at him, and Dan clamped his lips shut and looked away abruptly.

"Maybe not," Herb replied. "But the people living here did, and as soon as the vampires took one of their minds, they'd understand it just fine. That's the way these things are supposed to work, isn't it, Jeremy?"

Herb lifted his voice a little.

"They take us, and they know what we know, right?"

The group flinched as Herb raised his voice further still. He paused and listened intently. There was no sound from the interior of the house; nothing at all.

"Unless the texts got *that* part wrong, too."

Herb watched Jeremy carefully. Something had been off about the older man on the trawler, and now his behaviour was even stranger. He had spent the helicopter ride sitting behind Herb in tense silence, refusing to engage in any discussion.

Now that Herb came to think about it, what Jeremy

had looked, back on the chopper, was *scared*. Almost like he knew they were heading straight for a bad place.

Jeremy continued to back away slowly, his eyes fixed on the doorway, a look of horror on his face. A couple of the clerics began to follow him, and then stopped when they noticed Herb standing firm.

"We need to get out of here, Herb," he said, shaking his head.

"And go where? It will be dark in a little over an hour—"

"Anywhere," Jeremy snarled. "You can't seriously be considering going in there."

Herb returned his gaze to the reception room, trying not to focus on the monstrosity at its centre. The room was brightly lit by the huge windows, just as the rest of the house would be. He couldn't imagine the vampires staying in a place like that, not unless they were hiding in cupboards.

Indecision tore through him. His father owned an apartment in London that was rarely used, but it boasted few of the defensive capabilities that the mansion would once it was locked down. The apartment had been fitted with the same steel shutters as the buildings on the compound, but it lacked UV lights and, more importantly, thick stone walls.

Beyond the apartment in the city, he couldn't think where else he could possibly go. Fleeing blindly into the coming night without a safe destination would be asking for trouble.

"Anybody here?"

Herb yelled the words almost without realising he was doing it; bellowing them into the echoing silence of the mansion. He had to do *something*. The uncertainty was killing him.

He strained his ears to catch some response; any sound which might indicate that there was a presence in the house.

Nothing.

He turned to the group.

Opened his mouth with no clear idea how he was going to tell them that he thought they should go inside.

He didn't get the chance.

Somewhere behind him, a woman's voice broke the silence inside the mansion.

Crying.

Calling for help.

CHAPTER TWELVE

D an heard the woman crying, but he no longer saw the vast reception room spread out before him, or the grisly mountain of bodies.

Instead, he saw the face of the woman he loved, lit in the ghostly green of nightvision goggles. Her eyes wide and terrified as the talons hooked under her jaw and began to pull—

And then suddenly he was running forward on autopilot, following the sound of pitiful crying blindly, and his mind felt like it was short-circuiting, neurons igniting in all directions; a fireworks display in his skull.

He ran without looking back, without waiting to see if the others would follow.

He had forgotten they were even there.

He turned left into a large dining room, and the sound of the crying got louder.

He ran.

And the black river crashed over him.

For a moment, the only thing Herb could do was stare in amazement as Dan Bellamy bolted, tearing through the reception room without even pausing to glance at the pile of corpses, following the woman's scream for help.

Dan had already veered to the left, and out of his sight, through an archway that led to the main dining room, before Herb managed to persuade his own feet that they should follow.

He pulled out the two guns he had acquired on the trawler, wondering what good they would do him if he was actually required to use them, snarled at the others to follow, and chased after Dan. When he glanced back, he saw that they were all terrified, but all were following—with the exception of Jeremy. It looked like the older man hadn't even entered the mansion.

Herb hadn't picked him for a coward.

He reached the entrance to the dining room just as Dan disappeared through a doorway at the far end, running like his life depended on it. In the distance, Herb heard the crying get a little louder. The survivor—whoever she was—had to be in the main part of the kitchen. Herb led the group at a sprint, his heart hammering, following Dan through the doorway.

He slammed to a halt.

Bellamy was standing a few feet in front of him, shaking his head and blinking slowly, as though he had just woken from a deep sleep. Beyond him, sitting on the island in the centre of the huge steel-and-stone kitchen, Herb saw the survivor.

Her name was Zoe, he remembered. Zoe Yates. Her family had married into the Order generations ago. She was a few years older than Herb and, when he was a teenager, he'd developed a fearsome crush on her which had lasted for an excruciating couple of months.

Despite that, it took him a moment to place her exactly.

With all the blood.

Zoe sat on the island alongside a knife rack, clutching a blade in each hand.

Sawing.

Slowly cutting her own legs off.

For a moment, Herb's thoughts drained away, his mind unable to cope with the horror his eyes served up. He stared at Zoe's face, and crawling dread made his throat constrict. In her eyes, he saw a terrible awareness. She knew exactly what she was doing, he realised; she could feel every furrow that her hands were carving into her own flesh.

She just can't stop it.

Herb's jaw dropped.

And his mind snapped into action.

"There's still one here," he snarled, his muscles tensing involuntarily, preparing for the attack he was certain was incoming.

Before anyone could react, the house began to rumble around them, and the steel shutters started to close.

Someone had activated the lockdown.

No. Some*thing*.

It was under the bodies, Herb thought in dull terror. *Playing a damn game with us. We walked right past it.*

The light began to fade as the shutters rolled down.

It's sealing us inside.

In the dark.

His eyes widened. "Turn on the lights," he roared, and he ran from the kitchen back out into the corridor that connected to the dining room, flicking on the light just as the shutters closed, plunging the rest of the mansion into darkness.

Herb threw himself back into the kitchen and slammed the door behind him, locking it with an ancient iron key that had almost rusted into the lock, and flicked the nearest light switch on. With a faint buzz, fluorescent strips hummed into life overhead, flooding the centre of the kitchen with cold, white light.

The kitchen comprised several smaller rooms, and when Herb jabbed a finger at them, the stunned clerics fanned out quickly and lit the whole place up. There were two other doors into the kitchen: one leading down to the extensive wine cellar, and another that opened onto a narrow service stairwell which led up to a first-floor lounge and bar area.

He dragged a table across the door, jamming it into the wood, praying that it would hold, and motioned at the clerics to lock the remaining two doors. Outside, he heard the faint smashing of glass and knew immediately that the vampire had taken out the lights that he had just turned on in the corridor. The kitchen was an oasis of light in the mansion.

All exits and windows locked down, a vampire at the door.

No way out.

"It's okay," Herb said in a voice that came out high-pitched and tremulous. "It can't get in."

As if in response, the vampire charged at the door, impacting on it with a thunderous crash. Herb saw the table that he had used for a barricade wobble a little, and realised that if he didn't believe in his own words, he couldn't expect anyone else to, either.

"It can't get in," he repeated firmly.

Outside the heavy kitchen door, there was only silence. The vampire had charged it once, testing its strength, but now...

What the hell is it doing now?

Herb's heart hammered painfully, and he picked up the two handguns once more, and set them down again on a counter almost immediately. They weren't the weapons he needed. Where the hell *was* the weapon he needed?

He scanned the kitchen. Dan Bellamy had collapsed to his knees in a large walk-in pantry, and was gasping for air, with his hands gripping the sides of his skull. He looked like he was about to have another seizure, or perhaps even a heart attack.

Edgar was wrong about him.

Suddenly, the unmistakeable truth rolled out in front of Herb, and he saw it clearly. Even if Dan Bellamy was somehow special, it didn't matter. The guy couldn't actually *fight* the vampires. He was terrified and broken. Weak. His survival on the Oceanus had been a fluke, and Bellamy was coming apart at the seams because of it. So what if they couldn't take his mind? They would just tear apart his body while he cowered and whimpered.

Herb felt like a lawyer who'd built an entire defence on a gross miscalculation, and only realised his error when the judge began to laugh in his face. He had followed his heart, determined to do *something*, to fight back somehow —and his determination to act on impulse would end up killing them all.

He squeezed his eyes shut, and saw his father's face, twisted into a sardonic grin.

Who'll be the head of the Rennick family?
You?

Dan gurgled and choked, gasping for breath like he was drowning, and despair washed over Herb. He turned away.

Just in time to see Zoe throw herself from the kitchen island and drive a knife deep into the chest of the nearest cleric. Stephen gasped as the blade lodged between his ribs, and he staggered forward a couple of steps, passing Zoe on like a virus. She hurled herself off him and drove the other knife into Christian's neck, sending an arterial spurt across two other clerics before anybody could move.

When Christian crashed, gurgling, to the floor, Zoe went down with him as the legs that she had mutilated beyond comprehension buckled beneath her. She barely seemed to notice the fall. Upon landing, she instantly shot out a blood-soaked hand like a striking viper, plucking the knife from Christian's neck. It came free, and the blood came with it; a crimson fountain that finally put an end to the cleric's ragged panting.

Zoe began to drag herself toward the others, smearing a trail of gore across the tiles behind her. With every staccato lurch forward, she swung the knife with her left hand, each wide arc spraying thick crimson droplets across the room.

The attack took only seconds, and the sudden savagery of it rooted Herb to the spot. He watched in dumb fascination as the clerics retreated from the swinging blade, shrieking in terror. Only when one of them unlocked the door to the wine cellar, and they began to flee from the kitchen, did Herb finally snap out of his stupor.

"No!" he yelled, and he sprinted around Zoe, hurdling over the blade that she swung in his direction.

Already, two of the clerics had fled from the room, blind panic setting in and making them lose their minds. A third—Scott—was halfway through the door when Herb grabbed his shirt and pulled him back into the kitchen.

He slammed the door shut and locked it.

"That's what it wants," Herb snarled at the cleric, and he turned to face Zoe.

She was only feet away.

Still coming; still clutching the knife.

Still *crying*.

Herb wanted more than anything to turn and flee from the hideous sight, but he grimaced and darted forward, skipping around the knife and stooping to catch her arm. His fingers closed on her wrist and he twisted it violently. The knife fell to the tiles with a metallic clatter, but Herb didn't even hear it landing.

His entire focus was taken up by Zoe's eyes: wide and pleading, so terribly *aware*.

She's still in there somewhere, he thought, and felt a scream gathering in his lungs. *She's living every second of it.*

He pushed Zoe away and rose to his feet, taking a step backwards and kicking the knife away from her grasping fingers.

Zoe's eyes dropped to her hands in despair, and she whimpered as they began to drag her back toward the distant knife rack.

She won't stop, Herb thought. *It won't let her. It will use her until she is dead...or we are.*

Zoe's commandeered body was reaching up, straining

for the knife rack on the kitchen island when Herb picked up one of the guns he had left on the counter and put a bullet in the back of her head, slamming her into the floor.

Doing what was necessary.

Just like Dad.

Herb gritted his teeth, and shook away the grinning image of his father.

At his feet, Zoe's body was motionless at last, her eyes fixed and empty.

And as the echoing blast of the gun in the enclosed kitchen faded, and Herb tried to process the insanity of what she had been forced to do—what *he* had been forced to do—the vampire outside the kitchen door began to *chuckle.*

The sound coiled around Herb's nerves like razor wire, but even as his instincts howled at him, his mind was calling his attention to something else. A very important detail. The rest of the house remained quiet. The two clerics that had fled through the wine cellar in a panic hadn't even started to scream. Not yet.

Because it has been busy with us.

There's only one here, he thought.

Could it be that there *was* only one more vampire? According to the texts, the English nest was small, but was thought to number in the dozens.

Maybe that was a lie, too.

It made sense, didn't it? That the creatures who had decided to erase their existence from human history might exaggerate their own strength? They weren't immortal, that was for sure.

Herb frowned, and in the distance, he began to hear the shrieking of the two clerics, exactly as he had known he would. A flurry of terrified yells which cut off abruptly, until there was only one voice left.

And his screams were long, and slow.

Herb tried to tune out the horror of the noise and *think*.

One vampire.

If there are more out there, where the hell are they?

CHAPTER THIRTEEN

The absence of light made the noise all the more terrifying; a high-pitched scream that shredded Adam Trent's nerves like a hacksaw.

He froze, the wrench in his hand forgotten, and stared into the blackness. The cone of illumination cast by the light mounted on his hat dissolved after a few feet. Beyond it, the darkness was an abyss.

Sometimes the tunnels could play tricks on you—especially when you were working near an active line. The shriek of metal on metal could sound otherworldly in the dark, and most of the staff working the lines had let their nerves get the better of them at least once. It took some getting used to, working down there in the pitch black, tending to the roots of the city. The darkness and the isolation; the musty air and the dislocation from reality. It all took its toll, especially on those who were new to the job.

Yet Adam had been working maintenance on the London Underground system for ten years and counting. He was no rookie.

And that isn't metal-on-metal.

The noise which Adam heard, ricocheting around the cavernous tunnel, was a twisted fusion of terror and pain. Definitely *not* mechanical; it was unmistakably the sound of someone screaming. It rang out clearly over the clanging noise of Roni hammering at a stubborn section of the rusting track a few feet to his left.

It sounded like it came from a distance down the tracks, somewhere around the curve of the tunnel. Even if there had been light in that direction, Adam doubted that he would have been able to see what had caused the noise, and maybe, he thought, that was a good thing.

The scream spoke to him on an animal level, and his senses shifted into a state of high alert.

It lasted for maybe five seconds, rising in pitch.

Ending suddenly.

And then there was thunderous silence.

The two-man sub-team's work—routine repairs on a section of the *Northern Line*—ceased immediately.

Adam turned to face Roni, and flooded his colleague with light.

"You heard that?"

Roni nodded slowly, but both question and response were unnecessary: Adam knew that he hadn't imagined the noise as soon as he saw Roni's eyes; painfully wide, darting with incomprehension. He looked as unnerved as Adam felt.

Adam took a hefty flashlight from his belt, and aimed it down the tunnel. The other sub-team—Colin and Tarpey; good guys, whose easy banter generally made the long hours pass quicker—were a few hundred feet further down the line, working their way back towards Adam's position.

The scream had come from their direction.

It had to have been one of the two men that screamed, but Adam had no idea what could prompt a man to make such a noise.

Come to think of it, he wasn't sure he even wanted to know.

He tried not to notice the beam of light jerking as his hand trembled wildly. The flashlight's bulb was a good deal more powerful than the one attached to his hat, but it, too, was eaten by the void before it revealed anything out of the ordinary.

He saw nothing.

Heard nothing.

"You think one of them is hurt?" Roni hissed, and Adam flinched at the sudden break in the oppressive silence.

As it happened, yeah, Adam *did* think either Colin or Tarpey was hurt. Maybe even worse than hurt. He couldn't see how a man could scream like that and *not* be in terrible agony. Men had been injured in the tunnels before, plenty of times, and Adam had rushed to their aid without hesitation, tending to injuries that ranged from concussion to electrocution to—on one particularly horrible occasion—dismemberment. It was, he thought, part of the job description. He imagined that it had to be the same whenever people worked in places that were so inherently dangerous. You developed a bond, even with the colleagues you didn't much like. An unspoken code. *Look after each other down there.*

Further down the tunnel, it sounded like somebody needed looking after, all right, but this time, Adam found his feet unwilling to move and his skin prickling. Suddenly, he felt terribly afraid at the prospect of calling out to see if everything was okay. Frightened that he would draw the attention of something; some awful creature out there, sharing the shadows with them.

He wondered if he should shut off the light, and hope whatever was out there could not see him.

Sweat beaded on Adam's forehead as his mind ran to dark destinations. Whatever was out there, it had surely killed Colin and Tarpey, and it was crawling toward him at that very moment, unseen in the dark, licking its lips...

He willed his legs to move.

And then the whimpering started up; faint, but audible. The soft, gurgling cries of a man suffering terrible pain. The sound was somehow even worse than the screaming.

"We have to help him."

Roni's words.

High-pitched and breathless; the voice of a man out of his mind with fear.

Adam swallowed hard and nodded almost absently, his eyes fixed on the section of tunnel that he could not see. Someone was still alive, and they were hurt. He *had* to help. He lifted the wrench above his head, brandishing it like a club. Roni acknowledged the gesture, but there was no question in his eyes, and Adam knew, then.

It wasn't just him. Not his imagination. Roni felt it, too: the air in the tunnel, suddenly thick and syrupy; laced with danger. A nagging certainty that there was another presence in the tunnel with them, something foul and dangerous.

Adam advanced slowly, his heart hammering painfully, the wrench raised.

Ready.

Click.

He froze again, and this time the message his nerves tried to send was *run*, but fear had tangled the wiring in his brain. He felt like he was standing in quicksand.

He remembered listening to Tarpey talking about the time when he had seen a train heading straight for him in a tunnel which he had believed was inactive, and about the grey area between fight or flight; that rabbit-in-the-headlights paralysis.

Tarpey had called it *fight, flight or shite.*

It had been funny. Adam had laughed.

Click, click.

He swallowed painfully.

The noise was heading toward him, getting louder. Advancing a little and pausing. It sounded to Adam like the cautious movement of an animal. But there weren't any animals in the London Underground, not really. Rats, of course; maybe the odd stray dog. Yet the sound he heard wasn't made by any rat or dog. It skittered and tapped, and struck Adam as more like the noise an insect might make.

Yet for the noise to be that loud, it would have to be huge.

Or very close.

He felt his heartbeat ratchet up in intensity until he was sure his chest would burst open.

The shuddering beam of light gave up nothing. He frowned, and felt a dry panic squeezing his bladder. The noise sounded close enough that he was sure he should be able to see *something.*

Click, click, click, cli—

So loud, Adam thought. *Like it's right on top of us.*

Oh.

Shit.

Adam knew that it would be there even before he jerked his jaw up and illuminated the roof above his head with ghostly light. Some crazy intuition told him before he saw it.

Bursting from the shadows toward the two paralysed men, bewildering and obscene.

A creature born in a fevered nightmare.

It came at them fast, scuttling along the ceiling like some horrific spider; humanoid in shape and yet somehow insectile at the same time. Glistening skin that seemed to absorb the light. Angular limbs whirring in furious motion, eating up the distance at extraordinary speed.

Glowing red eyes.

Teeth.

It shrieked as the light spilled across it, and launched itself down onto Roni before he could react, opening up his body from shoulder to groin as it fell, cleaving him in two almost casually with a talon as long as a pocket knife.

Adam heard a tragic, surprised gasp followed by a wet *splat*, impossibly loud in the enclosed space, and realised with numb horror that the noise was Roni's *blood*. It sounded like there was so *much* of it, raining down heavily on the ground. A grisly downpour that fell not from storm clouds, but from an unfolding nightmare.

Blood, Adam decided distantly, made a *horrible* sound. It was a noise no human being should ever have to endure.

Roni's eyes flickered with piercing awareness for an instant as his guts began to slide from his abdomen. The oozing dark mass of innards looked almost alive in the bleak light, and the awful sight of his colleague's pulsing organs made the last functioning part of Adam Trent's mind shriek loud enough to break the spell.

Go!

The creature began to turn to face Adam even as he turned away, pounding his legs forward.

He only managed to take a couple of frantic strides before something impacted heavily on his back.

Searing pain.

Falling.

Adam crashed into the ground, and the air blasted from his lungs.

The light on his helmet smashed, plunging him into pitch-black darkness.

He rolled over onto his back, feeling something flapping around the base of his spine, and realised in horror that it was his own flesh, drawn apart like curtains. He gagged.

Hauled himself to his feet.

Heard guttural breathing in the void.

He tensed, trying to ready himself for the next attack.

It came from his left, delivering another tearing blow, and this time Adam was conscious of the fact that he was sailing through the air moments before he clattered into a wall with a dry and terrible *slap*. His skull rang, and for a moment he just laid there, with his eyes shut and his head spinning, waiting helplessly for the end.

Waiting.

Nothing.

His left side felt like it was on fire, and he dropped a hand to find that a sticky chasm had opened up in his love handle, a hole that felt gigantic to his probing fingers.

Again, he rose to his feet and began to stumble away, and again he felt the talons raking him, lifting him and tossing him away like rotten meat. Another hole. Another *leak*.

Another pause.

It was during that pause that Adam slipped into a dreamlike trance, and thought about his neighbour's cat; about the way he had once watched it idly batting a mouse around the garden, letting the poor creature believe it had a chance to escape, only to drag it back for another round of *fun with claws and teeth* at the last moment.

It's playing with me.

This time, Adam couldn't even bring himself to stand. He rolled onto his back and heard it moving toward him slowly, like it was savouring the moment.

"Please," Adam slurred, a bubble of blood and saliva popping on his lips, "please...just kill me..."

The thing laughed, and Adam let his head drop against the ground. He closed his eyes.

Prayed for oblivion.

And felt it crawl directly over him.

Tasted the rotten stink of its hot breath; blood and ancient decay.

He opened his eyes, and found the hideous face just inches from his own, terrible eyes burning like torches in the darkness.

Adam stared directly at those sickening crimson pools and felt something in his head snap; something that made his skull ring with a dull and nauseating permanence.

His sanity began to evaporate, making room in his mind for something else; worse than the pain had been; than any pain could *possibly* be.

The creature took what was left of Adam Trent's mind then, and in his final moment, he understood the terrible truth.

It wasn't going to kill him at all.

CHAPTER FOURTEEN

G rowling.
      Increasing in intensity.

Filling the dark space like the sound of idling American muscle.

Cornelia Stokes glanced at the rear view mirror and saw light brown eyes staring directly back at her. The rising growl became a bark.

Conny grinned and returned her eyes to the road, steering the van along Mornington Crescent toward Euston. Her day had been mapped out, and it was supposed to provide little in the way of drama: she and Remy had spent the early part of the afternoon in Regent's Park—keeping an eye on a rain-soaked and peaceful protest which certainly didn't *look* like it might turn nasty—when she got the call to respond to an emergency at the train station.

Remy barked again, louder.

To anyone who didn't know better, it might have sounded like the dog in the rear of the van was going crazy; growling and barking at nothing. But Conny had been Remy's handler for four years—most of her career with the British Transport Police's *Dog Unit*—and knew him better than she knew herself. The chaotic noise was his routine; his own way of preparing himself for the work he knew was to come. When he was placed in the van and the sirens began to wail, that meant only one thing for Remy. Time to put on his game face.

Time for action.

Conny couldn't have silenced him even if she had wanted to.

Remy's specialty was crowd control. Controlled aggression was his purpose, and he was the best police dog that Conny had ever seen, let alone worked with. Smart and obedient and completely harmless...ninety percent of the time.

The *other* ten percent of the time Remy was a snarling weapon, and on each and every occasion that the German Shepherd was called into action, Conny found herself astonished at the impact his bristling presence could have on a crowd of people. Even those who were armed *themselves* shrivelled in fear at the sight of him. A weapon with teeth, she concluded, reached right into the primitive part of a person's brain in a way that no knife or firearm ever could.

Remy represented a primal fear that could not be ignored, and often merely the sight of him—eighty-five pounds of coiled muscle, propping up snapping jaws full of sharp trouble—was enough to calm even the most aggressive of suspects. Conny had a long-standing love affair with firearms, but once Remy had given her his complete, unquestioning loyalty and trust, she wouldn't have traded the dog for a full-auto assault rifle. Guns jammed; they got misplaced or ran out of ammunition. Remy never did.

She swung the small police van onto Hampstead Road, nodding acknowledgment at the afternoon drivers who pulled aside to let her through, and Euston Station loomed ahead of her. She stepped on the accelerator.

Conny and Remy had been asked to provide backup to the security staff at the station: to help break up a scuffle which had broken out among several commuters waiting at one of the Underground platforms. In Conny's experience, most fights broke up as soon as Remy started to bark, and she expected that this occasion would be no different.

Her day could have been a lot worse, she thought. She could have been one of the poor bastards dealing with the massacre which had taken place in south London just a few hours earlier: a junkie who'd gone berserk in a supermarket, killing three people and wounding two others before taking his own life. When local police had responded to the incident, they had discovered the bodies of a further nine homeless people torn to pieces under a nearby bridge.

There was no weapon to deal with something like *that*, no shield that could keep the damage at bay, either. Sometimes, the world just erupted into madness and violence that was impossible to comprehend, and somebody out there had to face it.

This would be nothing like that terrible incident, though. The fight at Euston was almost certainly nothing more than a few commuters getting steamed up over having to wait too long for a train and lashing out. A typical London flashpoint. It would probably all be over in less than thirty seconds.

She glanced in the mirror again as she pulled the van to a halt outside the station's main entrance and killed the siren.

Remy was now dead silent, staring at her calmly with expectant, hopeful eyes. The siren had stopped wailing. The time for preparation was over.

Conny opened the door and began to step out of the van when she felt her phone vibrate in her pocket. She pulled it out, and a dreadful sickening sensation unfurled in her stomach. She sat back down heavily, staring at the *unlock* screen. Afraid to swipe her thumb across it. As much as possible, she tried to compartmentalise her life; to leave the personal stuff at home and focus only on the job when she was on shift. Anything else would be failing in her duty as a police officer. She rarely carried her phone with her while she was in uniform.

Today was different, of course.

The screen on her phone glowed for a moment before falling dark.

You haven't got time to just sit here, Con.

She unlocked the screen, and felt a scream building inside her, desperate to be free.

A text from Logan. *The* text. Just two words, steeped in bitterness which punched her in the gut like a professional boxer. No matter how much she had tried to prepare herself for seeing them, the words inflicted damage that she already knew would never heal.

Confirmed. Huntington's.

Conny placed the phone gently on the dashboard, face down, and stared through the rain-flecked windscreen at the exterior of Euston Station for several long moments, until Remy huffed impatiently.

You're on duty.

She blinked away the tears that gathered in her eyes, and set her mouth in a firm line. Remy was right.

Time for action.

At ground level, Euston Station was a huge, functional square space lined with overpriced shops, and a bar in which unoccupied seats were as rare as reasonable rent. Toward the front of the building, where the departure boards displayed the latest information for each of the eighteen platforms, a few hundred passengers clustered, waiting for the signal to board the trains that would take them toward the north of England.

Conny headed left, aiming for the escalators that would transport her down to Euston's separate Underground station, and glanced down at Remy. The dog remained silent and focused, his watchful eyes scanning, ears pricked up. She gripped his heavy chain leash tightly, as her own training dictated, but she would have been confident in unleashing him, knowing that he would have kept pace without the restraint.

Below ground level, the short escalator led to a small area filled with ticket machines and electronic barriers which barred the path to the subterranean platforms that were yet another level further down. There was no sign of a disturbance in the ticketing hall, but the tension in the space was palpable. The barriers to the platforms had been closed by staff, and the resulting crowd which formed simmered with uneasy frustration at *yet another delay on the Tube.*

Conny heard a loud voice informing passengers that

there was a 'security issue' down on the platforms, and that delays of around fifteen minutes were expected.

Not if Remy has anything to do with it, she thought, and headed toward the barriers, letting Remy carve a path between groups of commuters who parted silently to let them pass. When she reached the barriers, a portly and stressed-looking security guard waved her through with a nod, gazing warily at Remy.

The dog ignored him, his gaze focused on the next escalator. Much larger than the first; it speared down into the earth, providing access to the Northern Line's north and south platforms.

He growled softly.

Conny nodded, and quickened her pace. They were close enough now that Remy could probably hear whatever was happening down on the platform. Maybe he could smell blood and danger on the air.

The escalator had been switched off, so Conny and Remy took the steep metal steps leading down at a brisk pace.

When she was halfway down to the next level, she could hear the shouting at last, and Remy finally began to strain at his leash.

THE FIGHT LOOKED LIKE IT WAS STILL ONGOING.

Conny stepped onto the platform that served southbound trains, moving past some onlookers who had retreated to a safe distance, but couldn't bring themselves to actually leave and miss the excitement. Far to her right, at the very end of the platform, she saw a mass of bodies milling around, a couple of whom wore the distinctive hi-vis yellow jackets which marked them out as staff.

She broke into a trot, reaching the perimeter of the fracas in a few seconds.

Remy's growl grew louder; a rumbling thunder that cut cleanly through the noise of the scuffle. Several faces turned toward Conny and her partner, their eyes widening.

Once she had pushed past a few gawkers, Conny saw that there were a couple of people on the platform lying face down, unmoving. At least one of them was bleeding heavily, and both were either unconscious or dead.

She hesitated.

It looked a little more serious than just some fight.

Several other people had staggering away from the tussle, nursing minor injuries, and the two staff were struggling with a man who screamed and thrashed, resisting their attempts to pin him to the floor. Conny watched the man shrug off one of the staff and swing at him with what looked like a length of rebar, and decided she had seen enough.

She unhooked Remy's leash and pointed at the weapon.

"Go."

Remy approached steadily, barking furiously, and the two staff rolled away from the thrashing man, their eyes wide and fixed on the dog. Isolated with Remy, the man leapt to his feet, and Conny expected that he would immediately drop the weapon and either attempt to flee or surrender.

Instead, the man—who Conny noticed in surprise was also wearing a torn hi-vis jacket, its bright colour dulled by dirt and bloodstains—took a step toward the dog and lashed out, swinging the heavy metal in a savage arc.

Conny's breath caught in her throat as Remy took matters into his own hands, darting underneath the intended blow. He struck before his attacker had even finished swinging, leaping forward and clamping his teeth onto the guy's forearm.

Twisting.

The rebar hit the floor with a clatter.

And Conny's mouth dropped open in amazement as the man lined up a *punch* with his free hand, striking Remy in the neck. The dog clearly decided that enough was enough. It pulled hard on the man's forearm, twisting its thick neck violently to unbalance him, and brought him down hard onto the platform. He hit the floor face-first with a sharp *snap* that Conny thought had to be his nose valiantly attempting to cushion his fall.

Yet *still* he struggled.

Conny had never seen anything like it. Remy had brought plenty of people down over the years, and not once had anyone even tried to get up when the dog was looming over them.

The stricken man heaved himself back to his feet with the German Shepherd still attached to his arm—blood flowing freely around Remy's powerful jaws—and he began to stagger to his left.

Conny recognised what was happening immediately. The man—maybe drugged, who knew—clearly wasn't feeling the pain of Remy's teeth as he should be, and was using his superior weight to drag the dog across the platform.

Toward the tracks.

The live line, Conny thought in horror.

"Remy, release," she yelled sternly, and Remy obeyed instantly, glancing back at her with something like chagrin in his eyes.

When Remy withdrew his teeth from the man's forearm, he lost all balance. He might have fallen onto the tracks anyway, carried there by his momentum, but as Conny watched the man in the torn hi-vis jacket dive off the platform onto the deadly waiting track with a wince, she couldn't help but think that it looked, for just a fleeting moment, like he *wanted* his life to end.

Had he continued to struggle with Remy because he wanted the dog to *kill* him?

For several long seconds, a pregnant hush descended on the small crowd of people gathered on the platform, and Conny stared down at Remy, seeing her own confusion reflected in his big brown eyes.

CHAPTER FIFTEEN

---

*F*amiliar sensation
    Crawling up the back of—
"Dan...Dan? BELLAMY! Snap out of it!"

Dan coughed violently and sucked in a deep breath, trying to calm the raging vibrations in his head. The air stank of blood and shit and death, and it felt like his skull was fracturing.

Herb, he thought. *That's Herb. Focus on his voice.*

"Oh, fucking hell...*Dan?* Can you hear me?"

He took another breath.

Let it out slow.

And the world began to swim into focus.

Herb was standing over him, his face twisted in concern.

"It's okay, we're safe," Herb said. "For now, anyway. It can't get in."

Dan pulled himself to his feet, and his eyes widened when he saw the kitchen. The large group of men he expected to see suddenly wasn't so large at all. Two of Herb's followers were lying on the floor, one panting out rattling breaths and clutching at his bloody chest; the other was motionless, with a towel draped over his face. Still others looked to have disappeared altogether.

"What happened?"

Herb's brow creased.

"You didn't see?"

Dan coughed, spitting out the foul-tasting air.

"I get...blackouts. Panic attacks."

"Panic attacks?" Herb stared at him, bewildered. "Jesus Christ. How the hell *did* you survive on that ship?"

Dan glared back at him for a moment, and felt dark emotions bubbling, clutching at him; trying to pull him under.

—*hands in the darkness*—

He scowled. "Just bad luck, I guess. I tried to tell you. I'm not what you think I am. Not special. Not some sort of *vampire slayer.*"

Dan's words came out harsh, tainted with bitter sarcasm.

"No shit," Herb muttered. "I guessed that much when you decided to have a fucking breakdown instead of help—"

Dan punched him.

Actually *punched* him.

His right arm shot out of its own accord, fingers clenching into a bony fist, and he drove Herb's words straight back down his throat.

It was, as far as Dan could recall, the first punch he had thrown in his life. He doubted it was powerful enough to hurt; certainly as he threw it, his arm felt loose and elastic rather than taut, but the blow snapped Herb's jaw sideways, and a moment later the bigger man was sitting on the floor, staring up at him in surprise.

Dan stared back.

Stunned.

Mortified.

And Herb *laughed.*

He rubbed his jaw ruefully as he stood up, and he grinned at Dan, who could do nothing but gape at him.

"Well, all right, then," Herb said. "I guess that's more like it."

Dan had no response. At least, none that he could vocalize.

What the fuck is wrong with me?

"There are eight of us left," Herb said, and paused, staring at one of the bodies on the floor. The man with the bloody chest was no longer drawing in those rattling breaths. He sighed heavily. "Make that seven." He glanced at his watch. "I'd say we have about half an hour before it gets dark outside. We need a way out."

"A way *out?* Aren't we safe in here? I thought you said it couldn't get in."

Herb nodded.

"It can't get in *right now.* But once it gets dark outside, it will have no reason to leave those down."

He pointed at the shuttered windows.

Dan felt his stomach lurch. Herb was right. It was the vampire that had sealed them in. When the shutters were no longer required to keep the daylight at bay, it could simply reopen them and come through a window.

"Does this place have a cellar?"

"Yeah," Herb said grimly, and he pointed at a door to the rear of the kitchen. "Through there. The others went that way; made a run for the front door, I think. They didn't make it."

Dan searched Herb's eyes and saw the remembered

nightmare the younger man was trying to conceal. *He must have heard them screaming*, he thought, and for a moment Dan was back on the deck of the Oceanus, listening to a symphony of destruction being played out in the darkness. Cries of fear and pain and horror, all punctuated by the otherworldly shriek of the vampires.

"How long was I, uh, out for?"

"About ten minutes. At least this time you weren't screaming." Herb offered a watery smile.

No, Dan thought. *That part is still to come.*

"Ten minutes," he said absently. "An hour until sundown."

"Yeah. Ish." Herb nodded.

"How many exits are there?"

"From the kitchen? Three. But they all lead to open plan areas. It would run us down in no time."

Dan frowned. He couldn't see how they could possibly escape without further loss of life. Even if they could successfully leave the kitchen and somehow lose the vampire in the vast house, the place was locked down. The only exit that mattered was the one the vampire itself had blocked; the mansion's front door.

They could try to run, maybe, turning lights on as they went; try to lock themselves in another room, perhaps, one which might offer some means of escape he couldn't imagine.

It would be suicide.

"Maybe if we split up, we could—" Dan said, and fell silent when Herb stared at him, aghast.

"Split up? I take it you've never seen any horror movie, ever?"

He had a point. Besides which, Dan thought, he was the only one who didn't know the layout of the Rennick mansion. If it came down to fleeing blindly, he would surely be the first to die.

"Then we have to kill it," he said uncertainly.

"Yeah," Herb replied. "Why didn't I think of that?" he rolled his eyes. "Killing them is where *you're* supposed to come in, Dan. If you've got some grand idea on how to go about doing that, I'm all ears."

Dan searched his thoughts.

He *had* been lucky to survive his encounters with the creatures on the Oceanus. On both occasions, he had killed vampires that were preoccupied with murdering somebody else. It was like they were complacent, so sure that no human would dare attack them that they had let their guard down. He had landed sucker punches, no more than that. He remembered the moment of hesitation on the twisted features of the one that had killed Elaine; the way it almost seemed that the vampire couldn't actually believe what was happening as Dan attacked it with a cleaver.

But that had been in the swirling storm of chaos on board the cruise ship. Here, where the vampire was focused only on hunting the tiny group of men that had sealed themselves away from it, he didn't think that luck would hold.

"What do you *actually* know about these things?"

Herb opened his mouth to respond, but Dan cut in.

"And if you say anything about ancient fucking texts, I may have to punch you again."

Dan smiled weakly. A joke.

Isn't it?

"I can only tell you what is supposed to be true," Herb said. "They claim to be immortal; they live below ground. They sleep for centuries. They feed on humans. In their presence, humans lose their minds. We are powerless to resist them. They don't like light. Oh, and they don't burn. That wasn't in the texts. I saw that one myself." Herb rubbed absently at his bandaged arm. "I don't see how any of that can help us now, especially since any or all of it could be lies."

They don't burn, Dan thought. He stored that piece of information, and then irritably told himself that he didn't *want* that knowledge taking up space in his brain. If he could just get away from the mansion—away from the monsters; away from Herb and his rapidly diminishing group of followers—he would flee and gladly hand himself over to the police and confess to the murder he had committed in the Atlantic. He could spend the rest of his days in the safety of a cell, and he wouldn't ever have to think about the creatures that Herbert Rennick called *vampires* ever again.

He stared at the locked door.

Behind it, he heard soft snuffling sounds; wet smacking. It was a noise he had heard before. The vampire was sitting outside the kitchen. Feeding. Waiting.

Listening.

They are intelligent, Dan thought, *not mindless monsters. We know that much for sure. They can speak. They can understand.*

He clutched at Herb's arm, and pulled the younger man close, breathing into his ear softly.

"It's listening. We need to draw it away, up to the top floor, and make a run for the front door, you understand?"

Herb nodded, but he looked dubious.

He mouthed *how?*

Dan stared around the kitchen in mounting frustration. He saw counters, racks of crockery and pans, various foodstuffs. Some wine bottles. No way out. Nothing that might serve as a distraction.

His mind raced.

"Where does that dumb waiter lead?" he said loudly, and pointed at a patch of bare wall.

Herb followed his gaze and then stared at Dan, puzzled. There was no dumb waiter.

Dan mouthed *play along*.

Herb's confused expression softened, and he nodded vigorously.

"It stops off at all five floors," he replied, making sure that his voice was loud enough to carry. Trying to ensure that he wasn't being too obvious.

Dan nodded.

"If we can get to the top floor...is there a way we can access the roof?"

Herb grinned and shook his head.

"Yeah," he said. "A skylight in the attic."

Dan could tell from Herb's wide smile that there was no skylight; maybe even no attic.

"Then we'll go up," Dan said. "Quietly. If we make any noise once we've left this room, it will hear. Once we get to the roof, we run. Can any of you fly the helicopter?"

He expected them to shake their heads. Instead, *all* of them nodded—even Herb.

"The benefits of a Rennick home-schooling," Herb said with a crooked grin. "I can build an EMP bomb; I can strip and reassemble most any firearm you can imagine; I can fly a helicopter. I *can't* function as a normal part of society. That's the trade-off."

"Okay," Dan said, "so it's agreed?"

He looked around the small group of terrified men.

When did I end up being the one in charge?

The thought sent a thrill of dizzying anxiety coursing through him. He breathed deeply and forced it back before it put down roots. This was definitely *not* the time. If Herb was right, they might have only a matter of minutes before the sun started to dip below the horizon. If they didn't make it out of the mansion, their only option would be to lock themselves in one of the kitchen's windowless store rooms and pray.

If it came to that, Dan didn't think he would ever see daylight again.

I can be terrified later.

"Agreed," Herb said quietly, and he reached out to a nearby cupboard, sliding open the door loudly enough for the noise to carry beyond the kitchen.

A nice touch, Dan thought, and he tilted his head and listened.

Outside the kitchen, the faint, sickening sound of the vampire feeding had stopped.

Silence.

CHAPTER SIXTEEN

R emy sat and watched Conny with a slightly
puzzled expression, his head tilted a little to the
right.

He huffed.

Right back at you, Rem, Conny thought. *What the hell
was all that about?*

She leaned over the platform edge, staring down at
the prone body on the tracks.

Her brow furrowed.

Now that she had a chance to look at it properly, she
saw that the dead man's hi-vis jacket was very similar to
the ones worn by the staff at Euston. A blood-spattered
I.D. tag was pinned to his chest. She squinted at it, just
able to make the lettering out.

Adam Trent, senior engineer

Conny's frown deepened.

One of the staff?

"He...he came from the tunnel." A young woman's voice, her tone high-pitched and tremulous.

Conny turned to see a number of stunned commuters staring at her. Frightened, shocked faces. The woman who'd spoken took a step forward, jabbing her finger first at the distant tunnel and then at the bodies on the platform.

"He killed them."

Conny glanced at Remy. The young woman's aggressive gesture had his attention. Remy didn't discriminate when he was on duty. There was either *threat* or *no threat*. He growled softly.

"Easy, Rem," Conny said, and waved a *stop* gesture at the young woman. "What's your name, Miss?"

"Deanne." Her lower lip was quivering, her eyes wide. Remy relaxed a little at her tone. "I was standing right there...he was screaming. He came out of the tunnel, screaming like there was something chasing him, and then he...he just..."

Deanne's eyes filled with tears and she pointed again at the two bodies on the floor.

"Deanne, I'm going to ask you to step back, okay?" Conny lifted her voice. "I need *everyone* to step back, please."

The crowd shuffled backward a few steps, and Conny turned to examine the bodies on the floor. She could tell immediately that the nearest was dead; a middle-aged man in a suit whose face had been pulped, presumably by the rebar. It would have taken more than one blow to do the sort of damage Conny saw. The second victim, a young woman who looked roughly Deanne's age, appeared less seriously injured. Conny walked over and knelt at her side. She pressed a finger into the prone woman's neck, searching for a pulse, and nodded. Faint, but there.

She hit the button on her radio and called for an ambulance, before alerting her CO that Euston Station required the presence of a little more than a single dog handler, and then returned her attention to Deanne.

"Did he *say* anything?"

Deanne shook her head, and the tears began to roll down her cheeks.

"We brought him down when he attacked the girl," a man's voice said. Conny glanced at the speaker. A young man in a hoodie gestured to a small, disparate group of men around him. "We tried to hold him on the ground until the security guys got here. He...just kept swinging. He didn't say a word. He was...screaming. Like she said."

Conny nodded over her shoulder at the tunnel.

"And you saw him come from that direction, too?"

"Yeah. Sounded like a fucking train coming at first," he said, letting out a nervy laugh.

Conny returned her gaze to the tunnel, distracted by the buzz of her radio.

"Copy that," a crackling voice said. Conny's CO. "Hold your position, Stokes. We've got reinforcements en route. Secure the platform and await further orders."

Conny turned back to study the carnage that Adam Trent had caused. Several injured, at least one victim dead, but the platform *was* secure. She had just reported that very fact. Trent was dead.

Secure the platform from what?

Behind her, Deanne was talking again, softly; tearfully, but Conny wasn't listening. She was staring at Remy.

The German Shepherd had apparently decided that

Conny was in no immediate danger, and was no longer watching his handler. Instead, Remy was staring at the distant entrance to the tunnel.

And whining softly.

Remy didn't *whine*; Conny doubted that he had since he had been a puppy.

Squinting, she moved to Remy's side and squatted, following the angle of his gaze. She saw nothing. The entrance to the tunnel yawned; an impenetrable abyss.

"What is it, Rem?"

Remy's response was a low growl, and for the first time ever, Conny thought she detected a different note in the familiar noise, something that sounded a little like *fear*.

She gazed at the tunnel.

Saw nothing.

Couldn't quite suppress a shudder.

The London Underground Central Line was generally the most overcrowded on the rail network; hardly surprising given the easy access it offered to many of London's most popular tourist spots, and the fact that it passed through the shoppers' Mecca that was Oxford Circus. Travelling at rush hour on the Central Line was the last resort of the desperate and the crazy, in Petra Duran's opinion, which was precisely why she stepped onto one of the dreaded trains at around four in the afternoon, an hour before the offices of the city would spit out tens of thousands of weary commuters.

Even at that time, in what should have been a quiet

period, the train still felt crowded, and it still stank of sweat...and she *still* didn't get a seat.

She clung onto one of the handrails for balance as she travelled from Notting Hill Gate toward Liverpool Street, where she was due to catch an overground train that would take her out of the city towards Norfolk, and a family reunion that she was dreading. The whole journey would be a slow descent into eventual Hell, and it all began with the damn Central Line.

Petra figured she was something like three stops away from getting out of the Underground and heading to somewhere that might offer some actual fresh air, when her train began to slow down between stations for no good reason.

The old, familiar sinking feeling as the brakes squealed. It was the first of what would probably be many delays in her journey. The train crept along for a few hundred yards. She sighed.

Somehow, Petra decided, the train moving so slowly— surely at one mile per hour or less—was even more irri- tating than if it just came to a full stop.

Of course, as soon as *that* thought popped into her mind, the train *did* stop completely.

She peered at one of the tube maps which hung over the scratched, dirty windows that mocked passengers with a view of nothing other than pitch-black darkness. The train had halted somewhere between Chancery Lane and St. Paul's.

She checked her watch.

If the delay swallowed up more than ten minutes, she ran the risk of missing her connection at Liverpool Street. Petra cursed herself for leaving the house so late. That was the trouble with journeys you didn't want to make: you tended to eke out every last second before finally leaving home only when you absolutely had to, leaving no margin for error.

She began to daydream idly about calling her mother, and saying that she had missed her train.

There's no way I can get there now, Mum. I'll just have to meet your twenty-five-year-old boyfriend some other time. Such a shame...

Even if Petra had made that call, she knew her mother would have insisted that she find alternate transport. She hadn't been home in nearly two years, and that, as far as her mother was concerned, bordered on being a personal insult.

Still, it was nice to at least *think* about calling it off. Nice to linger on prospect of just turning around and returning to her studio apartment, spending the rest of the day reading a book and eating chocolate. It would be *so—*

BANG.

Petra jumped as a loud thump ricocheted around the carriage, snapping her back to reality.

A couple of passengers murmured and peered around in interest. Those, Petra figured, had to be tourists. True Londoners knew that the only place to point your eyes while on a tube train was the floor, or—at a push—the maps above the windows. Eye contact was a definite no-no.

BANG.

The second thump was louder—way louder—and it sent a ripple of tension rolling through the carriage.

Train protocol abandoned, Petra found herself staring straight into the eyes of an old man sitting near the middle of the carriage when a third thump rocked it; saw those eyes widening with a growing apprehension that she felt uncoiling in her own gut.

That third bang sounded much closer, and somehow heavy with *intent*.

The tube was grimy and slow and overcrowded and *shit*, but mostly it was predictable. Yet the thumps that Petra heard were entirely new to her. It didn't sound like an engine malfunction or even the wheels on the tracks. It didn't sound like anything she had heard on a Tube train before.

In fact, it almost sounded like somebody was walking alongside the train, banging their fists against the exterior, or perhaps swinging a baseball bat at it. But that couldn't be possible.

Another thump, though this one far more distant. A carriage or two further down the train.

Whatever was causing that noise, it was definitely *moving*.

Now, almost everybody in the carriage was peering around at each other nervously, each perhaps hoping to see a face that wasn't riddled with concern staring back at them.

Petra glanced at the door to her right, focusing her gaze on the strips of glass that were little more than pitch-black rectangles.

Suddenly, for the first time ever, she thought about how the passengers must look from the outside; beacons of light in the darkness, lit up like a bloody Christmas tree.

So vulnerable.

She shuddered.

Edged a little closer to the glass.

Holding her breath.

Did I see something out there? Something in the black-ness? Some darker shadow?

Is it looking at me right now?

Petra's heart pounded, and she leaned in further, until her nose was only inches away from the window. When the breath in her lungs began to feel like a serrated blade, she let it out softly, and it fogged the glass in front of her face.

She wiped at the pane, half expecting to reveal a face pressed up against the other side of the glass, something hideous and twisted and demonic; maybe some crazy cannibals that lived in the tunnels, like in those silly old movies her boyfriend loved.

Nothing.

Just darkness and delays on the Central Line. Every-thing oh-so ordinary. The strange banging was probably just the engine imploding. Most of the transport system in London needed replacing yesterday, if not four decades earlier. Most likely, the noises were just parts of the train dying at last, and ensuring that her journey would be slower, and just a little more hellish than it ought to be.

Stifling a nervous chuckle, Petra turned away from the door and faced the carriage once more.

Squuuueeeeeeeeeeaaaaaallllllllllllllllllllll.

The noise stopped everyone in the carriage like a freeze frame. It sounded like a rusting nail being scraped across glass. An obscene shrieking that made shoulders hunch and teeth grit.

Somewhere, a passenger whimpered.

Might have been Petra herself.

With the lights blazing inside the train, the windows were little better than mirrors, but through the distorted reflections of themselves, everyone in the carriage saw it.

Attached only to empty darkness; somehow all the more terrifying for being disembodied by the light spilling from inside the carriage.

A hand.

A single, terrifying hand.

It looked like it belonged to some enormous bird, or some prehistoric creature; long, thin fingers that ended in wicked talons.

The hand ran along the length of the carriage, scratching a line through the middle of each pane of glass, and the noise was dreadful and hypnotic. Petra watched, unable to look away, as the claw slowly drew closer to her position by the doors. Its movement was almost leisurely, like whatever unseen horror was attached to the fearsome talons was enjoying every second, and wanted to draw it out as much as possible.

The squealing stopped.

And then the lights went out.

For several moments, the darkness was so complete that Petra thought something had blinded her.

She listened to her breath, rattling like rusted chains, still hearing that all-consuming screech of the terrible claws on the glass, and let out a trembling yelp when emergency lighting kicked into life, bathing the carriage in a soft, orange glow. Suddenly, it was possible for her to see what the grotesque hand was attached to: a creature that she couldn't even have conjured in her worst nightmares was standing right outside the window.

More than one.

Monsters.

Petra saw them for only the briefest of moments, for barely a second—just a fleeting, chilling glimpse—before the windows imploded, and something—some *things*—hurtled into the carriage.

And the crowded space filled with the sound of screaming.

Conny secured the platform with the help of Remy and the two bruised security staff, guiding the small crowd of witnesses out to the bottom of the escalators which led up to the ticketing hall, explaining that medical assistance was on the way and that they would all be required to provide statements.

Almost as soon as she had shepherded the commuters away from the platform, she saw the first of the reinforcements arriving, clattering down the stopped escalator in single file, evenly spaced.

Her eyes widened in surprise.

Kevlar body armour. Assault rifles. Protective visors.

An armed response unit.

What the hell?

The first group of officers made directly for the tunnel that led to the platform without even looking in Conny and Remy's direction. A second group followed, and made their way straight toward her.

"You have been ordered to evacuate the station," a man wearing an Inspector's uniform said loudly, addressing the group. "Please leave in a calm and orderly fashion."

As if perfectly planned, the *up* escalator began to move again. Armed officers began to guide the shaken commuters toward the exit, telling them that they would be taken care of upstairs.

"Sir," Conny said, "these people are witnesses to a murder. There is an ambulance—"

"That will have to wait."

Conny blinked.

Murder will have to wait?

"The ticketing area has been cleared," the Inspector continued. "You'll need to go up to the main hall and speak to the CS."

"Chief Superintendent?" Conny repeated, surprised. "Here, at the station?"

He nodded.

"*Everybody* is here or headed this way. All hands on deck. Didn't you hear on the radio?"

Conny flushed. Her radio had been crackling during Remy's scuffle with Adam Trent. With all the noise of the man screaming and the dog snarling, she hadn't been able to pay attention to it.

She shook her head.

"Well, get upstairs." He looked down at Remy, who was still staring back toward the entrance to the platform. "I'm sure they will want you both up there."

The last of the commuters had disappeared from sight, and the Inspector gestured for his group to make for the northbound platform.

"Hey," Conny called, "it didn't happen in there, it was the southbound line."

The Inspector shook his head and grimaced behind his visor.

"It's *all* the lines."

CHAPTER SEVENTEEN

Herb's pulse thundered in his ears as he gripped one side of the table which he had placed across the kitchen door as a barricade. Dan held the other side, and when he nodded, they lifted together, moving the table aside as quietly as possible.

He stared at Dan. One minute the guy was having seizures on the floor, and the next, he was smoothly taking over as Herb's own courage began to desert him. At any moment, Herb half-expected him to collapse and start screaming, but Dan remained focused only on moving the table without making a sound. His head was bowed in concentration, his mop of hair matted with sweat. Herb noticed for the first time that he had a scar that began an inch or so above his right eyebrow, running up into his tangled hair. A surgical scar.

Before Herb could ponder the significance of that scar any further, Dan began to lower the table. Herb focused on making sure the legs didn't make a sound as they made contact with the tiles, and when he looked up again, Dan had already brushed his hair back over his forehead, and was moving to the door and pressing his ear against it.

After a moment, he shook his head.

Now, he mouthed, and Herb nodded, picking up the two guns from the counter and gripping them in palms that trembled wildly.

Dan began to turn the heavy iron key.

Slowly.

Quietly.

Wincing as he eased the ancient tumblers to the *unlocked* position.

Finally, after what felt like an eternity to Herb, Dan began to twist the handle.

And the door flew open, smashing him aside like a ragdoll.

He crashed across the table they had moved moments earlier, slamming into a cabinet. Going down hard, and disappearing from sight.

The vampire came in without hesitation, and Herb turned and fled blindly, throwing himself behind a counter.

The world became chaos.

The creature shrieking; the hideous noise echoing off the tiled walls, reverberating and multiplying until it seemed endless.

Glass breaking.

Lights winking out.

The sound of flesh tearing.

A strangled yelp.

Herb flipped onto his back as the room plunged into near-total darkness, and fired several rounds from the pistols wildly, aiming at nothing and everything in his terror.

One of the guns clicked.

Empty, Herb thought, and he tossed the weapon aside and put the barrel of the other against his temple, gasping at the searing heat of the metal on his skin.

It had been a desperate plan. Trying to trick a vampire like it was a child. Desperate...and doomed. Herb's command of what remained of the Order had lasted a matter of hours, and he had led them directly into disaster, making every wrong decision it was possible to make. All were dead, save for handful, and the man he had sworn he was going to save was instead going to die. Again.

I'm no leader, he thought, and his finger curled around the trigger.

He squeezed his eyes shut.

No hero.

Shreds of light bled through from the outside world, squirming around the edges of the shuttered windows, bouncing off chrome surfaces.

Half-illuminating the abomination as it moved with appalling purpose.

The creature charged into the centre of the room, raking its talons through the gut of one of Herb's followers. *Jay*, Dan thought, oddly detached from the unfolding horror. *I remembered his name, after all.*

The vampire leapt away from Jay's still-standing corpse as gunfire ricocheted through the kitchen: a deafening thunder that made Dan's ears ring. Muzzle flashes that threw bright, fleeting light on Jay as he began to fall, spilling something heavy and liquid from the gaping hole torn across his abdomen.

And it began.

As familiar anxiety at first; fear which hit him like an oncoming train, before twisting into something darker and less familiar.

With a roar, Dan hauled himself to his feet, striding forward and batting a gun from Herb's hand as he placed it against his own temple.

"Eyes *shut*," he snarled, his mouth delivering the command his brain hadn't been aware of, and he leapt for the knife rack, his fingers closing around a cold steel handle.

A cleaver.

Of course. That made sense.

Because the nightmare which had begun on the Oceanus wasn't over. He was still there, in the thick of it, thrashing; trying to break free of the madness. Locked inside a mind that was slowly crumbling to pieces as it tried to withstand the insanity of the world.

He turned, and saw the vampire attached to the ceiling like a dreadful, enormous insect, untroubled by gravity. It held another of Herb's followers by the neck, his feet dangling at least four feet above the ground, and before Dan could move a muscle, the monster sliced through the man's throat like ripe fruit. His body fell, an obscene torrent of dark blood pumping from the space where his head had been moments earlier.

The abomination snorted out something that might have been a laugh as it tossed the cleric's head aside.

And drilled its eyes into Dan.

He felt a sickening sensation erupt in his mind; a terrible sort of pulling, as if the creature had hooked invisible claws into his brain and was trying to wrench it from his skull. As Dan watched, transfixed, the creature's eyes seemed to glow, becoming strangely hypnotic, and the awful pulling in his head grew stronger, until Dan felt sure that his skull was about to explode.

The vampire dropped down onto the tiled floor.

Took a step toward him.

Click.

HERB WATCHED IT HAPPEN AS AN ORBITING satellite might observe the destruction of the planet: detached and distant; separated from the insanity somehow. He couldn't persuade his muscles to move, couldn't even draw a breath into lungs that burned with the desire to power a scream.

Dan Bellamy wasn't special at all.

The vampire stalked toward him casually, and Dan just...stood there. Staring at it; a huge cleaver dangling from limp fingers, his jaw slack; his eyes wide.

It has taken his mind, Herb thought in dull terror. *Edgar was wrong. I was wrong. And now we're all going to die.*

Click.

Click.

The vampire took another couple of steps forward on those hideous, angular legs.

And it *stopped.*

For a moment, Herb gaped, bewildered, as the vampire and Dan stared into each other's eyes.

And then Dan screamed.

Lifted the cleaver high above his head.

And *charged.*

His timing was off.

The creature whipped to the right as he swung the cleaver, and the blade landed only a glancing blow on the monster's neck. He switched his grip on the handle, and swung again; a sweeping backhand that a tennis pro would have admired, and a bestial roar erupted from his lungs as the blade carved itself a home in the side of the vampire's hateful head, lodging so deep in the thing's cheek that when the vampire began to fall, it was impossible for him to maintain his grip on the weapon.

Shattering pain erupted in Dan's belly.

He stared down, blinking stupidly.

Tried to process the sight of the three wicked talons buried in his stomach, and the awful tearing sensation as the creature's weight dragged the hideous weapons away from his flesh.

A spatter of blood hit the tiles.

My blood.

So much—

And then Dan, too, began to fall.

The darkness took him before he landed.

Herb watched in a daze as both Dan and the vampire crashed to the floor. The room looked more like an abattoir now than a kitchen; bodies and blood and death piled in every corner.

The remaining three clerics—Lawrence, Scott and Adrian—stared at the twitching monster in horrified fascination, watching as it reached up a hand with a snort, gripping the handle of the cleaver that had split its skull almost in two, and tried to pull the blade out.

It screamed, and thick, black blood oozed from the wound like treacle.

It took Herb a moment to realise that the creature wasn't dying, or if it was, it was doing so slowly.

That moment was long enough.

Adrian picked up a large carving knife from a counter and took a step toward the convulsing abomination, his face twisted in terror as he stared down at it.

"No!" Herb screamed. "Don't look at it!"

Too late.

Adrian lifted the wicked blade high.

Drove the business end into the side of his own head.

Herb looked away in despair as the cleric dropped to the floor, and the vampire began to roll toward the rear of the kitchen, still clutching at the steel that had penetrated its skull. It scrambled out of sight behind the island in the centre of the room, melting into the thick shadows.

"Get Bellamy!" he hollered, loud enough to shake Lawrence and Scott from their stupor, and he sprinted across the slick tiles to Dan's inert body.

You can't die. You can't.

There was no time to check Dan's injuries; to determine whether it was safe to move him. It certainly wasn't safe *not* to.

Herb grabbed a handful of Dan's thick sweater, trying not to notice how heavy and sticky with the man's blood it was, and began to heave, his feet slipping. Despite his slim frame, Bellamy was dead weight, and Herb made little headway until Lawrence appeared in front of him and grabbed the unconscious man's ankles.

Somewhere in the shadows to the rear of the kitchen, the injured vampire shrieked. In the metal-and-tile kitchen, the noise was impossibly loud, otherworldly.

It might have been a sound born of pain.

Might have been determination or murderous desire or rage.

Herb didn't want to find out.

"We have to *go*," he roared.

CHAPTER EIGHTEEN

W hen Conny reached Euston Station's main hall, her jaw dropped.

The hall was filling up with police officers: a dizzying vortex of uniforms representing a myriad of units and boroughs. She couldn't guess at exactly how many of her colleagues there were gathering below the departure boards, but it had to be north of two hundred.

This is a lot bigger than some guy going nuts with a length of rebar.

Yet it wasn't just the sheer number of police present that made her skin prickle: the atmosphere in the room itself was rotten with tension. As she moved away from the escalators, toward the bulk of the gathering force, Conny caught the eye of several officers and shot them a quizzical glance. Each time she received only an abrupt head shake in return. By the look of the confused expressions on the faces Conny saw, no one had much more of a clue about why they were there than she did.

Remy's chain hung slackly in her left hand. The dog should have been alert in the presence of so many police officers—curious at the very least—but Remy simply hovered at Conny's side, staring back at the escalator that led down toward the distant crime scene. His behaviour was unnatural, almost like he had been struck by some sudden illness. She couldn't remember ever seeing the dog so subdued.

Conny began to move toward the crowd and scanned the room, hoping to spot either somebody that she knew, or the Chief Superintendent that the Inspector heading to the platform had mentioned, but it was her ears that grabbed her attention, not her eyes.

A nearby constable, who looked like he'd only been on the job a year at most, muttered ominously that his brother worked out of Scotland Yard, and had told him that the army had been called in.

Someone else said they had heard of incidents in other cities.

"It started in Morden," Conny heard another voice whispering quietly. "The guy with the knife, you heard about that?"

Conny frowned. The spree killing at the South London supermarket a couple of hours earlier was a big deal, of course, and she was certain that the tragedy would dominate the national headlines for days to come, but she wasn't sure why that incident would prompt the Metropolitan Police to send such a large group of officers to the London Underground. Morden was the very last stop on the Northern Line, way out in zone six. Far away from Euston.

"He was the start. I heard there have been *other* incidents. And the news is talking about a cruise ship being attacked. Blown up. It's terrorists..."

A cruise ship? Conny hadn't heard anything over the radio about it.

She glanced up. Above the departure boards, a large television screen displayed the latest news. There was no volume, but there was indeed a stone-faced newscaster sitting in front of a picture of a huge cruise ship. Along the bottom of the screen, a headline read *Tragedy in the Atlantic*.

What the hell would that *have to do with* this?

A murmur rippled through a group of officers standing to her left, catching her attention, and when she tore her gaze away from the TV screen, she finally spotted some senior uniforms in the distance. Before she could move toward them, Conny saw the group exchanging troubled glances and quickly exiting the hall. They stood outside in the rain, talking animatedly in hushed tones. Lots of gesticulating.

The tension in the hall jacked up a notch.

Far to her right, Conny heard a loud bark and searched through the bodies, finally catching sight of the dog. His name was Jackson, and Conny knew his handler, Robert Nelson. Several weeks earlier, Nelson had asked Conny if she would like to go to dinner, and she had rejected him more bluntly than she had intended. He seemed like a nice guy, but he had terrible timing.

A conversation between them would be awkward. Conny sighed. Dogs were so much *easier* than people. She made a mental note to keep it brief, and she pushed through the crowd with Remy trotting along behind her, apparently happy to be on the move once more.

Robert looked like he was having trouble keeping Jackson calm. The dog was a German Shepherd, just like

Remy, but noticeably smaller. Jackson's specialty was his nose: he was one of the best sniffers on the Force.

Robert looked up as Conny approached, and his face crumbled into a weak grin.

"Uh, hi, Cornelia. How are you?"

"Robert," she nodded. "Do you know what's going on?"

His smile faded. "Probably no more than you, but whatever it is, it's big. And this isn't the only station involved. *All available officers*, right?"

Conny stared at him, baffled, and he frowned.

"You didn't hear it on the radio?"

"I was...busy."

"Well, you didn't miss much. All I know is that people have been going missing on the—"

A loud murmur passed through the crowd, cutting him off, and Conny turned to see the senior officers striding back into the room wearing stricken expressions. A man with a beard, who was wearing what Conny thought was a Chief Superintendent's uniform, gestured to somebody that she couldn't see.

A moment later, the murmuring of the crowd became a loud chatter.

Someone was handing out firearms, pulling them from a secure crate and distributing them to men and women who looked equal-parts horrified and excited at the prospect of arming themselves.

And all Conny could do was stare.

Heckler and Koch G36. Assault rifle. Thirty-round magazines. Five-point-Five-Six Calibre. Able to switch between semi- and full-automatic. A work of art.

MP5SF. Submachine gun. Capable of firing seven-fucking-hundred silenced nine-mil rounds per minute.

Single, burst or continuous fire. The MP5 was a stubby, hissing snake of a weapon, and Conny thought it was perhaps the most beautiful thing she had ever seen.

Some of the firearms were held casually, with the easy grip of familiarity. Others were clutched in hands that shook, just a little. Guns were not routine for British police, not even in the country's capital city. There would be plenty of anxious men and women there, Conny thought, facing the prospect of their first firefight.

Including me.

Many of the more senior police officers in the main hall took an assault rifle, and being surrounded by all that firepower made her feel dizzy with longing.

She blinked in surprise when a man wearing a Lieu-tenant's uniform stepped directly in front of her and pressed a *Glock 17* into her palm.

She stared at it, open-mouthed.

Moulded polymer casing. Seventeen nine-millimetre parabolic rounds. Under-barrel tac-light.

It was heavy; solid.

So beautiful.

The gun fit into Conny's palm like it had been custom-made for her.

"Have you been trained with automatic weapons?"

Conny shook her head slowly, her eyes distant; focused only on the Glock. She had developed a parent-troubling love of guns and weaponry at around the time that girls were *supposed* to be dreaming of owning ponies, and had fired automatic weapons on ranges on several occasions, but had never carried a firearm in the line of duty. Once, carrying that sort of firepower regularly had been her ultimate goal, but that was before she had been partnered with Remy, and had seen what a thinking weapon was capable of.

And now, here she was, being handed a pistol in the middle of a real-life situation that she had no grasp of whatsoever.

Damn, though, the gun did feel powerful. *Intoxicating.*

"Constable. Constable?"

Conny blinked and looked at the Lieutenant.

"You stay at the rear, you understand? The ideal scenario here is you handing that weapon back to me fully loaded."

She nodded.

The Lieutenant dropped his gaze to Remy.

"He a sniffer?"

"Crowd control, Sir."

"Hmm. Well, that might prove just as useful."

He began to move away.

"Sir," Conny said, blurting out the word before she had even realised she was about to speak. "What's happening?"

The Lieutenant arched an eyebrow and glanced back at her. She saw impatience in his eyes, and something else, too. Uncertainty, maybe.

"You didn't hear on the radio?"

Conny shook her head.

"We were dealing with a violent—"

The Lieutenant interrupted her with an irritated gesture. He nodded toward the front of the hall, and the group of senior officers gathering beneath the departure boards.

"Eyes front," he said. "Briefing any second, now."

He turned away before Conny nodded, and slipped into the crowd, searching for any other unarmed officers.

Moments later, a voice called out.

"Quiet!"

The excited chatter which had filled the hall as the weapons were being handed out died away immediately.

Conny moved forward and lifted to her tiptoes, peering over the heads of those in front of her. A bearded man of around forty-five with a grave expression held his left hand aloft. It was the man she had seen moments earlier giving the order to pass out the guns.

"Chief Superintendent Porter," the bearded man said. "Some of you know me. For the rest of you, I'm sorry we're meeting under these circumstances." He took a deep breath. "In the last hour, deaths have been reported at a number of Underground stations. Maintenance staff, working in the tunnels, have not returned from their shifts. At present, there are at least sixteen people unaccounted for. Three of the missing members of staff *did* return, and none of them have lived longer than a couple of minutes. All have committed suicide, usually after attempting—and in a couple of cases succeeding—to take the lives of others first."

Just like Adam Trent, Conny thought.

Porter finally dropped his hand, apparently concluding that he had everybody's complete attention. He lowered his voice a little.

"You've all heard about what happened in Morden earlier today. It looks like it was not an isolated incident."

There was an audible intake of breath around the hall.

"Most of the outer parts of the rail network have already been closed and evacuated. We have started moving toward the centre of London, shutting stations as we go. At this moment, there are more than twenty Underground stations out there full of officers just like yourselves, hearing this exact same information."

Porter drew in a breath and scanned the hall from left to right.

"In the past ten minutes, several trains have gone dark."

He paused for a moment, as if to give that information a chance to settle on everyone's mind.

Trains lost in the tunnels, Conny thought. *Civilians*. Dear God, the Chief Superintendent was telling them that virtually the entire London police force had been called out. Even himself. Was the Commissioner of the entire bloody *Met* out there somewhere, standing in an Underground station, delivering an identical speech and handing out guns?

"At this moment, we have to assume the worst."

Porter lifted his chin, staring around the faces that were fixed upon him.

"There is something in the tunnels; we don't know what. According to the powers that be, we had no prior intelligence suggesting that a terrorist attack on the trans-port system was imminent, but we must assume that we are dealing with a large, multi-cellular threat, here. Quite possibly, a citywide attack. I'm not going to lie to you, we're going into this blind, and our numbers are stretched across half of London. Our primary focus here is to find those trains and all civilians, and to secure these tunnels. To ensure that the stations are safe, and that whatever is happening down there does not spill out onto the streets. Engaging with any threat is strictly secondary until we know more about what we are dealing with, is that understood?"

A ripple of agreement passed through the crowd.

"We have a lot of ground to cover," the Chief Superintendent continued, and Conny thought she heard in his voice an echo of the sentiment she had detected in the eyes of the Lieutenant who had armed her. A wavering uncertainty. "You will divide equally between the Northern Line and the Victoria Line, and you'll split further to cover the northbound and southbound tunnels. There are already armed response teams waiting on each platform, and they are the tip of the spear, understand?"

The gathered crowd mumbled its acknowledgment of the order. Porter sucked in a lungful of air and continued.

"When the tunnels split, you will divide into groups of *no fewer* than seven. If you see anything that looks like a device—*anything*—you are to inform either your immediate CO or myself, and we all fall back and wait for the bomb squad. Your radios won't work once we're inside the tunnels, but these,"—he held up an oddly cheerful-looking walkie-talkie—"will give us limited range. We don't have enough for every one of you, but I want each group to be carrying at least three. I expect constant radio contact, and I mean *constant*. I can't stress this enough: if any of you deviate from these orders in any way, I'll have your arse in front of an inquiry before you can say *sacked*. I expect you all to come back here without a scratch on you, now do I make myself fucking clear?"

This time, the agreement was louder, almost a cheer.

Jesus, Conny thought, *this is all for show. Puffing up the troops before sending them into battle. What the fuck is this?*

The Lieutenant who had handed out the guns began

to wave officers toward the escalator leading down to the platforms. Conny fell into line behind the others, scanning the faces around her and seeing her own anxiety reflected in them.

And for the first time since Adam Trent had died, she felt tension on Remy's leash.

She looked down at the German Shepherd, and frowned.

The fearless dog was dragging his weight, his eyes focused intently on the *down* escalator, as if he was reluctant to approach it.

Like he was afraid of what might be waiting for him down there.

CHAPTER NINETEEN

Leon Mancini wasn't a religious man, not like most of the freaks back at the ranch in Colorado. If Jennifer Craven had ever harboured ideas about changing that fact —about *converting* him—she had wisely decided not to follow through on them. There were some people that even she understood that you couldn't just throw in a dark room and dose with acid and expect obedience.

Mancini was one of those people. He had been running operations in Force Recon when Craven was trying on her first training bra; there was no form of torture he hadn't been trained to withstand.

So Craven made him love her.

As it turned out, the torture would have been preferable.

Craven was sharp and dangerous; a knife sheathed in an expensive dress suit. Mancini didn't trust her an inch, and never would, but she had broken him in a way that military training could never have prepared him for.

For a long time, he told himself that he was working for the money the Craven family offered, and that was certainly true while Jennifer's old man had been running the show. As soon as Jennifer took charge and began aggressively expanding the Order, he began to harbour doubts. The threat to his life if he chose to leave the ranch was obvious, but Mancini had no problem with that. He'd lived most of his life under threat of one sort or another, and he knew when he signed up that his predecessor had met an 'untimely' end.

That didn't matter. If he left, and the Cravens came after him, they'd discover that he was pretty hard to kill, and they wouldn't be the first.

Just as he was preparing to get out, Jennifer came to him, and found a way to make him stay.

That had been years ago, and he still couldn't bring himself to leave, not even after she had rejected him so brutally.

Yeah, love was the worst torture of all.

Their affair lasted only a year. Not by his choosing.

When it was over, Mancini remained professional, and told himself that as long as Jennifer played it straight with him and paid well, things would go just fine between them, just like they had with her old man. The rest of the freaks at the ranch could carry on with their weird rituals and worship of their *buried gods*; Christ, they could dance naked under the moon waving severed cocks in the air for all he cared.

Old man Craven had told him the truth—or at least as much of it as Mancini cared to know—before Jennifer had taken over. The Cravens believed in vampires; that the monsters lived underground in hibernation, and occasionally a few popped up to the surface to eat some folks. They had turned their ranch into a twisted Disneyworld, and were slowly growing their cult by attracting vulnerable youngsters who didn't know better and *re-educating* them.

As far as Mancini was concerned, the Craven family's religion was no more bizarre than any of the others—and no less steeped in blood. And, much the same as every other religion out there, the people at the top rolled about in a seemingly endless pit of money, and were more than happy to spend some on having men like Mancini around to make them feel safe.

The rituals—the overtly, almost cartoonish devotion to a sort of Satanism—were mostly for show, but the show worked. A steady stream of miserable teenagers made their way to the ranch, either of their own volition or as a result of active recruitment, and numbers grew until the place more closely resembled a small town.

Mostly, Mancini's twenty years as an employee of the Craven family had seen him keeping peace at the ranch, and keeping unwanted visitors out. At times, he had been required to kidnap and ultimately murder scientists across a multitude of disciplines, everything from astrophysicists to botanists, as Jennifer Craven focused on hunting down the truth about the grave she had 'discovered' sixteen years earlier and the creatures that she had been born to serve.

At other times, on occasions when new initiates escaped the ranch and ran, either losing their minds or finally coming to their senses, Mancini and his team hunted them down.

One way or another, nobody left the ranch.

Over recent years, informed, no doubt, by the internet, a surprising number of desperate parents had found their way to Colorado's perfect middle-of-nowhere, searching for the children they believed they still had some claim to.

They didn't get to leave either.

Only once had the secrecy of the ranch been truly compromised on Mancini's watch; two years earlier, by a tiny documentary crew whose dream of headlines had blinded them to the fact that they weren't dealing with some two-bit religious wackos. Had the idiots in question restricted themselves to long-range surveillance, they might even had succeeded in making their little movie, but they just hadn't been able to resist getting closer for the perfect shot.

When that incident was finally resolved, Mancini watched the recordings they had managed to get. It was a little like watching one of those tired *found footage* horror movies that seemed to be everywhere in recent years. Just like those movies, the filmmakers' story ended in blood; in bones scattered across the plains.

It wasn't noble or glorious, but it was a job, and for twenty years, it had been a good one. Better to Mancini than the military had ever been.

He couldn't help but feel that England was going to change that.

Because it was almost dark already.

He wondered if he had an English counterpart. Maybe the Rennick family had their own Leon Mancini.

Maybe he, too, was scanning the countryside around the Rennick mansion through a rifle scope at that very moment, trying to spot some threatening movement in the last scraps of the afternoon light.

The Gulfstream which Jennifer had provided for Mancini and his team had touched down at a private airfield south of London almost an hour earlier. From there, they took a van southwest, driving for around thirty minutes to reach the land owned by the Rennick family.

There was a single overgrown road leading through thick woodland to the compound itself; there was no way they could take the van through there. If the Rennick compound was set up anything like the Craven Ranch—and based on what Craven had told him, Mancini was certain that it would be—the road would be under constant surveillance, and most likely rigged with auto-mated defensive measures.

He parked a couple of miles back from the road, and led his team the rest of the way through the trees on foot, keeping a wary eye out for bear traps and tripwires.

They moved in silence, like watchful ghosts. Each and every one of them had been a part of missions in terrain that was far worse than anything the English coun-tryside could throw at them, and they made quick progress through the forest.

After around ten minutes, during which period even Burnley and Montero had managed to stay silent, the compound loomed before them, huge and dark. Several smaller buildings gathered around a vast mansion that looked like something out of a TV show; one of those achingly dull period dramas that the Brits loved to produce.

Mancini scanned the compound through the M24's powerful scope, and felt the hair on the back of his neck rising.

Steel shutters looked to have been drawn across all

the windows of the main mansion building, but the front door stood wide open, gaping like a hungry mouth.

According to Jennifer Craven, the Rennick compound was home to a total of more than fifty people, yet there was no sign of movement anywhere.

"What do you think, Mancini?"

He ignored Braxton's question for a moment, concentrating on trying to focus his scope on the interior of the mansion beyond the doors. He thought he could see *something* in there, but the light was no good.

He lowered the rifle and sighed.

"I think whatever happened here, we missed it. But we have to be sure."

Braxton looked dubious.

"Yeah, sure. But we're gonna find some bad shit in that house. You know that, right?"

Mancini nodded. He knew it, all right. The combination of the closed shutters and the open door could only mean one thing: somebody had tried to hide from *something*, and they had failed. He would be leading his team into either a trap, or—if the Craven family was right about vampires after all—the scene of a massacre. There was no way around it. This was where Herbert Rennick had been headed, and Mancini had no other leads to follow up. If the Hermetic wasn't here, the team would be heading home empty-handed, and Jennifer Craven's rage would be fucking *biblical*.

"Didn't come all this way for nothing," he said grimly. "Tell the others we're moving in."

MANCINI'S TEAM WAS THE BEST OF THOSE AVAILABLE

at the ranch, which made them damn near as lethal as most any military unit in the world. Braxton and Montero had been SEALS, Rushmer had spent a decade in Delta Force, and Burnley's work in the Special Activities Division of the CIA was so classified that even she had no idea what any of her missions had been about. Or so she claimed.

The team was rounded off by its only member with a non-military background: Ed Bricknall, who was one of only a handful of westerners to have ever been invited to Shaolin Temple to study with the monks, if his tales were to be believed. The guy was practically a fucking *ninja*, with the fastest pair of hands Mancini had ever seen and an apparent inability to feel pain. He couldn't even imagine where Jennifer had dug *that* guy up.

They were badass all right, every last one of them.

Their presence should have made him feel safe.

Yet as he stopped at the threshold of the Rennick mansion, *safe* turned out to be the last thing Leon Mancini felt.

Jennifer's warning about what he could expect to face ran through his mind repeatedly, and though he didn't believe her, not *really*, her dire words had been delivered so earnestly that they had managed to burrow under his skin.

If you engage the vampires, you will *die. Trust me. Stay in the light.*

The power was out in the mansion, or the lights had been smashed, and with daylight quickly fading and the shutters down, the interior of the house melted into darkness within a few feet of the front door. Standing in the main doorway, Mancini pulled out a flashlight, and began to sweep it around a huge, ornate room that looked like the lobby of a fine hotel.

The beam made the shadows dance jerkily, and picked out sights worse than anything he'd seen in his long military career; an atrocity that was beyond his comprehension. Bodies smashed and broken like children's toys, organs strewn about the vast room like grisly confetti.

He shouldered the rifle and pulled out an MP5.

And all of the vampire bullshit which he had listened to from the Craven family for years came back to him. Creatures that couldn't be killed. Creatures that ripped your mind away from you and made you their puppets. Sadistic monsters that revelled in terror and pain. Evil fucking incarnate.

It was all true. Craven wasn't taking impressionable kids and brainwashing them to believe in some satanic nonsense. She was brainwashing them with the *truth*.

Evil lurked in the Rennick mansion. Mancini could feel it, radiating from the shadows in waves, rolling around him like dry ice. He had felt fear plenty; being an elite member of the military wasn't about not feeling fear, it was about not letting that fear slow you down for a second. Acknowledging it and having the courage to press forward regardless.

He hadn't ever felt fear like this.

Mancini had courage enough to take on most any objective, but he knew as he felt that evil washing over him, that taking another step inside the mansion would not be bravery. It would be stupidity.

Jennifer Craven, he thought, was not worth *this*.

"Back," he whispered urgently, "there's nothing here."

But there was.

His wavering light caught movement in the centre of the gigantic room, and for a split second he saw it clearly, rising from the pile of corpses on unsteady legs, a walking nightmare with the handle of a blade protruding from its cheek and a ragged strip of human flesh hanging from its hideous jaws.

Feeding, Mancini thought in horror.

With a screech, the vampire leapt vertically, disappearing into the shadows at the top of the room.

It didn't come back down.

Don't look up.

"Run!" he hollered, turning away and leaving the mansion behind at a sprint. He heard footsteps running with him, but they were quickly drowned out by gunfire. Mancini glanced over his shoulder and saw Rushmer emptying his whole clip into Ed Bricknall's gut, ripping the *ninja* to shreds, all his years of intense training and dedication punched out of him in seconds by large calibre bullets.

Rushmer's eyes were wide and horrified as he executed Bricknall, and Mancini knew exactly what his expression meant; knew it in his gut as sure as he knew his own name. The vampire had Rushmer's mind, just like Jennifer Craven said. It *was* Rushmer.

"Go," he snarled at the others, "before he can reload. *Don't look back.*"

He aimed for the trees, tossing his heavy sniper rifle aside and pouring every ounce of energy he had into pumping his legs. A hundred yards. Fifty. He saw Burnley disappear into the trees first—damn, she was *fast* —just ahead of Braxton and Montero. Both of the younger men were pulling away from him steadily.

Behind him, he heard the distant crack of automatic

fire, and the distinctive whine of bullets fizzing around his head.

He leapt the last few feet, hitting the deck inside the tree line and rolling, inhaling a mouthful of wet dirt and leaves.

When he scrambled to his feet, spitting and gasping for air, he saw Braxton and Montero taking up defensive positions, readying their weapons.

"Are you insane?" Mancini snarled, running deeper into the trees. "They're gone; there's nothing we can do for them, understand? Get to the van. Go!"

"What about the mission?"

Mancini slowed, glaring at Braxton, and ducking instinctively when he heard distant rifle fire split the night once more. It didn't sound like it was close, but it wasn't worth taking the risk.

"If Herbert Rennick came back, he isn't in *there*," Mancini snapped, and turned to run.

"You're right," an unfamiliar voice said, and Mancini whipped his body toward it, lifting the submachine gun. "You just missed him. But I can tell you where he's going."

The man who had spoken stepped out from the trees, his hands held above his head. A big man, with a hard stare; Mancini thought he had the look of someone who knew how to handle himself, but he didn't appear to be carrying a weapon.

Mancini lowered the MP5.

"Jeremy Pruitt," the big man said. "I believe I may have spoken to your boss on the phone."

CHAPTER TWENTY

The tunnel stank of age; damp and rust and decay. And fear.

Conny walked, as instructed, at the rear of the large group of armed police, listening to the soft shuffling of boots ahead of her. She figured there had to be more than forty of them in total, creeping along the southbound line.

No one spoke.

And with each step forward, the mood among the officers became a little more toxic, the apprehension ripening inside them just that little bit more evident. It didn't matter which unit the officers came from, she thought, or what experience they had. This was about as far from standard operating procedure as it was possible to get. They were *all* afraid.

We're going in blind, Chief Superintendent Porter had said, and it turned out he was being both literal and figurative. Most of the officers carried flashlights—either in their hands or affixed to their weapons—but the beams looked fragile in the suffocating darkness; they only lit so much. Wherever the flashlights were not pointing, the darkness became an impossible void. Shadows surged and retreated. As soon as the platform lights of Euston Station disappeared, just a few hundred yards into the tunnel system, Conny became painfully aware that the abyss was at her back; that all lights including her own were pointing forward. It felt like the blackness was chasing her, waiting for an opportunity to swallow her whole.

The tension in the group was palpable. It poisoned her mind, and grim fantasies began to unspool: killers closing in on her from behind, all-but invisible in the darkness. Drawing nearer with knives in their hands and psychotic grins splitting their faces. Or maybe the shadows were home to explosive devices that the police could not see, buried charges which would detonate and bring the tunnel roof down onto her head, crushing her bones and slowly suffocating the life from her...

A sensation which Conny hadn't experienced in more than thirty years came back to her suddenly and vividly. She remembered sitting up in her small bed, staring at the closet in her bedroom, certain that the door was opening...slowly...

...and that something monstrous waited inside.

Her grip on the Glock tightened until her knuckles ached.

It was just her mind playing tricks on her. The tunnel hadn't even split yet, and the only way anyone could be behind her was if they came from the same platform that she and forty-plus other armed police had used.

It was, Conny mused, incredible how quickly all the training and all the resolve just drained away when confronted with unknown danger and a lack of light. Some responses were primal; instinctive and unstoppable.

And the darkness was the most complete that she had

ever known. In the pitch black, with all her colleagues wearing dark uniforms, the world was reduced to floating points of light and half-stifled, fearful exhalations.

A bead of cold sweat ran down her back, making her flinch, and she tried to shake the dread settling over her away. She had been in plenty of threatening situations in her career; *life*-threatening on more than one occasion, but the tunnel was getting to her, crawling under her skin.

And that wasn't just the darkness' doing, she realised. It was Logan. Her poor boy, who needed her now more than ever, no matter how much he might deny it. Logan was going to require her support desperately in the coming months and years, just as his father had. As much as she tried to put her personal life aside when she was at work, there were some situations in which it simply wasn't possible. She was walking headlong into an unknown danger that made her stomach churn while her son was in the hospital, struggling to comprehend a terminal diagnosis. While she was all that he had.

If any harm comes to me, it will be Logan that suffers, she thought bleakly, and flinched when the group of police in front of her abruptly halted.

Conny craned her neck to see what their lights were trained on, and her stomach lurched.

The tunnel split into four directly ahead of them, and the Chief Superintendent was busy dividing them into smaller groups and pointing at each tunnel in turn.

As the fractured wall of light that had been ahead of her began to break apart, and the smaller groups moved away into the tunnels, Conny couldn't help but think that things had been bad moments earlier, but now they were so much worse.

Eventually, only her small group was left, led by CS

Porter himself. Along with Conny and Remy were half a dozen officers who looked like they *really* wanted to turn and run back through the tunnel, and a handful from the armed response units she had seen earlier. The *tip of the spear*.

The AR officers took the lead, moving down the far left tunnel with their assault rifles tucked against their collarbones, each weapon sending a beam of light thirty metres ahead of them. Behind them, Porter led the rest. He kept a Glock pointed at the floor in his left hand; a walkie-talkie in his right. For the moment, all Conny could hear was rustling and faint static, along with the occasional mumbled word, all rasping from the tinny speaker at a barely-audible volume.

The group pressed forward into the smaller tunnel with just a dozen flashlights, and the darkness that had felt dangerous when it was at her back embraced her like a live thing; a creature that swallowed up the lights cast into it with ravenous hunger.

She followed the Chief Superintendent, trying not to think about her son, and about how he would cope if she did not make it back, and her growing anxiety slowly boiled all her thoughts away, until just one was left.

Please, God, let this tunnel be empty.

Remy strained at his leash continually, trying to pull her back toward the platform at Euston, and Conny slowly began to fall behind. As a gap opened up between herself and the rest of the group, her nerves began to dance uncontrollably. There was no way she could allow herself to get separated from the others.

"Heel, Rem," she hissed, jerking on the leash, irritated at the note of panic she heard in her voice.

He continued to pull, turning every step into a battle, until finally Conny stopped. "Fine," she muttered, "if you want to go back, go back."

She glanced down the tunnel fearfully. Already the lights of the rest of the group were disappearing around a bend, threatening to leave her alone in the dark with only the Glock's tiny flashlight attachment to guide her. She had to let Remy go.

She loosened her grip on the chain, and Remy whined, but he didn't move. He didn't want to run away, she realised. Remy was far too loyal to leave her side.

He's trying to get me *to run away.*

A shudder rippled through her.

Remy whined again, very quietly, almost as though he was afraid of being heard.

She knelt in front of the dog and whispered sternly, "Remy. We're on duty. *Heel.*"

Remy lowered his nose miserably, accepting defeat.

Conny straightened and broke into a trot, closing the gap that had grown between herself and the flashlights of her colleagues.

Closing it too quickly.

Why have they stopped?

Her pace faltered, and she felt Remy give another hopeful tug on the leash.

The others were gathered around the Chief Superintendent, their expressions tense, all eyes pointed at the radio he held in his right hand. She jogged toward them and opened her mouth, drawing in a breath to ask what was happening, and Porter silenced her with a stare.

The radio hissed faintly, and a disembodied voice whispered, "I don't see anything. You?"

Another voice responded, "No, but I *hear* it. Don't you hear—"

The words dissolved in a meaningless blast of static that cut open the darkness in the tunnel like a blade.

Conny lifted her confused gaze to meet Porter's eyes. The bearded man was staring at the radio in open-mouthed horror.

Not static, she realised. *Gunfire.*

It lasted only a few seconds, but that was long enough for Conny to grind her teeth as she realised that what she was hearing was fully automatic, unsuppressed fire. The big guns.

In one of the nearby tunnels, a group of policemen had been forced to engage, and from the sound of it, they had emptied their entire weapons at something.

The clatter of shooting was followed by a sound all the worse; a sound that made Conny grip Remy's leash so tightly that the metal pressed painfully into the flesh of her palm.

Silence.

No one calling it in. No one shouting at their colleagues to get the cuffs, or to head this way or that way. No suspect's rights being recited.

Not even any groans of pain.

Just...silence.

It was the Chief Superintendent that finally broke it.

"Who fired?" Porter hissed into the radio. "Respond! Fitz? Stevens? Preston?"

A disembodied voice floated in the darkness, tinny and low.

"Not us, Sir."

It was followed swiftly by another; a voice that shook audibly.

"Clear here, Sir."

A beat.

Another.

"Dammit, Stevens," Porter snarled. "Respond. *Stevens?*"

For several long seconds the air in the tunnel was compressed by the awful silence, until the weight of it made Conny want to clap her hands over her ears. She squeezed her eyes shut and drew in a deep breath.

Let it out slowly.

This can't be happening.

Not today.

"Rendezvous back at the tunnel split," she heard Porter say, and when she opened her eyes, the lights of the group had already turned around, the others heading back the way they had come at speed. Moving in a daze, Conny turned to sprint after them.

And slammed to a halt as Remy tugged forcefully on the leash.

"Remy!" she yelled, and there was more than a note of panic in her tone now. Her voice was soaked in it. The damn dog had wanted to go back minutes earlier, and now he was trying to drag her deeper into the tunnel?

With a curse of frustration, Conny dropped the leash and took a step forward, trusting that Remy would follow.

And she let out a surprised yelp when she felt sharp teeth sinking into her flesh.

She stared down at her right calf in amazement. He wasn't playing—Remy almost *never* played, and certainly not when he was on duty—this was a *bite*, strong enough to break the skin.

She felt a stab of pain and let out a grunt, stooping to retrieve Remy's leash.

The dog began to pull on her leg and the pain spiked high enough to make her gasp.

"What the fuck, Remy?"

Remy whined and opened his jaws, the sudden release almost dumping Conny on her butt. He bumped his nose into her leg a couple of times and then bit again, gently this time, but persuasively, trying to pull her in the opposite direction to the one that Porter and the others had taken.

She focused on the distant group of flashlights. The others already looked far away, moving at a sprint. They would be around the bend and out of sight in moments. She wasn't one of the officers carrying a walkie-talkie. If she got separated from the group and somehow her flashlight failed...

She patted at her pockets.

She'd left her phone on the dashboard of the van.

Dammit, Remy!

Once more, she reached down to grab Remy's leash, intending to haul him along on his belly if necessary, and the tunnel behind her echoed to a sound that made her blood chill in her veins.

A hideous screech; a sound no human throat could possibly produce.

That's not terrorists, Conny thought bleakly. *It's something else.*

In the distance, Chief Superintendent Porter opened fire.

They all did.

The roaring guns spat gobs of light onto the tunnel walls, and Remy's plaintive whining became a frantic growl. He grabbed the cuff of her trousers firmly and yanked hard, but for a moment, all Conny could do was stand and stare numbly at the distant firefight. She saw no sign of return fire; just a group of police officers emptying their weapons into the darkness.

For several seconds, the thunder of the guns ricocheted from the tunnel walls, and then, in the distant, swirling pool cast by a half-dozen flashlights, she caught a glimpse of *something*; heard a dreadful *skittering*.

It moved fast, galloping along the underside of the fucking *ceiling* and launching itself at Porter.

Cutting through him like his body was made of smoke.

Conny watched the distant figure of the Chief Superintendent fall, and the tunnel filled with the noise of screaming; of wet ripping. She saw another figure collapse. Yet another—incredibly; impossibly—appeared to stuff the barrel of his G36 into his mouth and pepper the wall behind him with the contents of his own skull.

All of a sudden, Conny felt the pressure of Remy's jaws on her calf ease, and she knew what that meant. The dog had done his best to persuade her to run, but had decided the time had come for him to flee or die. He ran with a pitiful, apologetic whine.

More gunfire behind her. It looked like there were only five of them left now, and a couple were shooting wildly; hitting nothing. A hideous scream rattled along the tunnel, and another of Conny's colleagues went down hard, slammed into the ground by something that exited the shadows only for an instant.

It was all happening too fast.

I'm going to die down here.

With a glance at the Glock that now seemed tiny and

insignificant in her hand, Conny took the only option available. She *couldn't* die. Not before Logan did.

She turned away from the horror, following Remy's lead.

Running for her life.

CHAPTER TWENTY-ONE

I t wasn't following.

Either it was too busy tearing the rest of the police apart, or it hadn't noticed Conny and Remy hanging back further down the tunnel. Maybe it just didn't care. Perhaps it already had more than enough meat, and saw no pressing reason to chase after one retreating human and her dog.

Coward.

The word burned hot in Conny's mind. Her decision to flee had been instinctive, but that simply made it all the worse. It meant that despite all her years of training and experience, there had always been a danger threshold at which she would just turn and run, abandoning her duty. She had never been afraid of anything, not like this. When the creature had appeared, she hadn't thought about the safety of her colleagues or her oath as a police officer; only her certainty that her own death was imminent, and that her obligation to her dying son outweighed all others.

She ran without thought even for her direction,

focusing only on maintaining her balance on the uneven tunnel floor; on putting one foot in front of the other and opening up as much distance between her and that *thing* as possible.

What the fuck was it?

An animal?

If so, it moved like no animal that Conny had ever seen. In the brief glimpse she had managed to catch of the creature, it had clung to the ceiling like some gigantic spider, yet when it had dropped among the police officers, scattering them like a bomb threat, she was sure she had also seen it walking upright, just like a human. The brief snapshots her eyes had taken made no sense. Something as large as a bear, but wiry. Something that seemed to be made of teeth and claws.

Her mind ran to old horror movie scenarios. Maybe someone had dumped toxic waste into the sewer system, and some ordinary critter had been mutated into a hideous monster. London's very own *Godzilla;* crawling through the city's ancient basement, killing all who came across it.

Even in her heightened state of fear and confusion, that didn't ring true to Conny. If there were some dangerous animal living in the Underground, surely it would have been discovered years ago. But if it had successfully avoided discovery, why suddenly start killing people *en masse* now?

And how could this impossible creature have taken people from multiple stations in such a short space of time?

Because there is more than one. Maybe a lot *more.*

The answer uncoiled in Conny's mind, and she knew there was truth in it instinctively.

She slowed a little and hissed at Remy to stop. The dog looked back at her, wide-eyed, with an expression that Conny thought clearly conveyed *are you fucking crazy, human?*

The thought of fleeing, only to run headlong into more of the creatures was too terrifying to contemplate. Remy had sensed the thing long before it had appeared—either through its scent or the awful skittering noise it made as it moved—and it seemed unlikely that he would lead her straight into trouble, but panic was beginning to sink its claws into Conny's mind, muddying her thoughts. She found it hard to think of much beyond the fact that the dark tunnels could be teeming with monsters, and the only light she had was the tiny, hopelessly inadequate bulb mounted beneath the barrel of the Glock.

Every time she took the weak spotlight off Remy to ensure that she wasn't about to trip over some piece of debris or loose cable, she feared that he would continue to run, leaving her alone with the menacing shadows.

"Remy," she whispered, more sternly this time, and he pulled up with a soft grunt.

His willingness to stop had to be a good sign, at least. If there were more of the monsters in the Underground system, they couldn't be nearby. He trotted back and prodded her with his nose again, but Conny shook her head and put her hands on her knees, panting for air.

With adrenaline coursing through her, she had run faster and further than she thought possible. The pause gave birth to a raging inferno in her hamstrings, and suddenly she could feel the pain in her calf where Remy had bitten her.

"I need a minute, Rem."

Remy tilted his head inquisitively, but seemed content enough to hold their position.

Stopping didn't just give Conny time to feel pain and fatigue. It also afforded her an opportunity to *think*, but all her mind threw at her was guilt. She had stood and watched her colleagues being butchered, and then had fled, leaving the rest to die. She tried to tell herself that there was nothing she could have done; that most of the group were carrying weapons far more powerful than her handgun, and those weapons hadn't made a blind bit of difference.

I could have tried. *Should have done* something.

And then I'd be dead, too.

The remorse building inside her made Conny feel like screaming at herself in rage, and she gritted her teeth and swallowed back the urge. The time for self-recrimination was later. Right now, she had more pressing concerns.

Like, *where the hell am I?*

She summoned up a mental map of the tube system. After departing Euston, it should not have taken this long for her to reach the next station, King's Cross St Pancras. Those two weren't far apart. In fact, now that she came to think about it, she judged that she should have been damn close to St Pancras while Porter and the others had still been alive, yet she had run for several minutes without seeing a sign of either lights or platforms.

No sound of gunfire, either, she thought. *That's the good news.*

The bad news was that she was almost certainly in a service tunnel, or one that was not in regular use. There were plenty of abandoned tunnels all over the network; even some entire stations that had been left to gather dust. At that moment, even the sight of one of those so-called *ghost stations* would have been welcome. Anything would be better than the clammy claustrophobia of the tunnels.

I'm lost.

Instinctively, Conny began to play the Glock's light around her in a wide arc, hoping some sign or other means of identifying her location might have been helpfully left in the tunnel. There was nothing, save for featureless steel doors set into the wall at regular intervals.

The doors had to lead to maintenance areas, she guessed. Maybe even access points that would offer a route to the surface? Perhaps she could find a stairway leading up; hell, even a ladder would do. If necessary, she would find some way to carry Remy. All that mattered now was getting out of the tunnels quickly, and warning whoever was in charge at ground level that they needed to pull out of the Underground system; making sure that whatever was happening, it stayed below the surface, as far away from London Bridge Hospital—and from Logan —as possible.

She tried the radio clipped to her shoulder, but received no reply beyond a meaningless blast of static that sounded impossibly loud. Porter hadn't been kidding: this far underground, the radio was useless.

She paused for a moment, listening intently. Could she hear something screeching in the distance, the noise muted by thick stone walls? Had whatever was out there heard her trying her radio?

If so, maybe it, too, was holding its breath; listening. She could hear only silence.

Conny grimaced. She felt hopelessly exposed in the tunnel, especially whenever she flicked on the under-barrel light on the gun. The doors had to offer a better option.

"Come on, Rem. We need to find a way out."

Remy huffed softly.

―――――――

THE FIRST DOOR SHE TRIED WAS LOCKED, BUT THE second swung open at her touch.

Her heart sank.

It was just a junction room, no more than that. One of many meeting places for the thousands of miles of heavy cable that ran below the city like a vast spiderweb. The room was empty, and there was no other exit. There was no deadbolt on the door, but she saw a few lengths of rebar just like the one Adam Trent had crushed skulls with. She could wedge one of them against the door, and at least she would have a place to hunker down and feel safe for a while.

Coward.

She headed back into the tunnel.

Froze.

This time she definitely *did* hear screeching, and it sounded like it was in the same tunnel. Distant, but sharing a space with her.

It has finished with the others.

Now, it is hunting me down.

She flicked off the light immediately, and began to slide along the wall, feeling for the metal doors; listening to the pounding of her heart and praying it was the only thing she would hear.

Remy began to tug on the leash, urging her to move quicker.

She reached the third door.

Locked.

As was the fourth.

When she was halfway to the fifth door, the thing in the tunnel screeched again, and Conny almost screamed an answer. It was closer. *Much* closer.

She gritted her teeth, terrified of falling in the darkness, knowing that if she turned on the light she would paint a target on herself.

Click...click, click.

Blank terror soaked through Conny's mind, and she might have broken down altogether had her hand not found the door handle.

She twisted and felt tears of relief sting her eyes.

It wasn't locked.

Unable to breathe, she hurtled through the door behind Remy, closing it quietly.

She felt around for a deadbolt, and again found none. If there was something in the room for her to use to blockade the door, she didn't dare turn on her light to see it.

How well could the monster see in the dark? The question ripped through Conny's mind like shrapnel. If the things lived beneath ground level, it stood to reason that they would be able to see pretty well in the dark. But *how* well?

If it saw me...

Conny pressed her ear to the door, and heard the strange tapping sound the creature made as it approached. It moved forward and then paused, almost like it was searching for something, before moving on again.

If it *had* seen her, her chance of survival would be

determined by her physical strength; whether she could hold the door shut if the thing in the tunnel began to push from the other side. That did not seem likely.

Click.

Her eyes widened.

Right outside.

Click.

Conny clamped a hand over her mouth, praying that Remy would not make a sound. She didn't dare to look down at the dog. Didn't dare to move a muscle, afraid that even the slightest noise would give away her position.

For a sickening eternity, Conny stood at the door, listening.

And the clicking began again, growing fainter. Moving further away.

After a long time, Conny allowed herself to breathe again, and she flicked her light on, glancing at Remy. He stared up at her with wide, frightened eyes, visibly trembling. She scratched reassuringly at his ears, wishing there was someone who might scratch hers.

She swept the light from right to left and took in her surroundings: the room wasn't really a room at all; just the entrance to a small service corridor which she figured probably connected two of the main tunnels. The corridor ended at a short set of steps leading up to another door.

She peered at it uncertainly. On the one hand, putting another door between herself and the clicking thing in the tunnel seemed like the best idea anyone could ever possibly have; on the other, the corridor looked very old and little-used. There was every chance it would lead her even further away from civilization.

"What do you think, Rem? Is this a way out?"

Remy didn't appear to hear her.

He was staring back at the door that Conny had just shut.

Conny's jaw clenched, and she knelt next to the dog, placing her hand on his powerful shoulders. Remy's heart was pumping like a jackhammer.

"What do you hear?" Conny lowered her voice to a whisper.

Remy tilted his head, ears twitching.

And then he began to back away from the steel door.

It was all the persuasion that Conny required.

"Come on, Rem, let's go."

———

It didn't take long to cross the corridor; certainly not long enough for Conny to believe it could possibly offer a way out of the tunnels. She prayed that the steel door at the far end would not be locked, trying not to picture the result if it was: trapped in a dead-end corridor, with only the tunnel she had just fled from as an exit.

When she reached the door, she flicked off her light once more and put a calming hand on the back of Remy's neck. Wincing, she grabbed the cool steel handle and twisted gently, letting out a soft sigh of relief as the door opened, and stale air washed over her.

And not just air.

To her right, the impenetrable darkness melted away, and was replaced by a soft orange glow.

Light.

It was one of the missing Tube trains, sitting silently on the track like some eerie museum exhibit. The typical surgical-white lighting of the carriages was gone, and in its place there was what she guessed were emergency lights. The train must have suffered some sort of mechanical failure.

She dropped her eyes to Remy.

He was staring at the train curiously, but he looked relaxed enough.

Conny headed toward the train, keeping her gun levelled, scanning for movement. Approaching from the front, she had a long time to stare at the smashed front windows, and the torn corpse draped across them. A vast dark stain blossomed beneath the prone body of the driver, almost covering the nose of the train.

When she drew parallel with the front of the train, she peeked through the open door. The driver's controls had been smashed in, and the cab was a tangled web of ripped cabling and smashed circuit boards. It almost looked like the work of one of the creatures; a frenzied, animal attack. But why?

To disable the lights?

It made no sense. The things *were* animals, weren't they? Or monsters? She had no trouble believing that the creatures could have smashed their way into the train and killed the driver, but how would they know how to cut the lights...and why would they even bother? Without the driver, the passengers were sitting ducks, lights or no lights. If a group of armed police couldn't fight one of them, a bunch of terrified commuters trapped inside a stopped train would have stood no chance.

Despite that certainty, Conny's attempts to steel herself for what the rest of the train might contain fell short.

Way short.

A glimpse through the smashed windows of the first

carriage was enough for Conny to truly grasp that what was happening in the tunnels below London really was far above her paygrade. Shit, it had to be above *everybody's.*

The passengers inside had been slaughtered—no, *shredded*—by something. What was left in the carriage, pooled on seats and splashed up walls, looked more like a grisly stew than human bodies. Conny's eye fell on a dismembered foot here, an exposed jawbone there. Something sitting on a seat, which looked for all the world like a severed head with a human heart stuffed into its final scream.

Conny tore her eyes away and gulped for air, felt her stomach heaving, and then finally, when she drank in a breath and tasted the meat hanging on the air, she gave up the fight and let her breakfast out onto the track, loudly.

She heaved twice.

Spat.

Click.

Gasped for air.

Spat.

Click, click, click.

Conny froze.

Somewhere behind me.

Too late to run.

This is it.

She straightened, her nausea forgotten, and aimed her gun at the darkness, squinting; wishing that the light spilling from the train would just turn the hell off for a moment. The weapon shook wildly, and she figured her chances of actually hitting anything were around zero.

The clicking kept coming.

Closer.

Closer.

Conny loosed off her entire magazine, and the report of the Glock was deafening in the tunnel. When the echo of the gunshots faded, Conny lowered the weapon, drawing in a tremulous breath.

Click, click.

The shape emerged from the darkness slowly.

"Don't shoot."

The shape rasped out a wheezing chuckle.

Conny's jaw dropped. Robert Nelson shuffled toward her, his own gun held in listless fingers, pointed at his feet. He was pulling the trigger, over and over again. *Click, click, click.* In his other hand, Robert clutched Jackson's leash.

It looked like there were still parts of Jackson attached to it.

Robert stared straight through Conny, his eyes filled with tears that made his wide grin all the more unsettling.

"Don't...shoot," he gurgled again, thickly, and collapsed to the ground.

He was still pulling the trigger of the empty gun repeatedly, and when Conny knelt next to him and plucked the weapon away, his finger just...carried on. Firing the phantom gun that his mind still held.

Robert's eyes fixed on the roof of the tunnel, wide with fright and shock, and Conny knew as she looked into them that the roof would be the last thing Nelson saw. He was bleeding badly; choking out thick mouthfuls of blood.

Conny ran the light down across his body, expecting to see savage tears; half-certain that she would see his innards hanging out, just like the driver of the train.

What she saw was far worse.

A single bullet hole, punched into the base of Robert Nelson's throat.

Blood spurted from the wound at an obscene rate, and when Conny shrugged off her jacket and pressed it to the awful chasm in his neck, the heavy fabric soaked through almost immediately. She tossed it away and pressed her palm into that slippery, ruined throat, praying that she might hold his life inside him through sheer will.

She felt the pumping; the dreadful throbbing of blood.

Ebbing.

Slowing.

Stopping.

When Robert Nelson died, Conny couldn't help but let out a scream of despair. For that moment, the fearsome creature and the tunnel and the train of torn bodies ceased to exist, and there was only the fact that she had messed up everything, and it had cost a man his life. She screamed because she had to. Because there was no choice.

And somewhere in the darkness, something answered her.

The shriek that echoed through the tunnel ripped a gasp of horror from Conny's lungs. It was close. Jesus, in the silent darkness, the noise sounded terrifyingly loud.

She stumbled to her feet, and for a moment her legs just wanted to start running again, but she caught herself in time. The front of the train was almost certainly blocking the thing's view of her—but judging by how close the creature sounded that would only remain the case for a matter of seconds.

Have to get out of sight.

Conny stared about her frantically, and saw only two options: under the train, or in the train.

She could drape the bodies over herself, maybe; camouflage herself beneath the horror.

The prospect of lying in that lake of gore was numbing; something beyond terrifying, but there was no time to consider just how grim it might be. Right now there was only survival. Only those two options.

In the distance she heard it coming fast.

The hideous clicking.

Charging toward her.

Under the train.

Or in the train.

Conny grabbed Remy's collar firmly.

And made her choice.

CHAPTER TWENTY-TWO

I t didn't run along the ceiling this time.

Conny saw the clawed feet approaching, and her blood froze. She and Remy were wedged beneath the train, and most of her view of the tunnel was cut off by the tracks and the undercarriage.

But she saw the feet, and the sight of them dropped the temperature of her blood to zero. Each toe ended in a talon that looked like it belonged to some prehistoric predator.

Alongside her, Remy's body had gone alarmingly slack, like the dog was so scared it had slipped into a state of shock. She kept a palm pressed over his mouth, though it didn't seem likely that he would make a sound and give away their position, and she craned her neck.

The creature paused near the front of the train, and Conny's eyes widened with alarm as her mind tossed up a horrific possibility for the first time.

Can it smell us?

The creature took two quick strides toward Conny, and she almost screamed, certain that it would reach a clawed hand beneath the train, but suddenly, those terrifying feet were gone.

A thump above her made the carriage shudder.

It was inside the train.

She heard its clacking footsteps move from one side of the carriage to the other, and several quieter thumps, like the monster was tossing body parts around. Searching methodically.

Looking for someone hiding among the bodies, Conny thought, and she felt like vomiting again when she realised how close she had come to hiding beneath the corpses herself.

Above her, the creature continued to hunt.

They weren't just animals, she realised. They were *intelligent*; capable of considering their prey's thought process. It was surely just a matter of time before the thing decided to check underneath the train.

Run?

She felt despair well inside her. Just crawling out from beneath the train would surely make enough noise to alert the monster to her presence. And even if she did make it out, where was there to run to?

And what about Remy?

She couldn't run.

All she could do was wait, and pray.

Glass breaking.

Another thump; further away.

It went into the next carriage!

Conny felt a surge of hope rush through her. Was it possible that she could be so lucky *twice*? To have the creature right on top of her a second time, only for it to head off in the wrong direction once more?

She tensed her muscles, and listened. If the thing

moved even further down the train, she might get a chance to run after all.

It would mean leaving Remy behind. It had to: there was no way she could carry him quietly, and he was lying on his side, staring at her with abject, wide eyes; barely breathing. She doubted he could *stand*, let alone run.

She clenched her jaw.

It would break her heart to leave him.

It would break her heart *not* to.

She heard another series of thumps, even fainter still.

Now, or never.

She willed her muscles to move.

Wanted to reassure Remy; to whisper that she would come back for him.

She didn't dare.

Couldn't make a sound.

She stared into Remy's panicked eyes, her vision blurring, and turned away.

Just in time to see clawed feet landing heavily on the ground barely a yard in front of her face. She almost let out a yelp of surprise, and her muscles went rigid. She was too terrified even to shrink back into the shadows beneath the train.

Definitely more than one of them.

Another pair of feet appeared out of nowhere, just barely illuminated by the faint emergency lighting.

And then another. Another.

A lot more.

The creatures were making plenty of noise. Conny figured that she was at greater risk of being spotted than heard, and quietly eased herself alongside Remy, listening as the creatures—there had to be a dozen of them—leapt up into the carriage.

And began to feed noisily.

The horror of the sound was incomprehensible; meat being torn and chewed. Bones being snapped like bread-sticks. *Human beings.*

On more than one occasion, the carriage erupted in sudden grunts and shrieking, and Conny recalled nature show footage: animals feeding alongside each other suddenly going on the attack. With each shriek and each crash, her fear intensified until it almost felt unreal. The world began to spin around her, and she shut her eyes.

Perhaps I have gone mad.

Maybe I'm still sitting in the van.

Staring at my phone.

Those two words.

Huntington's Disease.

Incurable. Unstoppable. It killed usually within a couple of decades. Conny knew the disease and its cruel symptoms all too well. She'd known all about it even before Logan had been born, and she had prayed, every day since, that the hateful condition which had taken her husband would spare her son.

But prayers had a tendency to go unanswered. Logan had exhibited symptoms so *young*. He had been born to die, and she wasn't going to be around to make it right, and—

Her eyes flared open as she heard the carriage above erupt with a new noise. It sounded like the creatures were shrieking in unison, over and over. If it hadn't been a sound that could only have existed in Hell, Conny could have sworn that it was some sort of *language*, like a chant or prayer. Twisted and demented and terrifying.

She felt Remy begin to quiver alongside her, and reached out a hand gently to reassure him, stopping dead when she heard the creatures bellow a final shriek that shook the walls, and then there was silence for a moment, before they came crashing out of the train, their clawed feet once more slamming into the ground right in front of her.

The creatures charged away down the tunnel without pausing, almost as if answering some urgent rallying cry that she could not hear. When the thunderous clacking of their movement dissolved into silence, Conny remained frozen in place for a long time, her palm hovering above Remy's belly, her mouth open.

Still alive.

CHAPTER TWENTY-THREE

The London Eye was on its final rotation of the day. The vast Ferris wheel built at the turn of the century offered a magnificent, panoramic view of London from its slow-moving passenger pods, but to Hideo Kagome, the view had already been boring for at least twenty minutes.

Hideo's parents still seemed enthralled, though that didn't mean a great deal; Hideo thought they were enthralled by pretty much *everything* in London. It was, after all, the vacation the Kagome family had been waiting to take for several years, combining a visit to Hideo's older, UK-based brother Kasamo, with an opportunity to take in some of the most famous tourist spots in the world.

And it was all so *boring*.

Kasamo had barely been able to get any time off work, and so only saw them in the evenings when he was tired, and London? London was dusty old buildings and people with angry faces. Places where someone supposedly important had lived or died, like, *hundreds* of years earlier. Museums that took all day to trample around. Who cared?

At least the Eye had been an exciting prospect, like a giant fairground ride. It had even looked cool from a distance, sitting right on the south bank of the Thames, soaring high above the nearby buildings, all lit up like Christmas as dusk began to settle over the city.

But it was *so* slow. The egg-shaped pods, each large enough to hold twenty-five people—and which you couldn't even lean out of—sealed up for the duration of the ride, and that was it for the next forty minutes: crawling up into the sky inch by boring inch until the city was laid out below...and then crawling back down. Hideo's time would have been far better spent on his PS4, no doubt about that.

At least it was nearly over. He pressed his face to the curved glass, trying to look straight down. The pod was, he guessed, still at least a hundred feet above the ground. Far below, the queuing area was a functional square of concrete, spattered with token splashes of greenery. It was almost empty, most of the tourists having moved on.

Suddenly, his attention was taken by movement to his right. Something on the water. He glanced toward it, expecting to see yet another slow-moving riverboat, and frowned.

Nothing there.

He squinted into the last rays of the sunset, certain that he had seen *something* out there.

And movement erupted directly below him.

Hideo's mouth dropped open, his boredom forgotten.

So fast.

The thing—a dark shape that he could not even begin to identify—leapt from the water up onto the path that ran alongside the river with ease, landing with a fluid motion like an uncoiling snake. It took a couple of loping strides forward and then launched itself onto all-fours, galloping like a cat toward a small knot of people sitting outside a coffee shop which overlooked the river.

It barrelled into them at full speed, oblivious to their fearful screams...

...scattering tables and chairs like matchsticks...

...and began to tear them apart.

Hideo's eyes widened painfully as he saw an enormous splatter of blood—dark in the failing light—arcing across the pale concrete below. And then another. It looked like somebody had been ripped in two at the waist, the obscene *pieces* that they became tossed aside like garbage.

He screamed then, his mouth making the noise all by itself, and he stumbled backwards, away from the window, colliding with his stunned mother and sending her crashing to the floor.

He didn't even hear his father yelling at him as he helped her back to her feet. For a moment, all Hideo could hear was the noise of that distant splatter; inaudible and deafening at the same time. His eyes glazed over.

Somewhere below, a loud thump jolted him back to the present.

The thump became a shatter.

Glass breaking, Hideo thought in horror, and he scrambled to press his face to the window once more. The pod was closer to ground level now, ninety feet or less, and suddenly the giant fucking wheel was moving far too *fast*.

It's gonna deliver us right to it.

He searched, panicked, for some sign of the terrible

creature, but all he saw was the bodies it had left behind. Maybe, he thought, just maybe, it had already moved away from the Eye. Jumped back into the river, perhaps. Or it was in the pod at the bottom of the giant wheel, tearing the passengers to pieces...

Hideo gagged as he stared at the remains of the group of people who'd been enjoying their last ever cup of coffee, and began to offer silent thanks that he hadn't been down there when the monster had leapt out of the Thames.

His relief withered and died as the creature erupted from one of the pods directly below his, swinging easily on the frame of the Ferris wheel with long, gangling limbs, as comfortable climbing up the steel lattice of the structure as a primate.

Oh, no, Hideo thought. *Oh, no, please don't—*

With a screech, the creature swung up to the next pod, smashing the thick glass with a single blow and leaping inside, out of sight once more.

Distant, muted screaming.

Hideo turned to face his mother and father, and saw his terror reflected in their eyes. They, too, had seen it. He wasn't going crazy; the monster wasn't a product of his imagination. It wasn't what his mother would smile and label *teenage hormones running amok*.

It was real.

They were all about to die.

He opened his mouth to say something, though he wasn't sure what that might be. *My final words*, he thought numbly. How could a sullen fourteen-year-old boy possibly conjure up the right ones?

"Mother," he began to say, and the window behind him imploded.

The words, whatever they might have been, remained unsaid; there was just no room for them as the air thickened with terror. Suddenly, in the slow-moving pod, there was only enough room for screaming.

And dying.

———

Harold Birch patted at the air for a moment before his fingers landed on the cool, rough wood.

He gripped the bench and levered himself down onto it with a sigh, setting his stick against his right leg.

With his left hand, he reached out and ruffled the back of Brody's neck.

"Good boy. Take a break, Bro."

A moment later, Harold heard the soft *whump* as the dog's generous backside hit the ground.

Harold breathed in deeply, listening to the sounds of Hyde Park. He used to love taking Brody to walk there, and each time they visited, Harold would try to navigate to the very centre of the vast green expanse, judging that he was close to it when the sounds of the city—the background pollution that never truly dispersed—was at its quietest.

The middle of Hyde Park was the only place in central London, in Harold's opinion, where you could go and *almost* forget that you were in the city at all.

Increasingly, though, the park hosted noisy events; on most nights it seemed that there was some band or other performing there now. Even at times when the park should have been quiet, the relentless noise of London invaded. Kids playing godawful music through tinny speakers, or people chattering loudly—and constantly—on their mobile phones. The various pings, whistles and buzzes of information hitting the electronic devices the whole world now carried everywhere. Everything so damn *connected*. No way to escape any of it and just *be*.

Tonight, there was a rock band playing, and so Harold didn't make for the centre of the park. He skirted the edge of it for a while, just long enough to give Brody some exercise, and rested a while before heading back home. He could hear the music in the distance, the excitable murmur of the crowd.

The music itself was muddy and indistinct: it didn't travel well across the park; becoming little more than a dirge at distance. Harold didn't recognise the tune, though that didn't surprise him. Despite the winter chill in the air, it was still early, just late afternoon, and the stage would be home to a warm-up act at this time of the day. The crowds would gather in greater numbers for the main act in two or three hours. He probably wouldn't have recognised their music, either.

His ears were well-tuned, though: far closer, he heard the soft swishing of bicycles passing; there were always the fitness freaks lapping the park. Groups of joggers and cyclists, mostly. Occasionally, the heavier clatter of skateboards or rollerblades. The edge of the park was constantly shifting; home to those people for whom stillness and silence were reasons for discomfort.

The benches were set a way back from the wide path, and in the summer they bathed in the scent of flowers. During the warm months, the one that he usually sat on would be surrounded by the hum of insects, and Harold liked listening to their quiet little symphony being played out. Yet the park was so much busier in the summer, so much *noisier*.

In the distance, the crowd erupted in a loud scream, and Harold blinked into the unending darkness, surprised. The main act must have taken to the stage already.

At his left foot, Brody whined, and Harold tilted his head.

"What's up, Bro?"

The dog whined again; louder.

Harold frowned. Brody's communication skills were a minor miracle, but this was a noise that Harold hadn't ever heard the dog make before. A frantic, fearful noise, like Brody had seen something that terrified him.

Harold listened intently.

The bicycles had passed thirty seconds earlier, and he had heard nothing in his immediate vicinity since. As best he could tell, he and Brody were alone.

He reached out to pat Brody, and paused.

In the distance, the screaming intensified, but it sounded odd to Harold now, different in a way he couldn't place immediately. It took him a moment to figure it out.

The crowd was still screaming.

But the music had stopped.

Brody whined again, once, and then took off.

Harold had been holding Brody's leash in slack fingers—an unnecessary gesture since the dog was as obedient and even-tempered as a mutt could get—and he was too slow to react when he felt the cold leather slipping across his palm. By the time he closed his fist, the leash was gone.

And he heard Brody sprinting away.

"Brody!"

Harold stood uncertainly, stricken by a sudden anxiety. His stick clattered to the ground. Brody didn't slow at his call. If anything, it sounded like the dog was picking up pace.

And in the distance, the screaming seemed to be getting louder.

No, Harold realised. *Getting closer.*

Before the patter of Brody's fast-receding paws had faded, Harold heard another sound, like rippling thunder.

Footsteps, he realised, and felt a shard of icy fear lance his heart. *Lots of people, all running frantically. All screaming, heading straight for me.*

He crouched and patted the ground until he located his stick. Something bad was happening in the park, something that Harold couldn't even begin to understand. Without his sight, he relied heavily on his hearing, but right now his ears were filling with a dreadful, incomprehensible cacophony.

Someone rocketed past him.

Screaming the whole way.

Harold turned away from the noise of approaching footsteps, following the direction Brody had taken.

And suddenly, the air was knocked from his chest as someone barrelled into him at full pace. Harold went down hard, slamming a shoulder painfully into the bench he had sat on peacefully only moments earlier. Whoever had knocked him down didn't stay to see if he was all right; they didn't even *speak*. Harold listened in astonishment as they clambered to their feet with a whimper and took off again.

And then a wave of chaos broke around him.

Over him.

Feet running everywhere, trampling him, knocking him back down when he tried to get up. A million glancing blows that landed on his limbs as a tide of people broke around him. Screaming, all of them; wordless shrieks that sounded like panicked, primal terror.

Harold tried to get up one final time, and when a foot caught him on the side of the face, he gave up the struggle and curled up in a ball, hands held protectively around his head, and prayed for the madness to stop.

Somewhere beneath the thundering of feet and the piercing yells of fear, Harold heard another noise. Something that sounded like thick paper ripping. A sound that he thought was like branches being snapped, but slightly muffled somehow.

Bones, he thought, and his terror ratcheted up a notch. *That's the sound of bones breaking. And the ripping...it must be...*

Suddenly, the thunder of fleeing feet began to fade, and Harold lifted his head in amazement.

Whatever had happened, whatever terrible event had just unfolded in Hyde Park, it seemed to have flowed right past him. He heard some screams; perhaps people who had fallen like himself, but whose injuries were more severe.

The sound of fleeing people continued to move away.

They're gone, Harold thought, and let out a long, explosive sigh of relief.

Click.

Harold frowned at the noise. It almost sounded like a dog's claws tapping on a linoleum floor.

"Bro? That you?"

Click, click, click.

An animal of some sort exhaled loudly nearby; a snort that sounded far too *big* to have been made by a dog.

Harold froze, and the dreadful truth of his situation

unwound in his mind. Suddenly, it was like he could see again; like the thick veil that had been draped over his eyes for more than thirty years had lifted abruptly.

The people who were running were gone.

Escaped.

The thing that scared them is still here.

Click.

Click, click.

Harold swallowed; his throat felt like it was filling with broken glass.

It's right in front of—

Something large and heavy breathed onto Harold's face: a warm, moist wave of air that reeked of meat and blood. The creature grunted, and Harold thought the terrible noise, mere inches away from him, sounded almost like *confusion*.

He reached out gingerly, feeling the air in front of him.

And whatever was lurking out there in the syrupy darkness, beyond the reach of Harold's ruined eyes, *laughed*.

His mouth dropped open, and he had no idea whether the breath he drew in was intended to fuel words or a scream.

It didn't matter.

Harold's lungs were still inflating when something sharp punctured his chest. Huge; it felt like someone had just steered a train into his ribcage. He felt and heard the cracking of his bones, and then the terrible pulling sensation as something began to furiously rearrange his internal organs, before—finally—a new sort of darkness claimed him.

On the crowded, slow-moving streets of Camden, the lights were blinking on and the stream of daytime shoppers was slowly preparing to hand over ownership of the streets to the night-time revellers. Much of the expansive market was shutting for the day, the stalls trying to shift a few last items before the sun went down.

The vampire erupted near a railway bridge, spearing up from the ground into a crowd of people who were determined to spend the last few minutes of daylight sitting in a beer garden at the rear of one of Camden's most popular pubs.

It emerged from the dirt already swinging.

Its first victim didn't even have time to scream.

But others did.

In Oxford Circus, the traffic had slowed to a crawl as the evening rush hour began. Tourists moved in almost aimless herds, winding their way from one pedestrian-crossing to another, waiting patiently for the traffic to ease, or simply walking out in front of it and delaying the whole process still further.

The vampire rocketed from a manhole in the middle of the road, leaping onto the roof of a bus under the gathering darkness, and shrieked as it clawed a courier from his bicycle, sweeping him up and tearing him apart in a dull explosion of blood that spattered across windscreens and stunned faces.

In the distance, others answered.

With a roar, the vampire charged toward a group of

stunned pedestrians, impacting upon them like a speeding combine harvester, chewing up muscle and sinew as it carved through them before smashing into the window of a large department store.

THEY CAME FROM THE RIVER; FROM THE SOFT ground beneath parks and gardens. From the tunnels and stations of the Underground; scattered across the city, but rising as one.

Blood flowed across London.

And the last scraps of weak daylight dissolved.

Sundown.

PART THREE

CHAPTER TWENTY-FOUR

S *tay in the light.*
     Jennifer Craven's warning rattled in Leon Mancini's head like small arms fire as the van headed toward London.

It would be full-dark by the time the van reached the city, despite the fact that it was only around six in the evening, and it felt like reaching England's capital was taking forever. The roads around the south of the country were nothing like those back home: no wide, fast-moving highways here; instead, single-lane traffic crawled at infuriatingly slow speed through village after village.

And then there were the 'roundabouts.' Navigating them was logical enough, but the behaviour of the other drivers made each one a little hair-raising.

And slowed them down even more.

If Mancini had been able to speak to a local, they would have reassured him that the van was actually making short work of the trip to the capital; he wouldn't have believed them.

Still, the journey did give Mancini plenty of time to

absorb the story that Jeremy Pruitt told. The Rennick family had attempted to satisfy a vampire rising on a massive scale, unleashing the creatures on a cruise ship and then sinking it to bury the evidence.

Not a bad plan, all things considered, but somewhere along the way, one of the ship's passengers had begun murdering the monsters, and what was left of the UK arm of the Order when the dust settled was Herbert Rennick, an idealist in his twenties with more balls than sense, and a group of young clerics, most of whom, Jeremy said, had entered the mansion, but had never come back out.

But Dan Bellamy *had*, and Herbert Rennick had bundled him into a chopper, fleeing to the north just minutes before Mancini and his team arrived at the compound. According to Pruitt, the Rennicks owned an apartment in the city. It was there that Herb would head, the Brit was sure of it.

In a way, Pruitt's certainty made Mancini's heart sink. If Bellamy and Rennick had *really* disappeared; if they were on the wind, never to be seen again, he wouldn't now be heading toward the epicentre of the apocalypse.

Braxton drove, navigating the winding roads with only the occasional curse, and when Pruitt finished filling them in, Mancini held up a hand to silence him and pulled out his cellphone. He was only supposed to break radio silence in extraordinary circumstances.

He figured this counted, and punched in a number.

Jennifer Craven answered immediately.

"We're too late," Mancini said. "The vampires are already on the surface. By the look of things, they have been for a while. The Rennick compound is gone."

For a moment, Craven said nothing, and he wondered

if she was suppressing a smirk at his sudden acceptance of the fact that vampires did exist after all.

"What about the Hermetic?" she asked finally.

Mancini was sitting in the front passenger seat along-side Braxton. He glanced through the windshield at the sky ahead. Smoke was gathering over London, and several small fires lit up the skyline from east to west.

"Looks like he's in London."

"You know where?"

"Maybe. But London ain't looking so healthy right now."

"Yes. I'm watching the news. Tragic. Do you *know* where the Hermetic is?"

Mancini gritted his teeth.

"We ran into the guy who called you. Pruitt. He thinks he knows where Rennick took him."

"So what's the problem? Go get him."

"Half the team's already dead, Jennifer. I damn near died *myself*, and that was only coming up against *one* of them—"

"You *saw* one? What happened?"

"Some people died, some people ran. Defeat, Jennifer. *That's* what happened. Comprehensive fucking defeat. And now you want us to go into a city full of these things?"

Craven snorted.

"Like I said, I'm watching the news. They don't know what they are dealing with yet: reports are talking about sudden bouts of mass hysteria; people attacking each other or killing themselves. But they *do* know how wide-spread it is. So far, eight separate incidents have been reported across London. Which means eight vampires."

"Yeah," Mancini hissed, "eight *so far*. I doubt this is *all* playing out in front of the cameras, Jennifer. We have no idea how many—"

"It's a big city, Mr Mancini. I'm sure a man with your qualifications should be able to grab *one* civilian and get out in one piece. That is what I pay you for. No?"

Mancini pulled the phone away from his face for a moment, fighting back the urge to throw it out of the window. When he pressed it back against his ear, Craven was still talking.

"...chances of us stumbling across another Hermetic in this or any other lifetime are virtually zero. You do realise that understanding this Dan Bellamy could be the key to stopping the vampires once and for all? To understanding how they are able to live for so long? Their abilities? War is coming, Mr Mancini. The secret is out. In a few hours, there won't be anyone left on the planet who doesn't know about vampires, and humans tend to respond badly to threats. It doesn't matter whether the vampires come after us, or we go after them. The end result will be the same. We'll need to be able to defend ourselves with something other than walls. He is the *key*."

"Great," Mancini said. "And what if I *can't* get him?"

Craven paused.

"Then don't bother coming back. And pray for a quick death."

She hung up, and Mancini gripped the phone so tightly that he felt the plastic casing beginning to buckle.

He sucked in a deep breath, and focused on the burning city ahead.

Braxton shot a glance at him.

"Mancini? What'd she say?"

He slipped the phone back into his pocket.

"We go on," Mancini growled. "But at the first sign of

trouble—the first fucking sign—we're turning this piece of crap around and hightailing it outta here. I don't give a fuck *what* Craven says. I'll take her Gulfstream as severance pay. Fucking *gladly*."

Braxton glanced at him again, his eyes widening when he saw the anger written on Mancini's face, and apparently thought better of asking any more questions.

When the furious silence became too much to bear, Mancini leaned forward and flicked on the van's ancient radio, twisting the dial until he heard a breathless news reporter reeling off facts that they clearly had trouble believing.

There had been outbreaks of 'unexpected violence' across the centre of the city, and large parts of London to the north of the river were burning. All residents of the city were advised to evacuate immediately or to barricade themselves in their homes until the all clear was given. The military had been called in to restore order...

In the rear of the van, Montero and Burnley were bickering quietly, just as they had for most of the flight across the Atlantic.

Jeremy Pruitt just sat there, frowning at the floor, muttering to himself.

Mancini tuned it all out, and tried to persuade himself that Jennifer Craven wasn't worth it; that she hadn't been for a very long time. That the only rational thing to do was turn the van around and get the hell out of England immediately; find some way to disappear.

He said nothing, glaring at the road ahead, watching the miles creep by.

His gut told him that his entire world was about to be reduced to a single imperative.

Stay in the light.

CHAPTER TWENTY-FIVE

Conny only rolled out from beneath the train when Remy finally began to struggle. She released her grip on him, and he scampered out into the tunnel. It was the best indication she could get that it was truly safe for her to move.

She hauled herself to her feet, a little unnerved at how shaky her legs felt beneath her.

Remy was busy peeing. He glanced at her apologetically, and Conny almost laughed. She had damn-near pissed *herself* beneath the train. Under the circumstances, she thought he'd done pretty well to hold it in.

She left her flashlight switched off, seeing only by the soft glow of the train's emergency lights. Twisting her head left and right, trying not to look at Robert Nelson's body and failing miserably, she saw only darkness in either direction.

"Which way, Rem?"

Remy finished his business and trotted toward her, turning to face the left. The opposite direction to the one the monsters had taken. He looked up at her, tongue lolling out, and seemed relatively like himself for the first time in a couple of hours.

"Left it is," Conny said quietly, and smiled.

She detached Remy's chain leash from his collar, afraid of the noise it might make. She would travel in complete darkness, she decided, sticking to one tunnel and using her light only occasionally, if she needed to get her bearings. Ideally, she wanted to travel completely silently, too. She placed the chain gently on the ground, and Remy gave it a look of disdain.

"Now, stick by my side, right, Rem? No running off and leaving me down here, okay?"

Remy tilted his head and sighed indignantly.

Conny shot a final, despairing glance at Robert Nelson's body, and set off.

She moved slowly, listening to every sound. The soft whisper of her boots as she crept through the tunnel; Remy's claws, clacking occasionally on the concrete floor, making her heart leap. Something dripping somewhere. After around ten minutes, she heard faint scratching that made her pull up in alarm, until she realised it was probably just a rat. That was a good sign, she decided. Rats tended to flee from predators.

Like cowards.

Conny shook the thought away with a grimace.

She pressed on.

THE LIGHT HURT HER EYES, EVEN BEFORE SHE rounded the bend and saw the distant platforms and the signs, and finally knew exactly where she was.

Monument Station, on the north bank of the Thames.

It was one of London's less-busy stations, and by the look of the platforms, it had been evacuated and secured: the cavernous space was flooded with the same soft orange light that she had seen in the ghastly train carriages. The amber glow made the instantly-recognisable walls of the station otherworldly and threatening, barely keeping the shadows at bay.

She reached for the radio clipped to her shoulder, and thought better of it. She'd made it this far by moving silently, and she'd be damned if she was going to blow that at the last minute, when the exit was almost in sight.

Monument was very close to London Bridge Hospital. Once she reached the safety of the surface, she thought, she could radio for help and head directly to Logan. Get him out of the city entirely, if necessary.

She approached the light carefully, keeping a watchful eye on Remy, ready to turn and run if he so much as blinked. He trotted beside her as if there were nothing out of the ordinary, and she allowed herself to relax a little. When she reached the platform, she lifted Remy up onto it before clambering up herself. The station remained silent, and she glanced up at the CCTV cameras dotted along the platform, wondering if they were still operational and, if so, whether there was anybody monitoring them.

Probably not. The Chief Superintendent had said they were shutting down the whole rail network: Monument Station would have been completely evacuated like all the others, security staff included.

She groaned inwardly when she realised that if Monument was totally empty, the gates to the station would surely be shut. She and Remy would be locked in.

She quickened her pace, heading up the still escalator and into the small ticketing hall.

Dammit!

There were two sets of heavy iron gates at Monument: one in the ticketing hall itself, and another at the top of steps that led up to the street-level exit.

Both were locked.

She tested the inner gate. It looked like it had been locked electronically. There was some give in it, but there was no way she could open it manually.

Remy pushed his nose between the bars, sniffing at the fresh air, and looked up at her hopefully.

"Working on it, Rem."

She glanced back at the escalator, half expecting to see one of the hideous creatures following her. Nothing.

To the right of the escalator, she spotted a door marked *staff only*, and she headed for it, clenching her fist in triumph when it opened at her touch.

Beyond the door, a narrow corridor opened out into a small control room and a couple of offices and storage rooms. Somewhere in those rooms, she would find the button that would open those gates, she was certain of it. She waved Remy inside and closed the door quietly behind her, heading for the control room.

Inside, she saw four blinking monitors delivering the monochrome CCTV feed from the cameras dotted around the station, and a control panel.

She ran her fingers across the buttons until she spotted what she was looking for.

Inner Gate.

Outer Gate.

She hit them both, and sighed in relief when she heard the hum of the motor revving up out in the ticketing hall. Turning to the CCTV monitors, she saw the inner gate opening.

"Time to go, Rem," she said.

And she flinched.

Had she just caught movement on another monitor in the corner of her eye?

Something on the platform that she had walked across minutes earlier?

"Time to go!"

She ran, figuring she had thirty seconds, maybe less.

Burst out into the ticketing hall with Remy at her side.

Through the inner gate while it was half-open, up the tunnel toward the steps and—

The outer gate was padlocked.

The electronic mechanism had lifted the outer gate open a little way; less than a foot, she guessed, but further progress was prevented by a heavy chain and a sturdy-looking lock.

Remy scampered through the narrow gap easily.

Conny slammed into the unforgiving metal, jamming herself into the opening that was almost big enough to accommodate her. She pushed with her legs, wedging herself between the gate and the floor.

She wasn't going to make it.

She screamed in frustration, and once she started, she couldn't stop. Terror and grief and guilt; pouring out of her lungs until she felt sure she could never stop.

"Hey, hey, calm down. We'll get you out of there. Calm down, it'll be okay."

Her eyes flared open at the sound of the voice. Standing in front of the gate, with Remy at his side, she saw a British Army soldier wearing full tactical gear.

"It's behind me," she snarled, unnerved at the note of primal terror in her voice.

He lifted a flashlight, pointing it through the gate.

"There's nothing behind you."

Conny twisted, craning her neck to look back through the iron bars. He was right. The steps that led down to the ticketing hall were empty.

I'm losing my mind.

"Hang on," the soldier said. "We'll get you out."

He waved a *hurry up* gesture at someone that Conny couldn't see, and moments later she heard keys rattling.

When the gate opened, Conny fell out, collapsing to the ground, and began to scrabble away from Monument Station. The soldier who had spoken began to help her to her feet, and she heard another behind her, re-locking the gate.

"There are things in the tunnels," Conny gasped, "creatures—"

"Not anymore," the soldier said grimly, and he pointed up.

To the west, above the city's skyline, the night glowed amber.

London was burning.

"They're on the surface?" she asked weakly, already knowing what the answer must be.

He nodded, and took her arm, leading her away from the entrance to the station.

"First reported sighting was in Hyde Park around thirty minutes ago. There have been multiple sightings since then, all over the centre of the city. Nothing confirmed, but it's chaos out there. Lots of casualties."

"Thirty minutes," Conny repeated absently. "You guys got here quick."

"We were already on our way."

Conny stared at him, puzzled.

"The military was called in when we lost the police."

"Lost," Conny repeated slowly. "But that would mean..."

"You're the only one that has come back, yeah. As far as I know, anyway." His stern expression crumbled a little.

Conny's mind began to creak. It was just too much to process.

Somewhere in the distance, an explosion rocked the evening, and moments later a helicopter roared overhead, flying low.

"We're quarantining central London," the soldier said. "You need to evacuate."

She nodded at him numbly.

"The nearest evac point is across the bridge," he pointed at the Thames, "London Bridge Hospital. We have people there who will get you to safety. You know where it is?"

London Bridge Hospital.

Conny knew where it was.

Intimately.

CHAPTER TWENTY-SIX

Conny jogged across London Bridge with Remy keeping pace easily at her side, each stride setting off tiny detonations in her wounded calf. She paused around halfway across the river when a formation of jets streaked across the sky, heading for the centre of the city.

She turned to watch as the aircraft passed overhead, half-expecting that they were about to open fire on the city. Surely the situation hadn't become so bad in thirty minutes that the military were under orders to *bomb* the capital?

Apparently not: the jets continued north for several seconds and then banked left, disappearing from sight to the west.

A reconnaissance mission, then.

Now that she was able to see more of the skyline, Conny could see that the most severe of several fires raging in the city was two or three miles to the west, along the Thames. Knightsbridge, perhaps, or Kensington.

Above the city, she saw the spotlights of several helicopters surveying the streets below.

It would be a disaster zone in the most densely crowded areas, she thought, picturing the murderous creatures tearing through Trafalgar Square and Oxford Circus and Camden. The panic alone would injure many; it was, she guessed, probably the cause of the fires that she saw. There were likely a thousand car crashes occurring in the city centre at that very moment. Even without direct contact with the creatures, the chaos of the burning city would claim many casualties.

The southern bank of the river, by comparison, looked far quieter: no sign of fire, no helicopters.

She began to breathe a little easier. If the trouble—which Conny subconsciously labelled the *infestation*—was confined to the north of the river, then Logan was safe, and the army had already secured the hospital. He might even have been evacuated already.

The worst of it was over.

She turned her back on the burning centre of London and pressed forward, biting down on the pain in her leg and increasing her pace.

THE AREA OUTSIDE THE HOSPITAL WAS AWASH WITH light and people. There were three buses parked outside, engines running, and a group of soldiers were guiding a steady stream of patients and visitors toward them.

As Conny neared, two large military-looking trucks pulled up alongside the buses, and armed troops began to spill out of them. Around sixty in total, she guessed. They began to make their way to London Bridge, hauling pieces of equipment and sandbags. It looked for all the world like they were planning to set up machine gun emplace-ments on the bridge.

Quarantining the city with bullets.

She pushed through a crowd of bodies toward the hospital, flinching when a soldier grabbed her elbow.

"Hospital's being evacuated, Ma'am."

"My son is in there," she snapped, and shook away his hand.

He looked her in the eye for a moment, his expression impatient, and nodded, stepping aside to let her pass.

She moved through the entrance and into the recep-tion area.

London Bridge Hospital offered private healthcare only, and was small by the standards of most modern hospitals, with a little over a hundred rooms for patients. The reception area itself was plush, but cramped: a cosy waiting area and front desk opened out into a corridor containing elevators which transported patients and visi-tors to the treatment areas upstairs. The neutral decor was clearly meant to lend the place a cool, calming atmosphere.

It wasn't working.

The interior of the hospital was in chaos, and Conny's progress was slowed almost as soon as she entered the building.

The walls reverberated to the sounds of human anguish: cries of grief and disbelief; moans of pain and despair. The UK very rarely experienced natural disasters of the scale seen in other parts of the world: earthquakes were infrequent and lacked strength, and the weather almost never unleashed itself on the country with the sort of savagery experienced by those for whom tornadoes or tsunamis were simple facts of life.

The people streaming out of the hospital did not have disaster preparedness drilled into them, and it showed in the shock and confusion on their faces.

Two men in army uniforms holding exquisite M27s were trying to hold the tide of people back, in a futile attempt to keep the evacuation of the hospital orderly, and were failing pretty spectacularly.

Remy cut through the crowd like a hot knife, and Conny followed, making her way to the nearest of the soldiers. He looked stressed and afraid, almost like he was considering whether a short burst from his rifle might get everyone to just shut up and *listen*.

She glanced back at the hospital exit. At the rate that things were going, there would be a crush in the doorway.

This is going to get ugly, she thought.

"Wrong way, Ma'am."

She blinked, and turned to face the soldier. He nodded at the exit, and Conny shook her head firmly.

"My son is a patient. I need to find—"

The soldier waved a hand for her to stop.

"I don't know anything about the patients, Ma'am. We're just here to make sure everybody gets out. Your boy might be in there. Bottom three floors of the hospital have been cleared, I know that much. We have choppers en route for those who are too sick to get on the trucks and buses. ETA twenty-five minutes. Once they're gone, we're pulling back, got it?"

He met her eyes, ensuring that she understood.

Conny nodded her thanks, and turned away, guiding Remy toward the distant elevators. If the bottom three floors of the hospital had already been cleared, then Logan might still be in there somewhere. His room was on the top floor.

Twenty-five minutes, she thought.

She had plenty of time.

A BANK OF FOUR ELEVATORS WAS LOCATED IN THE corridor behind the reception desk, but Conny moved straight past them: all were in use, of course, and likely there were people on the top two floors stabbing the *call* button repeatedly.

She made for the stairs. They were narrow, and a trickle of those who weren't willing to wait for the elevators flowed down from the upper parts of the hospital.

Conny took the stairs two at a time, ignoring the ache in her muscles.

When she and Remy made it to the top floor, she stepped into tension so thick it almost knocked her backwards. The people who were already there—the top floor had to be still half-full of patients at least—were all clustered around the windows which faced the river, staring out quietly.

The silence in the place was putrid, and Remy huffed softly at her side, apparently coming to the conclusion that things might be better if they moved on.

"It's okay, Rem," she whispered, and she moved closer to the windows, unable to tear her gaze away from them.

Matters outside were deteriorating quickly.

The London skyline looked like a warzone of the sort that Conny had only ever seen previously on TV; the backdrop to a solemn news presenter reciting facts that were virtually impossible to comprehend. Tracer fire arced from the dark clouds, spat down onto the city from an aircraft that she could not see. At ground level, the fire seemed to be everywhere now, and pulses of light seared her eyes at regular intervals as small explosions rocked the city.

Her jaw dropped.

Without that newsreader to provide a reassuringly detached soundtrack, their place taken by the soft *whump* of the distant explosions, the sight of what was happening to London was mesmerising and terrifying beyond all reason.

How could things have fallen apart so fast that airborne attacks on the city had already been sanctioned? What next? Missiles?

Nukes?

The disastrous view from the hospital window meant only one thing.

We're losing.

The army had been called in and, just like the police, they were dying.

There wasn't time to consider how that was possible; how a bunch of creatures that killed with claws and teeth might be able to defeat one of the most advanced military forces in the world. Screw waiting for the military; she'd evacuate her son herself. Commandeer a car, point it south and just *drive*.

She began to move from room to room, searching for Logan. Typically, he was in the last room on the floor, near the fire exit. He was staring out of the window in shock, and didn't see his mother approaching.

Conny ran into the room, grabbing his arm.

"Logan, we have to *go*."

He didn't respond.

And when Conny followed his gaze, she saw why.

A helicopter.

Approaching fast.

Too fast, Conny thought, as she stared at the incoming vehicle in horror.

The chopper was big, but it was flying as though buffeted by the wind like a frail insect, veering crazily and lurching down toward the hospital. As it neared, Conny saw the blades stuttering.

It's out of fuel.

It was heading right for them.

"Get down!"

Conny wasn't even aware that she was shouting. She hit the deck, grabbing a handful of Logan's hospital-issue nightgown and pulling him down beside her. The chopper roared toward the windows, and the top floor of the hospital filled with screaming...

...and it disappeared from sight.

Moments later, a crash shook the building, rattling the windows in their frames. Conny could clearly hear a loud, metallic squeal as the downed helicopter scraped to a halt on the roof.

Fine dust rained from the ceiling.

Remy sneezed.

Conny stumbled to her feet, helping Logan up. She clasped his cheeks in her palms, and couldn't keep the tears at bay.

"Are you okay?"

Logan flinched away, his lip curling.

"Not really. I'm dying, didn't you hear?"

Conny recoiled at the bitterness in her boy's voice. She hadn't told him about the disease that had claimed his father, nor the possibility that Logan might inherit it, not until three weeks earlier.

When he had woken up one morning to find that he could barely move his left hand.

He had hardly spoken to his mother since she told him that Huntington's might be a possibility. For those three weeks, he retreated into his shell and refused to come out, speaking monosyllabically and keeping his eyes pointed at the floor. When the option to spend three nights at London Bridge Hospital while he underwent tests had been offered, Logan had jumped at it, and Conny knew it was because he couldn't stand the sight of her.

It broke her heart.

"Logan, I—"

A crash somewhere behind Conny cut her off, the noise followed immediately by screams of surprise. Conny spun around, her nerves blazing; expecting to see that one of the monsters had smashed its way into the building.

She blinked.

The crash had been the noise of someone kicking open a door labelled *roof access*. The *someone* was actually four men: two, who looked no older than twenty, carried a third—who appeared to be unconscious—draped across their shoulders. The last of the four men brandished a pistol as he moved out in front of the others.

"Looking for a doctor," he growled, waving people back from the exit and moving inside the hospital.

Remy immediately began to snarl when he saw the firearm, and a space opened up around Conny as the people crowding into the corridor moved away anxiously, their eyes fixed on the gun. She grabbed the dog's collar with her right hand, holding him back, and held her left arm protectively across Logan's chest.

The man with the gun stared down at the growling dog, surprised.

"Remy, *hold*," she said firmly. She glanced up at the man with the gun. "I could let him go," she said evenly. "He's dealt with firearms before. He's *fast*. I'd rather it didn't come to that, because people might get hurt. I need you to place that weapon on the floor. *Now*."

The man with the gun lifted his gaze to Conny.

"And what? You'll *arrest* me? You do know what's happening out there, right? In fact, fuck it, throw me in jail. A steel cage would probably be the safest place to go right around now, anyway."

Conny frowned, confused, and felt her cheeks burn. In a way, he had a point. Was she even a police officer anymore? After abandoning several of her colleagues to die—and then killing another herself?

I should be the one in prison.

"We're not here to hurt anybody," he continued. "I absolutely do *not* want to have to shoot your dog. Please, I've had a rough couple of days. Don't make me do that."

Conny's eyes narrowed.

"Then why *are* you here?"

The man lowered the gun a little and beamed at her.

"To save the world, of course."

CHAPTER TWENTY-SEVEN

I t was the burning bus that did it.

One of those distinctive London double-deckers, painted a bright and cheerful red. It rolled along slowly, almost of its own accord, with fire and thick black smoke pouring out of the windows.

Mancini stared at it, transfixed by the incredible spectacle and the grisly narrative it threatened to tell.

Was it full of people when the flames took hold; all of them now just meat cooked in a giant metal oven? Were the blistered remains of the driver still hunched over the wheel, his charred foot still pressing the gas pedal?

Mancini couldn't suppress the shudder that ran through his body at the sight.

And he couldn't stop watching.

That was the trouble.

If it hadn't been for the almost hypnotic sight of the burning bus—if they had been just thirty seconds earlier or later; if they'd taken a different turn as they approached the River Thames—none of it might have happened.

What did happen, in the first instance, was that everybody in the van was so transfixed by the eerie sight ahead of them that nobody saw the truck coming from their right, and they had time only to turn their heads at the last moment as it smashed into the side of the van.

The world span like someone had dropped it into a washing machine.

Inside the rolling van, Mancini heard someone yelling, and someone else loose a round from their weapon, before a lamp post abruptly killed their forward momentum.

Along with Braxton.

The van came to a rest on its roof, all windows smashed and most of the right side of the vehicle caved in. The driver's seat had been all-but obliterated as the solid stone post drove half of the engine backwards into the cab. Most of Braxton wasn't visible. He was smeared across the exposed engine like red paint.

Mancini looked away from the dead driver and checked himself for injuries. His head was bleeding, and he was pretty sure the seatbelt had cracked a rib or two, but he'd been lucky. He unclipped the belt, grunting as pain arced through his chest, and fell out of his seat. He twisted awkwardly to see into the back of the van.

"Everybody okay?"

"Burnley fucking *shot* me," Montero snarled.

"Grazed you," Burnley muttered. "Sheesh. And I didn't *shoot*; the gun went off. If I'd 'shot' you, you'd be dead."

"Yeah, whatever, Burn—"

"Keep your damn voices down!" Mancini hissed. "Pruitt?"

The Brit hadn't been wearing a seatbelt; he was crumpled at the rear of the van, looking pretty beaten up.

"I'm fine," Pruitt grunted. "The worst part is having to listen to Laurel and fucking Hardy back here."

Mancini grimaced.

"Yeah? Try spending six hours on a plane with 'em."

"Fuck you, Mancini," Montero said. He lifted his voice. "Hey, nice driving, Braxton."

"Braxton's dead," Mancini said flatly. "Like the rest of us, if you don't quit hollering."

He squatted low, peering out of the windows. The street outside the van looked quiet. In the distance, the fiery bus had come to a stop at last, crashing sedately into the side of a building and setting it alight.

"I think we're okay," he whispered.

"Tell that to Braxton."

Mancini flicked his eyes to Montero, letting his gaze burn some silence into the man. "We have to move," he said, not breaking eye contact. "Quietly."

He reached into the rear of the van, helping Jeremy clamber over into the passenger seat as the others fumbled at their seatbelts, and crawled out onto the road through the side window.

In the distance, he heard heavy weaponry being fired; a sound he hadn't heard since his days in the military: helicopter gunships raining death down onto the city. No wonder a single gunshot hadn't drawn much attention. Somewhere overhead, a jet engine shrieked, crossing the city in seconds. Mancini couldn't see it.

Jeremy hauled himself out of the window with a grunt, and pulled himself to his feet, refusing Mancini's offered hand. Almost as soon as the Brit was out of the way, Burnley slipped through the window smoothly.

Somewhere in the van, Montero let out a muffled curse.

"I only grazed him." Burnley shrugged.

Mancini ignored her, turning to Jeremy.

"How far away are we from Rennick's apartment?"

Jeremy scanned the streets, his expression thoughtful.

"We're not far from the London Eye," he said, "so it's just a couple of miles east, along the river. Maybe less."

"You know the way?"

"More or less." Jeremy glanced around fearfully. "It's a good thing it's quiet on this side of the riv—"

He fell silent as an unearthly shriek split the night.

Mancini span toward the direction of the noise. Somewhere near the giant Ferris wheel, he thought.

Not only on the south side of the river, but probably in the next damn street.

Montero finally hauled himself through the van's broken window, still muttering curses. Mancini clamped a hand over his mouth and hauled him to his feet.

He stared at Jeremy.

Jeremy stared back blankly, his face twitching in terror.

"Which way?" Mancini breathed, and Jeremy blinked, pointing down a dark street.

"See that building?"

He pointed at a skyscraper which loomed far above the nearby buildings.

Mancini nodded. At least they would be moving away from the creature, he thought, and finally released his grip on Montero's flapping jaw.

"Move," Mancini hissed. "Eyes open. *Quiet.*"

Without another word, he turned and set off for the street which Jeremy had pointed out. It looked dark and quiet, but with each stride forward, Mancini felt his nerves tightening. The others fell into line behind him, moving single-file, and even Montero looked focused.

After about three hundred yards, Mancini stopped, hunkering down next to a parked van.

"Which way?" he glanced at Jeremy.

"Straight ahead."

Mancini gritted his teeth. They would be crossing a wide intersection, bathed in the glow of streetlights. Completely exposed. He scanned left and right, and then turned to shoot a glance behind. There *was* a vampire in that direction somewhere, but he saw no sign that it was following them. The road to the right would take them south, back in the direction they had just travelled, and though Mancini desperately wanted to head that way, it wasn't an option. The road to the left headed toward a distant bridge.

The British Army would almost certainly try to establish a beachhead along the river, but it wouldn't do any good. At least one of the vampires was already south of the Thames.

There was nothing for it. Going forward was the only option.

Mancini waved a beckoning hand at the others and set off at a controlled run, cradling the MP5, his eyes open and alert for any movement. He was halfway across the intersection when he heard screaming to his left and he spun, raising his weapon.

A small group of people were fleeing from the direction of the river, chased by another: a man wearing a *peace is love* T-shirt and brandishing a huge knife.

Mancini lowered his weapon a little, gawping as the guy with the knife ran down a middle-aged woman, leaping onto her back and driving the knife into her head. Before Mancini could react, heavy gunfire rained down from above, and the guy with the knife damn near *exploded*.

With a deafening roar, a large chopper swung low overhead, turning back toward the other side of the river and heading back into the city.

Jesus, Mancini thought, *they don't even know what they're fighting against. They think* people *are doing this.*

The vampires weren't even showing up for the fight. They were staying in the shadows, turning humans on each other, revelling in the chaos. To the authorities, it probably looked like half of the city's population had gone completely berserk. *Throw in some far-fetched sightings of monstrous creatures*, he thought, *and you have a recipe for madness, and bad decisions.*

The British military was doing the work of the vampires for them, killing the wrong species indiscriminately. Yet every time they mowed down some poor bastard with a knife, the real enemy would simply take control of another puppet, and the wheel of insanity would continue to turn.

He blinked as his thoughts reached a troubling destination.

If one of the monsters' puppets had been that close; no more than fifty yards away...

"Move!" Mancini hissed, and took off at a panicked sprint.

He had taken no more than five steps forward when he heard a shriek split the night behind him.

CHAPTER TWENTY-EIGHT

D*arkness.*
Pain.
The hands in the darkness have him.
They carry him along helplessly, tossing and thrashing him.
The whole world is cascading black water.
Seeping through his skin.
Poisoning his soul.
And when it roars, he hears it clearly, and understands that it is not the sound of a river at all.
It is the sound of a voice.
Bellowing in the void, vast and incomprehensible.
Beckoning him forward.

CHAPTER TWENTY-NINE

The journey in the helicopter had become bloated with pounding anxiety almost as soon as the vehicle reached the outskirts of London and the *fuel low* light began to flash.

Herb had taken the pilot's seat, not trusting either Lawrence or Scott with the task, and his rusty skill with the controls had made the journey *interesting* even before the fuel began to run out.

When the warning light caught his attention, he had instinctively searched for a place to set down, but the city below seemed to be made of darkness and fire. Any landing could put them in immediate danger, and at the very least would mean that they would have to travel the rest of the way on foot. He had considered the prospect of carrying a comatose man through territory that was quickly becoming vampire country and dismissed the idea of landing. He didn't fancy their chances of surviving long down on the streets. They would make it to the hospital; they *had* to.

Besides, if the chopper was anything like a car, he thought, the fuel warning probably wasn't *urgent*. The tank probably still had plenty of miles left in it.

Apparently not.

Their destination was in sight, silhouetted against the burning city to the north of the river, when the engine began to wheeze out its last breaths, and setting the chopper down became a matter of crashing rather than landing. The final descent, as the rotor blades began to stutter, had been steeped in fear that should have made his soul shrivel, but he had remained oddly calm. Herb had decided, as the roof of the hospital lurched toward him like an uppercut, that you knew you were having a bad day when crashing a helicopter into a building was only the second most frightening thing to happen.

Or was it the third?

He couldn't be sure anymore.

Now that he was safely inside the hospital, with a doctor checking Dan, the adrenaline which had kept him upright for more than thirty-six hours steadily leaked away, and a wall of fatigue collapsed on top of him. It felt like he had been terrified forever, and the constant, draining fear and lack of sleep was making his thoughts unstable and skittish.

He hadn't eaten either, he realised, not since before boarding the Oceanus. Increasingly, he was finding it hard to think straight.

He shook his head and rubbed his eyes, trying to focus on what the woman who had examined Dan was saying.

"It's not his injuries," the doctor said.

Herb blinked slowly, switching his gaze from Dan to her.

"Not," he repeated dumbly.

"That's right. He has a lot of bruises and lacerations, and the wounds to his abdomen are deep, but not life-threatening. Not serious enough to render him comatose. I've stitched him up, though it was a rush job. He'll need to get to another hospital in the next day or two to get his wounds redressed, and—"

"Wait...it's *not* his injuries? Then why isn't he waking up?"

She shook her head, looking a little irritated.

"He is in shock, perhaps. A fugue state. Or he has a pre-existing psychological condition that I am not aware of. Look, I really—"

"You don't have his medical records?"

The doctor shook her head impatiently. "I'd have to request them from his current doctor. That tends to take a few days when the world *isn't* falling apart. He's not dying, but he's not waking up, either. I'm sorry, that's the best I can do. Do you need me to take a look at your arm?"

Herb blinked, and stared down at his bandaged arm. He'd forgotten all about it.

"No, it's nothing. You're *sure* it's not his injuries?"

The doctor nodded curtly.

"Quite certain. Now, please, I have other patients that I need to prepare for the evacuation..."

Herb nodded absently, returning his gaze to Dan as the doctor left the room.

Out cold yet again, he thought, and felt a stab of envy.

He was *so* tired.

He rubbed at his eyes once more. It felt like his eyelids were made of grit.

Lack of sleep. An empty stomach.

As problems went, they were so ordinary; so mundane.

Yet, despite his exhaustion, Herb wasn't sure he could ever sleep again. Certainly, if he had been forced to kill the police officer's fucking *dog* on top of everything else, he was sure he wouldn't sleep *well*. No, sleep was out of the question.

But at least he could eat.

He turned to leave Dan's room, and flinched in surprise when he saw the policewoman leaning on the doorframe with her arms folded across her chest. The dog sat at her feet, regarding Dan's inert body with an expression that struck Herb as *cautious interest*.

"Who is he?" she asked, as Herb made his way out into the corridor and headed for a vending machine a few rooms away. When he passed by her, she turned and followed. A moment later, the dog did likewise.

"Nobody," Herb said ruefully, "according to him, anyway."

He chuckled when he reached the vending machine, patting at his pockets. "No cash," he said with a weary smile. "Would you believe I didn't think I'd have to stop for snacks? Sorry about this."

The police officer frowned, and then her eyes widened in surprise as Herb pulled the gun from his waistband and blew a hole in the glass front of the machine.

Somewhere further down the hallway, someone screamed, and Herb yelled an apology.

He reached inside the vending machine and began to pluck out chocolate bars and tiny bags of peanuts. He ripped a pack of nuts open, pouring the entire contents into his mouth, and smiled happily at the policewoman as he chewed.

And chewed.

"Herb Rennick," he said finally, swallowing the last of the nuts and tearing the wrapper off a *Snickers*. He took a large bite and stuck out his right hand.

She shook it uncertainly, apparently disoriented by the sudden, formal gesture.

"Cornelia Stokes. Conny," she said. "You know what's going on out there, don't you?" Her eyes narrowed. "I can see it on your face."

"You must be a good cop, to get that just from looking at me," Herb said with a chuckle as he reached back into the smashed vending machine to pluck out a juice box. He popped the straw and sucked on it noisily, nodding his head at the smashed glass. "You gonna arrest me for stealing?"

"And vandalism, and threatening behaviour, and discharging a firearm in a public place, and being a shit pilot," Conny said. "Yeah, maybe later. For now I'll settle for knowing what you know."

Herb drained the juice box and grabbed another, offering it to Conny. She started to wave the offer away, but apparently thought better of it. She took the drink with a nod of thanks.

At her feet, Remy huffed softly, and Conny pointed at the vending machine.

"Grab some of that jerky, too. For Remy."

Herb grunted, raiding the machine once more and dropping his eyes to the dog.

"Hey, Remy. This jerky makes you an accessory to the crime, right? Or guilty of receiving stolen goods.

Either way, we're on the same team now, buddy. No teeth, understand?"

Remy tilted his head, his eyes wide and alert as Herb tore open a pack of jerky and held it out. The German Shepherd looked up at Conny pleadingly, and she nodded.

Within seconds, the jerky was gone.

Herb began to open another pack, and returned his gaze to Conny.

"I can tell you the truth—or as much as I know of it at any rate. But in my experience, people have a hard time believing it. In fact, those people I *do* tell generally seem to end up punching me. Hmmm."

Conny glared at him.

"Just tell me."

"The city is being overrun by vampires," Herb said breezily, heading back toward Dan's room, dangling a piece of jerky from his hand for Remy to follow. "This is the part where you say 'vampires? Are you crazy?'"

"Do you always talk so much without actually saying anything?"

Herb paused for a moment at the entrance to Dan's room, and his face split in a wide grin.

"Yeah, I think there are people who'd agree that was accurate."

He walked inside and sat heavily on the edge of Dan's bed, trying not to think about how much he, too, wanted to lie down.

"They're not vampires like you see on TV," he said. "The vampire myth is a fabrication; disinformation that the passage of time has given a veneer of truth, understand? Different civilizations have different interpretations, but they all have some version of the vampire myth, and it is all built on the same memories: creatures that live in darkness, and feed on humans. That's where the truth ends and the myth begins. The vampires hibernate underground for centuries, for so long that their very existence becomes a fairytale. When the time comes for a nest to rise, the humans who serve them offer up a sacrifice, and then erase the whole event from history."

"And how do *you* know all this?"

Herb took another bite of chocolate and chewed slowly, staring thoughtfully at Conny.

"Is that your kid in the other room?"

She looked surprised at the sudden change of subject.

"Logan, my son, yes," she nodded.

"He looks like he's pissed off with the world."

Conny's gaze hardened.

"He's...angry. Confused." She lowered her voice a little. "He found out today that he is dying." Her jaw dropped a little, as if she couldn't quite believe she had offered that information so freely to a complete stranger.

Herb snorted.

"So did a lot of people," he said around a mouthful of chocolate.

She stared at him evenly.

"You didn't answer my question. How is it that you know so much about these vampires?"

"I don't know enough." He returned her gaze without blinking. "I'm one of the people that served them the Oceanus."

He popped the last of the chocolate into his mouth.

Conny frowned, as if the word was familiar, but she couldn't quite place it for a moment. Her eyes widened. "The cruise ship?"

Herb nodded.

"The deal with these things is that they are meant to be immortal. Our choice was to do what they say or risk an entire nest rising—maybe even *all* the nests—and wiping us out."

"'*Was?*'"

Herb arched an eyebrow. The police officer seemed no more perturbed about the existence of vampires than if he had just informed her that it was raining outside. She picked up on the vital part of the information he was attempting to convey almost instantly.

He pointed at Dan Bellamy.

"He killed at least two of them. They die, all right."

Conny's gaze settled on Dan for a moment.

"How many are there?" she met his eye. "How many vampires?"

Herb's eyes narrowed.

"Gotta say, you're taking the news that vampires exist pretty well."

Conny shrugged.

"I saw them. In the Underground. *Vampire* isn't the word I would choose, but it serves just as well as *monster*, I suppose."

"You saw them? And survived? How?"

"I ran."

"You were lucky."

"Luckier than the rest of the police. You're avoiding the question. Again. How many vampires are there?"

Herb frowned.

"In total? Nobody knows for sure. According to records we have, which have proved to be...unreliable, each nest is structured so that there are several females for every male. Best estimate for that ratio is around nine to one. But even if that is true, we don't know how many males there are in any given nest, and we don't know how many nests there are out there; not for certain."

"Like lions," Conny said thoughtfully.

"Huh?"

"A pride of lions is matriarchal," Conny said. "Usually, around three or four females for every male. Males are for hunting and breeding. They don't tend to last as long as the females."

Herb stared at her, his eyes widening slowly as realisation dawned.

The Three.

The question of why only three vampires had been sent to feed had nagged at him for hours. The vampires which had been unleashed upon the Oceanus were *males*. They had to be. They had even looked a little different from the vampire he had seen at the mansion; slightly bigger, their bodies more heavily packed with sinewy muscle. *Males*. Why else would a bunch of creatures that had slept for centuries only send up three of its kind to feed?

Because the Oceanus wasn't about satisfying hunger. Well; not entirely. It was about something else.

The revelation banished all thoughts of fatigue, and Herb felt adrenaline beginning to course through him once more. Could the Three have been sent to the surface to feed because they were about to enter a breeding cycle? What other explanation could there be? It was so simple and so glaringly obvious that the truth hit him like a slap.

The vampires lived for thousands of years. If their breeding cycle was anything at all like that of people, the creatures would be *everywhere*; it would be they who ruled the surface of the planet, not humans. But the vampires *weren't* everywhere. In fact, it seemed that there were comparatively few of them for a species which claimed immortality. As far as the Order had been able to estimate, there were likely no more than a few thousand across the globe.

And suddenly, Herb knew why.

Their ability to procreate had to be severely limited. Maybe they could only breed every few hundred—or thousand—years. When the time came, the nest sent its males to feed, to gather the strength they needed to service the needs of the females and create the next generation.

If it was true, it meant that the Order had spent centuries helping the vampire species grow *stronger*. Feeding and nurturing an enemy whose number would eventually grow to the point where wholesale slaughter of humans was inevitable.

"Twenty-seven," Herb said softly.

Conny frowned.

"If the information my family has is correct—and that's a big *if*—that's how many there are out there. Twenty-seven. At least."

He strode to the nearest window and stared out across the river, lost in thought.

"That doesn't sound like many," Conny replied. "And if your friend managed to kill two, I'm sure the army will be able to deal with the rest."

Herb shook his head grimly.

"These creatures are smart," he said, "of at least equal intelligence to us. They won't just offer themselves up to be shot at. They move underground, they stay out of sight. They know how to remain undetected. That's the one thing I *am* sure of."

Conny frowned.

"I spoke to a soldier who told me there had been multiple sightings in the centre of the city. They obviously don't care *that* much about being seen."

Herb lifted his gaze to the London skyline, lit by raging flames.

The vampires didn't burn, he knew that much for certain, but the fire spreading across central London meant light. A lot of light.

"They came from the Underground system," Conny continued. "In fact, this all started because they were letting people *go*. It's more like they wanted attention. They drew the entire Metropolitan Police Force down into the tunnels."

Conny's voice cracked a little on those final few words. Herb didn't ask for details on what had happened to the police. There was no need. The answer was written in Cornelia Stokes' clouded eyes, as plain as day. She ran. The rest of the police didn't get the chance.

It's more like they wanted attention.

Some slippery awareness nagged at Herb's subconscious, clamouring for his consideration.

Multiple sightings.

"How many do you think there were?" he asked distantly. "In the Underground, I mean?"

Conny shrugged.

"Around a dozen, I think."

"Attacking the most visible part of the country that they possibly could," Herb muttered, almost to himself. "The middle of the city; all that light. They knew they would be seen. That's what they wanted."

"But *why*?"

Herb shook his head.

"I don't know. But if there *are* only a dozen in

London, it's because they want our focus here. As for where the rest are? I have no idea, but wherever they are and whatever they are doing, it won't be good for us."

Before Conny could respond, right on cue, the night erupted to the sound of gunfire.

CHAPTER THIRTY

Conny sprinted back to Logan's room, reaching it before the first rattle of gunfire had faded.

Logan kept his eyes deliberately averted from hers; a typical teenage sulk with a heart-wrenching undertone of finality. Her son's rejection felt like broken glass lodged deep in her chest, tearing into her flesh with every breath she took, but she refused to acknowledge it. Logan could hate her when they were both safe. For now, Conny needed to know where the danger was located.

"Did you see who fired?"

No response.

"*Logan!* Who fired, dammit? Was it the soldiers on the bridge?"

Logan looked shocked at the sudden vitriol in his mother's tone. He gave an affirmative grunt, and Conny focused her gaze on the bridge as Herb jogged into the room behind her.

"It didn't come from the south, as far as I can tell," he said.

Conny turned around, nodding, and pointed at the window.

"Logan saw it. It came from the bridge. Think they were shooting at vampires?"

At the mention of vampires, Logan looked like he *really* wanted to speak, but the rage and grief and confusion that twisted inside Conny's boy kept his lips clamped shut. Her heart ached, and she switched her gaze back to Herb.

"I doubt it," he said, and moved closer to the window.

"Then what were they firing at?"

"I don't know, but they're not firing now. I heard one gun, that's all. If they were shooting at a vampire, I have a feeling there would be more than one person shooting."

Conny nodded slowly, remembering the response of Chief Superintendent Porter and the others to the appearance of the creature in the tunnels. They had opened fire in a blind panic, shooting indiscriminately; *wildly.*

Just as I did.

That same fraught, instinctive response to the presence of vampires had cost Robert Nelson his life back in the tunnels. The memory was like a thorn in her soul. She tried to shake it away, and almost succeeded. There wasn't time to wallow in her remorse; not yet, but the grief was there, lurking somewhere in her rear view mirror, gradually closing in on her.

She focused on the dark bridge.

The soldiers might be more prepared for combat than the police had been, but Herb's words had a ring of truth: she couldn't imagine a group of armed men idly standing by while one of their number opened fire on a monster. After all, the creatures were beyond terrifying in appearance. Anybody holding a gun when one appeared, she thought, would either start shooting or start running.

The soldiers were little more than stick figures at this distance, but Conny could clearly see that they were having a heated discussion about something, one of them waving his arms and jabbing a finger at the other side of the bridge.

She tried to make out what he was pointing at.

On the far side of the bridge, she saw a single person walking steadily toward the soldiers. Whoever it was, they seemed to be in no rush to reach the apparent safety of the south bank of the Thames. Judging from the way they strolled forward casually, they weren't afraid at all.

She pointed, drawing Herb's attention.

"See that guy?"

As Herb squinted, Conny noticed the soldiers on the bridge raising their weapons, pointing them at the approaching man.

"Shit," Herb growled. "I think he has a knife." He turned to face Conny, his eyes wide. "We have to get out of here, right now."

"What? Why?"

"The vampires. They take minds; control people like puppets."

He returned his horrified gaze to the window.

"They're using people as weapons."

The man on the bridge suddenly broke into a sprint, heading straight for the soldiers. Conny watched them take a couple of uncertain steps backwards, aiming their weapons, and then finally, one opened fire and put the sprinting man down with a short burst of automatic fire. Before she could even begin to frame a question that might make sense of what Herb had just told her, she saw it.

And her nerves howled.

It had been crawling along the underside of the bridge: a dark, wiry shape that crept up behind the soldiers, who were focused only on the body of the man in front of them.

"A decoy," Herb said in an awestruck whisper.

As Conny watched, unable to blink, the creature reached the first of the soldiers, grabbing him and spinning him around to face it. Moments later, the man hoisted his weapon and began to execute his brothers in arms.

And the vampire was already gone, back over the side of the bridge, melting back into the shadows.

The 'execution' deteriorated quickly, becoming a messy, panicked firefight. When it was over, there were just three soldiers left standing. One dropped to his knees with his head in his hands, bellowing out a roar of despair that carried through the night almost as clearly as the chatter of the guns.

He doesn't even know what happened, Conny thought, and she shuddered.

But she couldn't turn away.

This time, when the vampire leapt from the underside of the bridge, it closed in fast, swinging its arms, and the remaining three soldiers exploded in a storm of blood. They didn't even get off a shot.

Didn't even see it coming.

When the last of them fell, his body ripped almost in two at his midriff, the monster on the bridge turned toward the south bank of the Thames.

And headed straight toward London Bridge Hospital.

Shit!

She grabbed Logan's arm firmly, ignoring his cry of irritation and surprise.

"Get your things," she snarled. "*Now!*"

Logan stared at her for a fleeting moment, apparently considering whether to make a big deal of her request or not, but when he finally looked her in the eye, she saw him register the fear his mother felt. He nodded, and began to slip on a pair of jeans, and Conny turned away.

Herb was already gone.

When Conny peeked out of the door, giving Logan a moment of privacy, she saw that the strange guy was back in the room with the unconscious man, holding an empty bottle of water from the vending machine over his sleeping friend's head. Tipping out the last few drops. It didn't appear that throwing water on him had worked, and it looked almost like Herb was debating whether or not slapping his friend might wake him.

"Scott, Lawrence," Herb barked. "Time to move."

Herb's other two companions, both of whom had sat in the corridor with a shell-shocked look on their faces ever since they had arrived, leapt to their feet on Herb's command, and ran to the big man's side. Together, the three of them hoisted the unconscious man from his bed.

And froze.

More frantic gunfire, right outside the hospital, followed by a rising chorus of horrific screams.

Inside.

THE SCREAMING CAME FROM THE GROUND FLOOR AND was muted by the hospital's five storeys, but it was no less terrifying for its lack of volume. All of a sudden, the fatigue which had threatened to overwhelm Herb evaporated, boiled away by the heat of an all-too familiar dread.

It's in the building.

Was there a fire escape leading down the exterior of the building from the roof?

He tried to remember the hospital roof as he had seen it from the cockpit of the helicopter, but the building was just a dark smear. He hadn't been landing. He'd been *crashing*. There hadn't been time to take in his surroundings.

If there's no way down from the roof, he thought, *we're all dead.*

Lawrence and Scott looped Dan's arms around their necks once more, carrying him like a drunk. Herb winced when he thought about the damage they might be doing to the guy. The stitches in his belly were a temporary fix, and the last thing Herb needed was for Dan to start bleeding again. The helicopter's interior had been drenched in the guy's blood; Herb doubted that Dan had all that much left to lose.

There had to be a fire escape. *Had to be.* Even if there was just a ladder leading down from the roof, they would be able to come up with something. If necessary, Herb would find some way to haul Dan down himself.

If it comes to that.

He listened intently, trying to gauge whether the monster was making its way up through the building. London Bridge Hospital was all-but empty according to Conny, its patients and staff evacuated almost entirely. If the vampire planned to search the hospital, it wouldn't take long before it found its way past the deserted floors below.

Or it might just decide that the building is empty and move on.

He ran back out into the corridor, just as Conny and her son exited their room and began to head for the stairs.

"We won't be able to sneak past it," he said, waving at them to turn around. "Go for the roof, and *listen*," he grabbed Conny's elbow, making sure he had her full attention, "these things are like Medusa, right? You know the story of Medusa?"

Herb glanced from Conny to Logan. Both were nodding.

"Don't look directly at them. If you lock eyes with one of these things, your mind is gone, understand? Kill yourselves before you let that happen."

He tightened his grip on Conny's arm until she flinched.

"I'm *serious*. These things like to play with their food when they aren't hungry, and I'm betting they're pretty well fed right now. Head for the roof, look for a fire escape. I'll be right behind you. I have a place nearby. If we can get to it, we'll be safe."

He released Conny's elbow.

"Well, safe-*ish*."

He wished he could tell her more; explain that if she needed to, she should take her son and run without looking back, but there just wasn't time. He sprinted to the double-doors which led to the stairs and elevators, and recoiled in horror.

Glass.

He hadn't even thought to check. The doors to the stairwell were two panes of thick, floor-to-ceiling *glass*. He could bar the handles, but that trick had barely worked once before. And *then* the door had been made of sturdy wood.

Gently, he pushed the left door open, prodding it with a shaking finger.

He heard it immediately.

The clicking of talons on the marble floor somewhere below him.

It was in the stairwell, and it sounded like it was coming up, moving floor by floor.

With a strangled yelp, Herb slammed the door and searched desperately for something to put through the handles. His eyes landed on a forearm crutch, and he snatched it up, his heart sinking in disappointment at how lightweight it felt. Flimsy aluminium; even as he slipped it between the door handles, he knew that it would not hold for long.

Somewhere at the back of his mind a faint, nagging voice muttered that if his best plans always amounted to makeshift deadbolts, he would eventually run out of doors altogether. He ignored it, and scanned the rooms. Many were glass-walled, and he could see that there were still patients in several of them; those whose poor health made fleeing a virtual impossibility. There were a handful of fearful doctors and nurses, too, all of them staring at Herb like he was holding a bomb.

There was no time to explain.

"It's coming. *Run*," he snarled, and he took off toward the roof exit, not pausing to check whether anyone had heeded his warning. He had done all he could.

The lock on the roof exit was smashed beyond repair where Herb had kicked it to get into the building. There was no way to seal or barricade the door from the outside. If there was no other way off the roof, he and the others would be faced with a stark choice: jump to their deaths, or be torn apart.

Or *taken*.

A violent shudder ran through him. Back on the Oceanus, he had been fully prepared to take his own life rather than let one of the monsters break into his mind, but that had been before he met Dan Bellamy. Now, Herb wasn't sure he had it in him to jump from the roof if the vampire cornered him. There was too much at stake.

Outside the broken door, three steps led up to the small helipad which Herb's chopper had briefly 'landed' on before ploughing across the roof and finally coming to a halt only when it collided messily with the low wall which ran around the perimeter.

He searched for the others frantically, and for a moment, when he couldn't see them, his hopes rose a fraction. Maybe they had found a fire escape, and were already heading down to street level.

He sprinted to the nearest edge, peering over it. The hospital overlooked the river, but it was a five storey drop, and the wide path below meant that even if they did jump, hitting the water was extremely unlikely. He turned away, and headed for the other side of the roof.

And that faint flicker of hope crumbled.

Conny's voice, calling to him from the other side of the ruined helicopter toward the rear of the building.

"There's no way down," she yelled.

Herb paled, and sprinted toward her. Lawrence and Scott were standing alongside Conny's kid, propping up Dan with fear plastered on their faces. Remy was staring up at Conny with an incredulous look in his eyes, like he was wondering how his human had managed to lead them to such a disastrous bolt-hole.

Conny pointed toward the chopper, and after a moment, Herb saw it.

The wall that he had crashed into had been home to a black metal ladder.

A ladder which now rested where it had fallen on the street far below, mocking him.

No way down.

CHAPTER THIRTY-ONE

Stay in the light!

Mancini rocketed away from the intersection, aiming for the intermittent glow of streetlights, too afraid to look back. He trusted his ears to tell him whether the monster was gaining on them.

His ears were full of bad news.

Judging by the thunderous sound of the pursuit, he was trying to outrun a creature that could move like a damn cheetah. The team had a significant head start, but it sounded like it was eroding by the second.

The vampire shrieked, the sound making Mancini's blood freeze in his veins. The noise was an attempt to draw attention, he knew; the creature's bid to get the fleeing humans to look in its direction.

No chance.

"This way," he snarled, unwilling to turn to check whether the others had heard him, and he loosed a short burst from the MP5, shattering the front window of a restaurant which occupied a corner plot dead ahead.

Inside, the lights were blazing cheerfully over empty tables and booths. It all looked so *normal*.

Mancini pumped his legs, running like he was a teenager again, and when he was close enough, he threw himself forward, vaulting over the waist-high window sill and crashing across a table and into the warmly-lit dining area. His momentum carried him on.

With a grunt, he rolled into a chair, and saw stars as one wooden leg impacted on his ribs. He gasped the pain away and hauled himself to his feet, throwing the flimsy furniture aside.

As Burnley threw herself into the restaurant behind him, Mancini took off again.

The lights of the restaurant might slow the vampire down. They wouldn't stop it.

He charged through the dining area into the kitchen to the rear of the building, slamming into a fire exit that led back outside.

Kept running.

Further ahead, across a narrow side street, he saw a car dealership. More lights, reflecting off the polished surfaces of eye-wateringly expensive sports cars. He fired the MP5 again, making straight for the shattering window, grimacing as he heard gunfire behind him. It sounded like someone—Montero, most likely—was laying down some covering fire, probably trying to dissuade the creature from following.

He was wasting his time, and his bullets.

Their only hope was to find somewhere that offered a sturdy wall to hide behind.

He burst into the showroom, darting around a black Ferrari, and blasted out the next window. Beyond it, he saw something that gave him faint hope: an old church, standing at odds with the sleek glass skyscrapers that had sprung up around it. The church had to be several hundred years old; its walls looked like thick, solid stone. Even better, the ground-level windows looked narrow—maybe even too narrow for a vampire to squeeze through.

Burnley shot past him. With a clear run, she was the fastest by far.

"The church," Mancini panted as she passed, moving with a smooth fluidity. If anyone was going to make it, Mancini thought, it would be Burnley. He cursed his bulk, and tried to ignore the fire slowly building in his muscles.

"On it," Burnley yelled, and tore away from him, eating up the ground. Somewhere further back, Montero was still shooting, and Mancini risked a glance behind, his eyes landing first on Jeremy Pruitt, struggling to keep his sprint going. Behind Pruitt, Montero was firing wildly back through the car dealership, peppering the showroom with automatic fire. Maybe, Mancini thought, he was trying to hit one of the car's fuel tanks and trigger an explosion, like in the movies.

But this wasn't a movie.

Mancini didn't glance at Pruitt as he huffed by him.

"Get in the church," Mancini muttered absently, his gaze fixed on the roof of the car dealership. He could have sworn he saw movement up there in the darkne—

The vampire launched itself down onto Montero with a shriek.

While Montero had been attempting to slow it down, the monster had simply scaled the building, traversing it in a matter of seconds. Montero was shooting at nothing.

Mancini turned away as the creature landed on the man and the gunfire stopped abruptly.

He didn't wait to see the former SEAL die.

He was already running.

Fifty yards to the church entrance.

He saw Burnley holding the heavy wooden door open, waving at him frantically.

Forty yards.

Saw Jeremy Pruitt disappear inside.

Thirty yards.

Saw Burnley's eyes widening in horror as she began to close the door.

Twenty yards.

"No!" Mancini shrieked, and he emptied the submachine gun blindly over his own shoulder, praying that he might slow the monster which he knew was bearing down on him, closing with every stride.

Ten yards.

Click, click, click, click clickclickclickcli—

With a desperate scream, Mancini hurled himself forward, aiming for the narrow gap as Burnley finally threw the door shut.

His hip glanced off the wood painfully, and he landed heavily on a cold stone floor as Burnley barred the door and something heavy crunched into the other side a fraction of a second later.

Mancini rolled onto his back, still screaming, slammed another magazine into the MP5 and scattered bullets at the inside of the door until the weapon clicked apologetically.

When he released the trigger, and the echo of gunfire receded, he heard only silence.

Mancini leapt to his feet, reloading and scanning the interior of the church.

"Vampires, right?" Burnley said in a shaky voice. "They...uh...can't go inside churches...right?"

Jeremy Pruitt snorted.

"Don't bet on it," Mancini replied, casting a glance around the huge interior of the church. The stained-glass windows looked too narrow for one of the vampires, but...

The glass shattered as he looked at it, and he had the briefest impression of a dark shape and glowing red eyes peering in before he tore his gaze away.

"Don't look at it," he roared, and ran for the back of the church. "Keep moving!"

He felt the monster's deadly gaze burning into his back the whole way.

The church—or maybe cathedral was more accurate—was huge, much bigger than it had looked from the outside. Far above, delicate arches propped up a decorative ceiling, and there had to be seating for five hundred, at least. Lots of fabulously intricate and expensive ornamentation lined the walls, images depicting violence and bloodshed and reverence. In some ways, it wasn't so different to the ranch back in Colorado. Different gods, same worship.

Mancini led the others down the centre aisle, panting for air.

To the rear of the building, there was a raised altar beneath a huge wall, filled with carved statues representing various bishops and saints. To either side of that were two wooden doors. Mancini slammed into the one on the right. Some sort of private chamber; a place for the bishop to relax between sermons, perhaps. More importantly, there was no way out. He turned, barging past Pruitt, and made for the opposite door. It opened onto a narrow corridor, with several smaller rooms and hallways branching from it, at least one of which looked to lead up to a bell tower.

Mancini grimaced. It wouldn't be long before the vampire made its way up there, and found a route into the church. He slammed the door to the base of the tower shut, searching for a key to lock it.

Nothing.

"Keep moving," he snarled again, and ran through the gloomy corridors, searching for an alternative exit. He ran frantically from room to room, his fear increasing with each door that he tried. There surely *had* to be another way out.

Somewhere above him, muted by thick stone walls, he heard the bell in the tower clanging, and adrenaline flooded his system. In a panic, he burst through several featureless doors blindly, until at last one spat him out into the night.

And headlong into the site of another atrocity.

He was standing across the street from the main entrance of a hospital, and there were corpses *everywhere*, chewed up and scattered across the street. Some wore uniforms marking them out as healthcare staff; others were clearly patients. Still others wore military clothing. The British Army, clearly, was having no more success when confronting the vampires than Mancini himself.

The scale of the slaughter was almost incomprehensible. Mancini's mind wanted to recoil in horror at the sight of so many torn bodies; to retreat to some warm, safe place and pretend that Hell wasn't opening up all around him, but his instincts drove him on. He charged forward, feeling the terrible burning ache caused by the extended sprint beginning to weaken his thighs, and made straight for the hospital, with Burnley and Pruitt behind him.

And a monster somewhere behind them.

Beyond the hospital, he saw the building which Pruitt had pointed out as their destination looming. The Rennick apartment. Just a few hundred yards away.

If they were lucky, Mancini thought as he streaked across the bloody road, the vampire might take a wrong turn in the church's narrow labyrinth of stone corridors. Maybe it wouldn't even be aware that they had found an exit, and would waste time searching the building, giving them enough time to lose it on the streets.

If they were lucky.

Mancini sprinted through the bloodbath with his jaw clenched, trying not to look at the corpses that littered the ground.

Luck looked to be in short supply in London tonight.

CHAPTER THIRTY-TWO

Herb heard a soft *thump* somewhere behind him, and knew instinctively that the noise had been caused by Scott and Lawrence dropping Dan's comatose body onto the flat roof.

He could hardly blame them, really.

He didn't turn to check whether Dan was okay. His entire focus was taken by the doorway, and the steps leading down to the corridor beyond. He couldn't see as far as the glass doors which he had barricaded, but the top floor of the hospital looked—and sounded—quiet. Those who remained—the most severely ill patients in their rooms and a handful of doctors and nurses—were apparently unharmed.

So far, at least, there was no screaming.

Herb turned away and scanned the rooftop again in growing frustration, hoping that he might see an adjacent roof that they might be able to jump to. There was nothing.

"We have to go back inside," he snapped at the others. "Find some other way down. Maybe the elevators—"

"Too late," Conny said.

Herb turned to face her. The policewoman had one arm wrapped tightly around her son—who looked like he desperately wanted to struggle away from her—and pointed at Remy with the other.

"Remy can sense them, or hear them. I don't know. But it's close. Getting closer."

Herb dropped his eyes to the dog. Remy stood at Conny's feet; muscles tensed, startled eyes fixed on the same open doorway that Herb had studied moments earlier. As Herb watched, Remy began to edge backwards, and shot a pleading glance up at his master.

The dog knew something was close, all right. The mutt looked as terrified as he thought it was possible for a dog *to* look.

"Found a drainpipe!"

Herb flinched as Scott hollered from the other side of the roof. When he turned to face the cleric, he saw that Scott was already swinging a leg over the low wall.

There was, he supposed, little point in remaining quiet now.

"We can't get Bellamy down a fucking *drainpipe*," Herb roared, but Scott simply shook his head and kept on climbing down. Herb could see Scott's intention written across his face, and he didn't hold it against him. The cleric simply wasn't prepared to die for Dan Bellamy. Why should he be? The brainwashing that all those who were inducted into the Order underwent clearly wasn't comprehensive enough. When faced with imminent death at the hands of one of the creatures they were supposed to worship, all that manufactured belief and loyalty just...crumbled away.

His father would have been mortified at just how

quickly the tiny empire he had built up had fallen apart. At any other time, that thought might have made Herb smile.

Not now.

Seething in frustration, Herb turned away and sprinted back to the *roof access* door, peering back down into the hospital. It still seemed quiet. The vampire hadn't come through yet. Was it possible that the glass was strong enough to stop it?

Why was nobody screaming?

He crept halfway down the steps, and stopped dead, his heart hammering.

At the far end of the corridor, the doctor who had stitched up Dan's belly was walking toward the glass doors slowly, her arms outstretched, moving unsteadily, as though in a daze.

Oh no, Herb thought, *don't do that—*

The doctor slid the aluminium crutch out from between the handles obligingly, and pulled the door open.

Welcoming the monster like an old friend.

She was still holding the door handle for a second or two, even after her innards had been lanced like an abscess; punched out through her back and splattered across the wall behind her in an instant.

Herb felt his own stomach do a backflip.

The doctor collapsed to her knees, and fell forward onto what was left of her stomach, and *then* the other patients and staff started to scream.

Herb gaped, and watched it unfolding in a terrifying sort of slow motion; his brain mulling over the twisted images that reached it, and telling him in no uncertain terms that he should be running or screaming or both. For a long moment, all he could do was stare.

The sound of breaking glass.

The light above the doctor's head winking out of existence as a fire extinguisher flew into the corridor and crashed into it, plunging the far end of the top floor into semi-darkness.

An impression of a large shape hurtling from left to right, crossing the hallway in a flash and disappearing into one of the rooms.

Another light cut out.

Another.

It was moving toward him, room by room, killing as it went.

At last, Herb tore himself away and fled back up the steps, pulling the broken door shut behind him and praying that the creature might overlook it.

If not...

There weren't many potential victims on the top floor of the hospital. Nothing much to slow the vampire down. If it was coming, it would be on the roof in a minute. Maybe less.

No time.

He caught Conny's eye as he burst back onto the roof.

She shook her head grimly, opening up a well of despair in Herb's gut. He didn't even need to ask; it was obvious from Conny's expression that they had found no other way down. Even if they *could* all clamber down the drainpipe and carry Dan somehow, their progress would be too slow. Too loud. As soon as the vampire reached the roof, their presence on the drainpipe would be unmissable.

He flicked his gaze to Dan, still unconscious on his back in the middle of the roof.

I can't leave him behind.

I won't.

Somewhere behind Conny, at the far end of the building, Herb heard a loud crack, followed by a surprised scream which ended with a sound like a gunshot, and he realised the flimsy option of fleeing had been removed altogether. At the edge of the roof, he saw Lawrence hauling himself back up over the wall, flushing and petrified. Apparently he, too, had decided that the drainpipe was the best option, and it hadn't been able to take both his and Scott's weight.

Lawrence gasped as he pulled himself upright, and peered behind him, leaning out over the street far below. When he turned away from the sheer drop, Lawrence's eyes were wide, his expression sickly, and Herb knew what the cleric had seen splattered on the ground, five storeys down. The drainpipe wasn't the best option anymore. It never had been.

It was hopeless.

All they could do was hide, like frightened children whimpering beneath their blankets, waiting for the monster to come for them.

"Get behind the helicopter," Herb hissed, "out of sight. If it comes for us, don't look at it. Jump if you have to. At least you'll get a quick death."

His eyes landed on Logan. The kid looked at his mother with fearful, disbelieving eyes, but Conny kept her gaze firmly on Herb. She nodded, her own eyes clear and focused, and Herb knew the message had got through. Conny's boy might be dying, but not at the hands of a monster. Not today. She would do what was necessary.

Will I?

Herb ran to the chopper, reaching it just after

Lawrence, and hunkered down behind the ruined vehicle as best he could, pulling Conny and Logan down alongside him. Conny began to call for Remy.

Herb clamped a hand over her mouth as his eye caught movement beyond the broken door.

Remy charged from one side of the roof to the other in a frenzy; running to the edge and peering over it, desperate to jump. Finally, he howled mournfully, and settled down on his belly in plain sight, not far from Dan. The dog was too terrified to think, Herb realised. It had given up all hope of survival, and opted to simply wait for the end. Maybe it was hoping for mercy, or it believed that if it offered no threat, the vampire might not bother to attack.

Herb shifted his attention to Dan Bellamy. Comatose in the middle of the roof. Maybe the vampire would assume he was already dead.

Unlikely.

Lying on his back in the cold evening air, Herb clearly saw Dan's breath pluming; his chest rising and falling. The vampire would see it, too. Dan would die without ever waking up, and his death would be the stark result of the latest in a series of Herb's bad decisions. Bellamy was important. Far too important to be left in the care of someone like Herbert Rennick.

Herb squeezed his eyes shut, feeling despair wash through him.

I led him into this. I led them all here.

To the place where we die.

CHAPTER THIRTY-THREE

The vampire crept out onto the roof slowly, swivelling its terrible red eyes until it spotted Dan lying on his back.

Herb watched it through the debris of the crashed helicopter. He wanted to look away, to block out the terrible sight of the abomination stalking toward the unconscious man, but he was transfixed; the fear knotting his stomach and deadening his muscles like a powerful narcotic. Almost impossible to resist.

The vampire paused, staring nonchalantly at Remy. Judging by how disinterested the creature seemed, and how still Remy remained under its gaze, Herb figured the dog must have finally passed out in sheer terror.

He risked a glance at the vampire from the corner of his eye, and saw its head swivel toward Dan. His fingers tightened around the grip of the gun, and he wondered how many bullets he had left. He hadn't thought to check since crashing on the roof minutes earlier. It was all happening too fast. No time to think. For all he knew, the gun might even be empty already.

Maybe I fired the last bullet at a vending machine.

An idiot, just like Dad always said.

If he did have ammunition, Herb thought he would get one shot, if he was lucky. If he could somehow aim the weapon without attracting the creature's attention, it would have to be an instant kill. The head? Herb had no idea where the creature's heart might be located—if it possessed such a thing. A perfect headshot was surely the only option, but Herb wasn't sure even that would be enough, given how hard their skin was, and how slowly they seemed to bleed.

In any case, Herb was a decent shot, but he didn't think he was *that* good. An image flashed in front of his eyes: lurching out from cover and trying to line up a head-shot, only to hear the click of an empty weapon.

Knowing that it would be the last thing he *ever* heard.

He wanted to scream in frustration.

The vampire hadn't noticed the small group cowering behind the crashed helicopter yet—or it knew they were there, but didn't care. Herb began to lift his gun, but it felt so terribly heavy in his hands, and aiming it would mean looking directly at the horror approaching Dan's position. If the creature swung its eyes toward him, Herb knew that his mind would be lost in an instant. He would probably wind up executing the others himself.

Alongside Herb, Lawrence whimpered. It was a plaintive noise; an animal noise, and Herb knew exactly what it meant. The cleric had reached his breaking point.

Before Herb could reach out a hand to silence him, Lawrence broke from cover with a yelp and bolted toward the opposite side of the roof.

He's going for the river, he thought, and, though he was certain the cleric would not make it, Herb felt a rush of adrenaline powering through his veins, almost like watching some era-defining sprinter trying to break a world record. He wanted to yell and cheer Lawrence on, but settled for clenching a fist until his nails began to dig into the flesh of his palm.

The cleric was *fast*.

He rocketed along the edge of the roof, covering half the distance before the vampire even had time to react; building up speed for what Herb knew would have to be the jump of the man's life.

Lawrence reached the edge of the roof and hurled himself forward into the night air—

And let out a sickening cry as the vampire hurtled after him, closing the gap between them in an instant and snatching him right out of the sky.

It smashed the cleric back onto the roof, and Herb heard something snapping. Lawrence's back, perhaps. The young man let out a bloodcurdling scream, howling pathetically for his mother, and the vampire buried its face deep in his gut, sending a spurt of blood shooting up into the air. It pulled back with something meaty clamped between its jaws.

Lawrence was still screaming, and continued to do so for a lifetime as the vampire ate him alive.

Behind the helicopter, Herb was paralysed by the sight. He prayed that the others would stay quiet, but with each passing second he knew that the dreadful noise of Lawrence's slow death would be lighting up their minds like fireworks. The others, he was sure, felt the same impulse as him: to dash for the door leading into the hospital while the vampire was distracted.

Herb finally persuaded his arm to move, and he rested

a hand on Conny's shoulder, shaking his head almost imperceptibly.

The door was temptation.

The door was death.

Maybe, Herb thought, as the cleric finally stopped screaming, the distraction that Lawrence had provided would persuade the vampire that there was nobody else on the roof.

Except Dan.

The creature tossed Lawrence's ripped remains aside, apparently bored now that the cleric had stopped convulsing, and made its way back toward Dan. It crawled directly over the unconscious man on all-fours, staring down at him with something like curiosity on its fearsome face. Thick blood dripped from its maw, spilling over Dan; running across his cheek like tears.

And it *stopped*.

Began to *back away*.

Herb's brow creased, and he felt Conny grip his arm tightly. He flashed a glance at her, and saw the confusion and terror wracking his own mind reflected on her face. Alongside her, Logan looked very sick, like he might pass out at any moment.

Herb aimed for a look which might reassure them, but he could tell from their expressions that he missed the mark by a distance.

Out on the roof, the vampire retreated a few steps, moving away from Dan. It stood upright, its hideous gaze still fixed on him.

And, as Herb watched in mute astonishment, Dan opened his eyes and rose unsteadily to his feet, staring directly at the creature, just as he had back in the mansion's gore-drenched kitchen.

Except this time, Herb thought dimly, *he has no weapon. No way to fight.*

He watched in horror as the vampire began to lift its sinewy arms, flexing out fingers like blades.

Dan took a step forward.

Toward the creature.

His eyes never leaving it.

And Herb's mouth dropped open as the vampire drove those wicked talons deep into the side of its *own* neck, and tore out its throat, pulling away a strip of flesh and tossing it aside. The monster's feverish red eyes were wide with something that Herb thought might—incredibly; impossibly—be *fear,* as it drove the talons into its body once more. Deeper, this time; twisting and gouging; ripping its life away in messy chunks.

Somewhere in Herb's mind, beyond the layers of fear and revulsion, there was revelation. Dan Bellamy wasn't just able to *resist* the psychic onslaught of the vampires; he wasn't just immune to their particular type of poison. It was far more than that.

He can do what they do.

Dan fell to his knees, coughing violently.

The vampire fell more slowly, its neck in ruins, eyes wide and blinking stupidly. Thick, black blood oozed from the enormous hole it had torn in itself, and when it hit the roof with a thud, it continued to scrape away feebly at itself, pulling away wet pieces of its life almost absentmindedly.

Weakening with each grisly furrow it carved into its body.

It took almost a full minute for it to finally die. Herb didn't think he managed to breathe for the entire time.

When the vampire's chest rose and fell for the last

time, Herb exploded into motion, running to Dan's side, his mind trying to frame a question—*any* question—and coming up *way* short.

Blood leaked from Dan's eyes like he was crying, and when he coughed again, he spat out a large mouthful of the red stuff. He looked ill, Herb thought. *Really* ill, like the people that he had seen on news footage, suffering the effects of some terrible illness or poison. Dan swayed, his eyes rolling in their sockets. Blood vessels had burst in each.

He looked like he was going to die.

"What's wrong with him?"

Herb jumped. He was so focused on Dan that he hadn't even noticed the others approaching him. He glanced up to see Conny staring at him in confusion.

"He's not normal," Herb replied absently, remembering Dan's own answer to that same question.

Dan coughed again. More blood on the wet rooftop.

"Fuck you, Herb," he whispered weakly.

Herb grinned broadly.

"He's *important*..."

He couldn't remember waking. All he knew was that when the lights in his mind flicked back on abruptly, he was standing upright, and he was outside somewhere. Cold rain. Biting wind.

And a vampire standing in front of him, trying to push itself into his mind.

Before Dan could even understand what was happening, instinct had taken over: fear at the attempted intrusion and rage hot enough to melt steel, and he *pushed back*.

It felt as he imagined it might feel to drive his thumbs through a person's eyeballs, burying them to the knuckles in the wetness.

The creature barely resisted at all.

When he took the vampire's mind, Dan felt an intangible pop in his skull, and all of a sudden he *was* the monster. Looking at himself. Taking a couple of steps backwards; tearing out flesh that felt like it belonged to him.

Adrift on the terrible black river.

Staring up at himself as he fell; feeling his hideous body dying as black blood spilled slowly.

Staring down at himself.

Up at himself.

I'm dying.

It's dying.

What am I?

Lost in shrieking madness.

Until, after a howling torment which lasted seconds and lifetimes, the presence in his head was gone. He was on his knees, and the world was a dark, spinning blur. It took several full rotations for him to remember his name.

Dan.

Dan Bellamy.

Dan stared down at the monster in front of him, coughing up blood and trying not to scream at the savage pain that arced through his skull as the roaring river in his mind retreated.

He almost laughed when he heard a sound which, in hindsight, he should have expected to hear.

Herbert Rennick's voice.

"...AND HE KNOWS IT."

Herb turned to face Dan, beaming proudly.

"Don't you? You believe you're special now, right? You see why I have to keep you safe?"

Dan coughed and wiped at his mouth, staring without emotion at the blood that stained his hand.

"You're doing a great job," he said weakly. "Don't let anybody tell you otherwise."

Herb laughed, and Dan couldn't help but warm to him a little. It was as if Herb had no ego, or he simply recognised his flaws and accepted them for what they were. He had the self-confidence to let a jibe like that wash right off him. Dan felt a stab of envy.

"Hey, you're still alive, right?" Herb said with a grin.

"Barely."

Dan glanced around Herb's companions. Somewhere along the way, he had lost several clerics and gained a policewoman, a dog and a teenage boy with a surly expression. It looked like the Rennick family cult was a thing of the past.

"What do you remember?" Herb asked.

Dan tried to piece his memories together.

"The mansion. The pile of bodies. Screaming—"

"Uh huh. There was a vampire inside."

Dan's eyed fogged up.

"The kitchen," he said softly. "Yeah, I remember. Did I...kill it?"

"Almost. You made it hesitate. Put a blade in its face." He pointed at Dan's belly. "Took a blow yourself."

Dan lifted his sweater and saw a thick bandage wrapped tightly around his abdomen.

"You have some stitches under there," Herb said. "Temporary. Better try and avoid ripping them out, if you can. The doc—"

Herb paused, his eyes suddenly foggy and distant, like he was looking at some terrible memory.

"The doctor said your injuries aren't life threatening, but I'd say she wasn't taking into account the possibility that you'd start bleeding from every orifice. Can you walk?"

Herb reached out a hand, and Dan hauled himself shakily up to his feet. He nodded.

"I can walk. But if I have to run, I'm not sure it will end well. Listen, Herb, while I was...with the vampire...I, uh—"

Herb grimaced, lifting a hand to stop Dan as gunfire sounded in the distance.

Followed by shrieking.

"We can't stay here," Herb said. "We have to move, *now*." He switched his gaze to the policewoman. "You're welcome to come with us, Conny. My father's apartment is close."

"How close?"

It was the first time the policewoman—Conny—had spoken since Dan's world stopped spinning. She had been studying him carefully; warily.

Just like the dog at her feet.

"A few hundred yards."

"I don't suppose it happens to be a fortress?"

"Not exactly. But it will be a hell of a lot safer than the streets."

Herb pointed up into the night sky.

"And it's got a hell of a view."

CHAPTER THIRTY-FOUR

Herb led the others down the stairs with Conny at his side, and Remy walking a yard ahead. The dog could sense the presence of vampires—Conny had been very clear about that—and Herb decided he'd be a fool not to listen. As far as he was aware, nothing in the texts had indicated that dogs—or any other animals—had any extrasensory perception when it came to vampires, but that didn't surprise him. More and more, the texts were looking like millennia-old propaganda. Of *course* the vampires wouldn't publicize their weaknesses.

As they made their way past the empty floors of the hospital, Conny kept dropping her eyes to Remy, and Herb watched her carefully. She was, apparently, satisfied that the dog sensed no immediate threat.

Herb wished he could say the same of himself. To him, the hospital was *alive* with threat, and death lurked around every corner.

The fourth and fifth floors were barren and stark; they looked almost as though nothing had happened there at all, save for a few beds which had been overturned, presumably as a result of the creature checking that nobody was attempting to hide beneath them. Those floors had been empty, according to Conny, with most of the hospital's patients either having already been evacuated, or making their way down to the ground floor to await transport.

Herb paused at each level as he descended, staring beyond the thick glass doors which led to consulting rooms and operating theatres, until he was satisfied that they were as quiet as they appeared.

With each pause, he felt his tension increasing. It already felt like they were taking too long.

Down on the third floor, the blood began to appear.

Streaky spatters of it, winding up the stairs to meet them.

Herb gestured at the others to halt.

He peered over the rail, scanning the small section of the ground floor that he could see. Somewhere below, one weak light still flickered. The rest of the ground floor stood in darkness. Yet that one light was enough for Herb to see: it looked like there had been plenty of people down there when the vampire came through.

It was exactly the same as it had been at the mansion: manmade light appeared to slow the creatures a little, but it didn't stop them entirely—and they were intelligent enough to disable lights as a priority. The hospital's reception area would surely have been brightly lit, but the vampire had come in regardless. Most likely, Herb thought, it had taken the lights out first, and then hurled itself into the crowd, ripping and clawing—

His nerves jangled, and he pulled Conny close, breathing into her ear.

"It's a massacre down there. And it's *dark*. You sure we can trust the dog on this?"

Conny glanced at Remy, who sniffed at the smeared blood on the floor nonchalantly.

"We can trust him."

Herb nodded, and lifted his voice a little for the others to hear.

"Okay, we're headed toward London Bridge Station. Once we get past it, we'll be right at my father's apartment. These things are burrowers. I'm hoping they won't want to stray too far above ground level, and with any luck we can hold up there until morning. Just follow me, okay? And stay *quiet*. If we get separated, find somewhere to barricade yourself in. If you survive until sunrise, get the fuck out of London and keep running. Above all: don't *look* at them. Got it?"

They all nodded, their expressions fearful as they considered Herb's words.

If you survive.

Herb decided that it was better not to let them dwell on that, and began to creep down the last couple of flights of stairs.

Eyes straining at the stubborn shadows.

Certain that he would see something looking right back at him.

When he reached the ground floor, he got to see the catastrophic results of a vampire bursting into a crowded room up close, and was perturbed by how quickly he was getting used to the sight of human bodies which had been torn to pieces. He did his best not to look at the corpses littering the floor, focusing only on the exit. The hospital's front door was propped open by the gore piled in the entryway, and Herb approached it in a half-crouch, gazing intently at the street.

Beyond the slaughter outside the entrance, he saw no sign of army evacuation trucks, though he did see a few military uniforms dotted around the lake of blood and gristle. Perhaps other soldiers were, at that very moment, on their way back to the hospital to pick up another load of people, but Herb knew he didn't have the patience to wait and see. Much of the hospital was glass and large, open rooms. No good hiding places.

If his father's apartment had been far, he might have suggested trying to find a secure room in which to lock themselves—maybe the hospital even had a basement— but they were only a few hundred yards away from a place that offered a real shot at safety. They had to keep moving.

He stepped outside, his neck twisting left and right.

In the distance to the right, somewhere in the direction of Southwark Cathedral, he heard screeching. He set off to the left at a fast trot, desperate to break into a run, but certain that if Dan Bellamy exerted himself too much more, the guy would surely pass out again—or worse.

He aimed for London Bridge Station—one of the city's busiest, and usually heaving with people; now just a hulking dark shape on the horizon.

And rising above it—rising above everything—his destination loomed.

───────

THE SHARD, DAN THOUGHT WRYLY, AS HE TRIED TO keep pace with the others. *Why am I not surprised?*

Herb was making straight for London's tallest building. It figured that a family with the sort of wealth the Rennicks had accrued would opt for just about the most expensive apartment that money could buy, and not even bother to use it.

He was falling behind the others as anxiety turned their trot into a jog, and then a run. He stumbled after them with every muscle in his body howling in agony.

The Shard dominated the skyline; an arrowhead which rose more than a thousand feet above the ground to pierce the clouds that routinely hung low over the city. It wasn't just the tallest building in London; it was one of the tallest buildings in the world. Dan recalled that he had read some piece of trivia which claimed that the smattering of apartments near the top of the Shard were the highest human living space in western Europe, as far away from the ground as it was possible to get.

He wondered if it would be far enough.

He tasted blood in his mouth again, and spat it out between gasps for air, feeling his vision start to swim.

And suddenly, he wasn't running after the others. He was *chasing* them. Desperate to taste their blood; to rip apart their pitifully weak bodies. To let them know what the top of the food chain *really* looked like. He sprinted after them, shrieking, lifting a hand, ready to tear at their flesh.

Kill them all.

The urge to tear human flesh was so strong in his mind that for a moment, Dan felt his consciousness flicker. He wasn't aware that he was falling until he hit the ground hard, rolling into something solid that stopped him painfully and sent stars shooting across his vision. He felt a wrenching sensation in his gut, and knew immediately that he had reopened his wounds.

All of them.

His head felt like it was on fire, vast areas of his mind reduced to charred embers. His brain pulsed with a fizzing, unstoppable energy which he hadn't felt since the months immediately following the knife attack. The black river, surging more ferociously than ever, as though it was trying to pull him to pieces. A sensation like endless falling.

"I've got him."

Reality snapped back into place.

Herb's voice.

Of course.

He felt strong arms lifting him; someone throwing him over a broad shoulder and setting off at pace.

Carrying him toward something terrible.

Dan Bellamy must have weighed roughly the same as the average teenage boy. Herb threw him over his shoulder with surprising ease, and caught up with the others as they reached the base of the Shard.

The front entrance of the enormous building was all glass; lit like a diamond commercial. Herb had been there once or twice with Edgar, but mostly the city apartment was viewed by the Rennicks as a place to retreat if the need arose, and as a place to meet and conduct business with representatives of the Order.

He remembered the way well enough.

"Call the elevator," he grunted, as he pushed through the revolving glass door, following the others into the lobby. Conny's son obliged, and by the time Herb arrived, the elevator was almost there.

He turned to scan the street outside. Everything still looked dark and quiet.

We might just get away with this.

The elevator was on the tenth floor, descending smoothly. It hadn't quite reached the ninth when Herb noticed movement in the corner of his eye. A dark shape approaching the front of the building.

Shit, shit, shit.

The vampire out front threw itself into the glass wall of the Shard, and a spiderweb of cracks formed across it.

The glass wouldn't take another blow.

Bing!

Herb let out a yell of relief when the elevator doors slid open. The others threw themselves inside.

"Thirty-three!" Herb yelled, and heard a cheerful beep as someone pushed the button.

The monster crashed into the lobby.

Herb stepped into the elevator, unable to turn around; knowing that the vampire was charging toward him, praying that the doors would close before the snapping jaws reached him.

He squeezed his eyes shut.

And then, when Herb expected to feel talons puncture his back, tearing at his innards...soft, soothing music began to pipe into the elevator, and the ceiling—a huge display screen—started to cycle through pleasant, relaxing images of lakes and clouds and beautiful summer days.

Conny let out an explosive gasp, and bent double, clutching her knees. Her son's face was red with fear, and what Herb thought looked like shame. Doubtless, he'd pissed himself. Herb couldn't blame him.

"Everybody all right?" Conny said. "Nobody looked at it, right?"

Everyone in the elevator shook their heads.

She glanced at Herb, who still had Dan slung over his shoulder.

"This apartment of yours. It's on thirty-three?"

Herb shook his head. "Thirty-three is where you have to cross over to one of the upper elevators. Once we get there, call them all. Soon as the first one arrives, someone hit sixty-three. We can lose it when we switch elevators. I hope."

With a grunt, he heaved Dan from his shoulder, setting him down on unsteady legs. "You okay, Dan?"

Dan nodded shakily, but kept his eyes fixed on the floor and said nothing.

"Nearly there, buddy." Herb turned back to Conny. "It will want to keep coming, but this is a big building. Gotta be a thousand locked doors in here. Even if it does find us, the apartment is secure. It will hold until sunrise."

He checked the elevator readout. Just approaching level thirty.

The vampires were fast, and verticality didn't trouble them. The only question in Herb's mind was *how fast*? The elevator moved quickly—surely too quickly for any living creature to keep pace—but still, as the readout ticked around to thirty-three, he expected the doors to open and reveal fangs stained crimson and eyes that would melt his soul.

Bing!

Herb's heart hammered.

The doors slid open.

Empty.

He let out a gasp of relief.

"Go!" he hissed, and hit the button for the twenty-fifth floor, sending the elevator back down. With any luck, he thought, the vampire wouldn't even realise that there was another set of elevators servicing the top half of the building. Maybe it would assume they got out on twenty-five. *Maybe.*

The thirty-third floor was home to a lavish Chinese restaurant and a bar area, but also served as a junction between the upper and lower parts of the building. An artist's depiction of the River Thames was painted on the floor, and it led around a corner to the next set of elevators. By the time Herb got there, Conny's son was already inside the nearest of them, holding the chrome doors open and waiting impatiently to hit the button marked 63. He waved Herb and Dan inside, and stabbed the button with a relieved sigh.

It took around three seconds for the door to close.

Each one felt like a lifetime.

The elevator lifted away serenely from the thirty-third floor, and Herb allowed himself to breathe easily at last. The apartment wasn't the stronghold that the mansion was—or was supposed to be—but the windows and door had been fitted with the exact same electronically operated steel shutters as the mansion. Except that this time, there wouldn't be a vampire inside with its hands on the controls.

I hope.

When the elevator announced its arrival with a cheerful *bing* once more, Herb stepped outside and hurried the others out. Once it was clear, he reached inside, and sent it back down to thirty-three.

"This way," he said, and led them to the right, along a wide glass-walled corridor, to a door which nestled alongside the exterior of the building, offering an incredible view across Canary Wharf and, on a clear day, as far as the east coast of England. Herb paid the dark panorama laid out before him no attention, and turned to face the apartment's front door. He flipped open a panel next to it, revealing a palm scanner, and placed his left hand against it.

The scanner was coded only to accept senior members of the Rennick household.

Like Jeremy Pruitt, who Herb saw standing in the apartment when the door swung open.

Behind a large man with a hard, bloodstained face, who aimed a stubby submachine gun directly at Herb's forehead.

CHAPTER THIRTY-FIVE

"Inside," Mancini growled, shooting an anxious glance down the hallway toward a distant door marked *stairs*. He kept the gun trained squarely on Herbert Rennick's forehead, and stepped aside, waving the small group at the door into the apartment with his free hand.

Somewhere behind him, he heard a click. Burnley readying her weapon.

Rennick was travelling with a woman wearing a police officer's uniform, and what Mancini guessed was a police dog, along with a teenage boy and a man who looked like he'd just undergone a savage round of chemotherapy. Dan Bellamy wasn't what Mancini expected at all; he looked frail and sick, his eyes ringed with blood. He didn't look up; didn't even seem to notice Mancini or the gun he held at all. It was like Dan Bellamy's eyes were somewhere else, staring at some horizon that only he could see.

He kept a watchful eye on the dog as the disparate group filed into the apartment, but the animal didn't look like it would give him trouble; it seemed focused on the distant stairwell, just as Mancini himself had been.

He closed the door and locked it.

"Hi Jeremy," Rennick said amiably.

Jeremy Pruitt sighed heavily.

"Hi, Herb."

"Better put the place on lockdown," Herb said. "There's one in the building."

Mancini felt the blood draining from his face, and glanced at Jeremy. "Do it," he growled, keeping his eyes on Herb.

"Weapons on the floor," he said. "All of you."

Herb slipped a handgun from his belt and tossed it at Mancini's feet.

Mancini stared down at it, confused.

"That's *it*? One gun?"

"Yeah," Herb said with a smile. "Not even sure it has any bullets, but do feel free to check. Oh, and hey: who the fuck are you?"

"I called the Americans, Herb," Jeremy said heavily, and he popped open a panel near the door, punching a code into a keypad. Moments later, steel shutters began to descend, covering the interior of the windows and the apartment's front door, erasing the view of the burning city.

"Yeah," Herb snapped bitterly. "Still working for Dad, huh?"

Jeremy shook his head and started to reply, but Mancini had heard enough. He gestured at the couches in the open-plan living room, glaring at Pruitt until he closed his mouth.

"Take a seat, Rennick. The rest of you, too. Burnley,

keep your gun on Rennick. If you decide his mouth is too smart, *do feel free* to shut it for him."

Burnley nodded, her eyes never leaving Herb.

"You don't need to do that—" Jeremy said, but Mancini waved a hand to silence him, and stepped back to the front door. He put his ear against the metal which now covered it, listening intently.

Nothing.

The sheet of steel which had fallen over the apartment looked thin, but he didn't doubt that it would hold. The vampires were strong and resourceful, but punching through tempered steel was a stretch, even for them. For the first time since he had arrived at the Rennick apartment—barely two minutes before Rennick himself did—Mancini allowed himself to relax. The vampires couldn't get in. The only way harm could come to those inside was if the monsters found some way to take down the entire building. It didn't seem likely.

Mancini checked his watch.

Still several hours until sunrise.

He lost himself in thought. Craven only wanted Bellamy, and she would have no problem with him killing Rennick if he deemed it necessary. Hell, she'd probably applaud it.

He shot a glance at Rennick. The guy looked like he was just *itching* to start talking again.

Firing a weapon with a vampire somewhere in the building was asking for trouble—steel shutters or not. If Rennick was determined to cause problems, Mancini would have to find quiet solutions.

Knifework, then

He glanced toward the distant kitchen.

"Okay," Herb said brightly, clapping his hands

together and rising from the couch. "Who wants cocktails?"

The policewoman grabbed his shirt, and hauled him back down into his seat, keeping her other hand firmly on the mutt's collar.

"Smart lady," Mancini said, making his way into the living room. "I'm not here for you, Rennick, but I have no problem killing you, if that's what you want. When you're running your mouth, all you're doing is making me change my mind about *how* I'm going to kill you. Capiche?"

"I recommend slightly overfeeding me and ultimately inducing a fatal heart attack," Herb said with a serene smile. "Should only take about forty years, and the police will never catch on. I eat plenty of junk food alrea—"

Mancini darted forward quickly and swung a left hook, connecting firmly with Rennick's flapping jaw, and the kid finally shut up.

Mancini kept walking, his nerves racing, heading for the apartment's plush kitchen.

And the knives.

He selected a large carving knife from a rack, and turned back toward the living room, coming face to face with Jeremy.

"You don't need to do that," the Brit said. "He's a good kid."

Mancini shrugged.

"Sure. They all are. But I have a job to do, and I've already lost most of my team getting this far."

"So, take Bellamy!" Jeremy thundered. "He's what you're really here for."

Mancini strode back into the living room, pointing the knife at Herb.

"He's a loose end, Pruitt. Come to think of it, there are an awful lot of loose ends in this room. Like you said, I only *need* Bellamy."

He lifted the knife, and Jeremy faltered, taking a half-step backwards. For a moment, the room bathed in tension, the air crackling with the threat of impending violence.

"I just wanted to go home."

Mancini blinked at Dan Bellamy's small voice. He glanced at him and laughed bitterly.

"Yeah, good luck with that, buddy. Where I'm taking you, you're going to be a long way from home."

"I have a condition."

Mancini frowned.

"I'm sick. Getting worse all the time. I just needed to go home and take my medication. Not even sure I'm...*me* anymore."

Dan kept his eyes pointed at the floor, and spoke in a soft monotone. Mancini couldn't even be sure that the guy was actually talking to him. He didn't even look like he knew exactly where he was.

Mancini walked around the couch, trying to attract Bellamy's attention. The scrawny guy just kept staring at the floor, his face buried beneath a mop of hair.

"What's wrong with him?" he asked dubiously, looking at Herb.

Rennick just stared back mutinously.

Dan giggled. "That's the funniest thing," he said. "I used to wonder the same thing myself. Now, I'm not sure it was ever me. It's the *world*. The question is: what's wrong with everybody else? Why don't you all hear it? The *river?*"

Dan lifted his chin and met Mancini's gaze.

Burning eyes.

A scream caught in Mancini's throat as invisible thorns punctured his mind, putting down roots. Taking away control.

His world became a tunnel, and all he could see was Dan Bellamy's searing pupils, ringed by blood, boring into his soul.

He hoisted the MP5, pressing the cold barrel into the side of his own head.

Bellamy rose from the couch, his eyes blazing, and Mancini dropped to his knees in front of him.

Worshipping him like a god.

His finger began to curl around the trigger.

And suddenly, the world was plunged into darkness.

The presence in his mind was gone, releasing him like an unclenching fist. Mancini fell forward, gasping for air, clutching at his throat.

"What happened?" a woman's voice snarled. Not Burnley; the policewoman.

Mancini heard a low rumble fill the room, and moonlight began to wash into the apartment. The steel shutters were opening.

"Power cut," Herbert Rennick said, with a rueful chuckle. "Lockdown didn't last long."

"They cut the power to the whole damn building?"

"Take a look outside, Conny. They cut the power to the whole damn *city*."

Mancini squeezed his eyes shut.

Should have run when I had the chance.

CHAPTER THIRTY-SIX

Herb strode over to the choking American and scooped up the machine gun which he had dropped on the floor. He checked the magazine, and nodded to himself. It was full.

The American woman—Burnley—still had a pistol trained on Herb, but she looked uncertain. Probably, Herb thought, Burnley was thinking about how close she just came to being the last one standing, and what the hell she was supposed to do next.

Join the fucking club, lady.

"I think we've got bigger issues right now, don't you?" Herb said amiably, gesturing at the American woman's gun. She nodded slowly, lowering her weapon.

"Conny," Herb said, "would you mind taking her gun? And any others she might be carrying."

Conny nodded, and headed for Burnley, who gave her weapon up with a sigh and opened her jacket to show that she wasn't otherwise armed. Conny turned the gun over in her hands, gazing at it intently as she moved back to the window.

Herb offered a hand to the man gasping on the floor in front of the couch.

"You never did tell me who the fuck you are."

The American glanced up at him, his eyes wide and angry.

"Mancini," he growled, staring at the gun in Herb's left hand. After a moment, he lifted his gaze to Herb's eyes and nodded, taking the hand that was offered and hauling himself to his feet. "What did he do to me?"

Herb grinned.

"He does what *they* do, Mr Mancini," he said, and struck out with a solid right, connecting sharply with Mancini's jaw and knocking him straight back onto the floor. "That makes us even. I'd prefer it if we could stay that way for a little while. *Capiche?*"

Mancini wiped at his lip and grunted.

Herb left him on the floor and strode over to the window, moving to stand alongside Conny and her son.

Far below, the city of London was a dark stain, lit only by fire and headlights.

"I don't get it," Conny said. "How could they cut the power to the whole city?"

Herb frowned.

"They cut the lights as a matter of priority," he said absently. "I should've guessed. But at least we know where the rest of them were, now. Power stations. London isn't served by just one. The city draws energy from several, all over the south of England. You don't just pull a plug and cut the power to a city of this size. While the whole world is looking at London, the vampires have been busy disabling the whole *country*. A few here to attract attention, the rest spread around Britain, dismantling our infrastructure. Taking out power stations, and who knows what else. They won't even have to engage with the military. They can pick us off at their leisure, and let our reliance on electricity do the rest. Without power, they own the night."

Conny shook her head in despair.

"I thought if I could get Logan out of London, things would be fine..." she trailed off, gazing out across the dark city.

Herb glanced at the terrified boy, and his expression hardened.

"We're gonna have to get him a little further than that," he said.

Conny smiled weakly.

"We?" she said. "*You're* going to help? I've got pretty serious doubts about you getting out of this room alive, let alone out of the city."

"You and me, both," Herb said with a wink, and he turned away.

"Hey, Captain America? What was your extraction plan? *Please* tell me you had an extraction plan."

Mancini glowered at him.

"We have a Gulfstream waiting at an airfield south of the city."

"Sounds good. Any firm ideas on how to get there?"

"Yeah, just one: wait here until sunrise," Mancini spat bitterly.

"Looks like your plans are about as useful as mine," Herb said. He glanced at the window dubiously. They were a long way from ground level, but if the vampires *did* venture up the building, they would be able to break in with ease now that the shutters were out of action. *Besides which*, he thought, *there's the small matter of the one that's already in the building...*

Staying might get them killed.

So might running.

Herb thought about the decisions that had led him to the dark apartment; the wrong choices he seemed to have continually made. At every turn, he had acted on his instincts, and people had died as a result.

"I guess we stay until they give us a reason not to," he said uncertainly. "They might not even come up here."

Dan coughed and shook his head, drawing all eyes in the room back to him.

"I tried to tell you, at the hospital," he said, his voice little more than a rattling croak. "When I was inside the vampire's head, I...wasn't alone. There was something there. Something...looking back at me."

Herb frowned.

"A vampire?"

Dan shook his head. "I don't think so. Something else. More like something the vampires worship. Like their version of God. It...guides them, I think. Communicates with them. The black river..."

"Okay," Herb said, lifting a hand in a *stop right there* gesture. "I'm not following."

Dan shook his head like a dog, trying to clear it out.

"Whatever it is, it knows where I am, Herb. Or: it knows where I *was* when I killed myself." He flushed. "Uh, when I killed the vampire."

Herb stared at him, confused. "The hospital?"

Dan nodded.

"They're all headed in this direction," he said quietly. "Every last one of them; following the black river. I think they're coming for me."

DAN WATCHED THEIR MOONLIT FACES CAREFULLY AS he delivered the news. Everyone in the room looked at him with a fearful expression that he knew was only half the product of him telling them that the immediate vicinity would likely soon be swarming with vampires.

The rest of their fear, well, that was reserved for Dan himself. It was plainly written on their faces—even Herb. They were all scared of him.

And shouldn't they be?

Dan focused his gaze on Mancini.

Was I really going to kill him?

The big American glanced at him furtively, and looked away. Dan knew why. For a moment there, he had *been* Leon Mancini, and a moment had been long enough to peer around in the dusty cupboards of the man's mind. Mancini had killed dozens in the name of country and money, and more than once for little reason at all. A mercenary.

Mancini didn't want to be in London; he was there, incredibly, to appease a woman he hated and loved in equal measure, and his fear at the events unfolding around the city hadn't quite broken his resolve to bring the prize that she demanded back to America.

Me, Dan thought bleakly. *I'm the prize.*

A surge of bitter resentment rose in his gut.

This will never end. If it's not Herb or Mancini, it will be someone else. Or the vampires.

Or the river.

He stared at the stocky American.

"Jennifer Craven," Dan said absently, and Mancini looked at him with wide, fearful eyes.

Herb glanced at Dan, surprised.

"Craven? What about her? And how do you even

know that name?"

"From inside *his* head." Dan pointed at Mancini. "His name's Leon."

Herb's jaw dropped, and he stared at Mancini, who in turn focused furiously on the window.

"Jesus Christ," Herb said, his voice soft with wonder, "...uh, stay out of my head, Dan, okay?"

"Jennifer Craven wants me," Dan said, through a rattling wheeze. "She's the one that sent Mancini. The head of the Order in America. She's a murderer."

Herb chuckled.

"Aren't we all?" he waved an arm around the room. "Well, maybe except Conny and her kid."

Conny kept her eyes on the floor.

"Yeah, maybe," Dan said, "but Leon over there thinks Craven *enjoys* it. Don't you, Leon?"

Mancini glared at him, his face a mixture of revulsion and barely-contained fury.

"He's afraid of her," Dan said, and began to cough violently.

Herb's brow furrowed. "When Craven starts to matter, we'll figure it out. First, we have to live that long. The hospital is right around the corner. If they start searching this whole area...if they find us? We won't survive the night in here without the shutters. Not up against all of them."

Dan felt the ripple of tension as it ran around the room at Herb's words. They all knew it, Dan thought, but hearing somebody *say* it was a whole different matter. *We won't survive the night.*

"How many more times do you reckon you can do your little *X-men* trick?" Herb said.

Dan shook his head.

"I don't know. I don't even know if it's *me* doing it. But each time it happens, I feel like a little less of me comes back. I'm not entirely sure that I'll...come back at all."

"Okay," Herb said, "We have to figure this out, you're right, but now isn't the time—"

It is, Dan thought, and blistering pulse of white-hot rage coursed through him. *It's exactly the time. In fact, it's long fucking overdue.*

I'm not anybody's fucking prize.

The strength of the emotion which rolled through Dan took him by surprise. Like all who live in fear, he had dreamed all-too often about asserting himself and taking charge of his own destiny, yet even in his dreams, the crippling anxiety had always been there, lurking in the background like a shadow.

Now, it was absent.

In its place; seething, boiling outrage.

Determination.

"Mancini," Dan said, his voice gritty. Mancini turned his head, but refused to meet Dan's gaze directly. "Jennifer Craven doesn't want to *kill* me, does she?"

"I don't honestly know," Mancini admitted with a sigh. "But I'd guess whatever she had in mind involved your death somewhere down the line, yeah."

"Hmmm," Dan grunted. "I suppose I'll just have to see if I can change her mind about that. So do what she pays you for, *Mr Mancini*. Extract us. Take me to Colorado. Take *all* of us."

"Sure," Mancini said sourly. "No problem. Other than the skyscraper without power that we're at the top of, and the city full of vampires, and your friend Rennick over there pointing my own gun at me. I'll get right on it."

Dan stared at Mancini for several long seconds, before finally nodding.

"Let him have his gun back, Herb," he said.

Herb looked dubious.

"What are you doing, Dan?"

"It's like you said. Home doesn't exist for me anymore. How could it? Where else *should* I go now? I've been running and hiding for the last two years. No more."

Herb's brow furrowed.

"It's okay," Dan said with a weak smile. "Let him have his gun. Leon won't get any funny ideas, will you, Leon?"

Herb stared at Dan for a moment, and then at Mancini. Finally, he shrugged and slid the machine gun across the floor to the American.

"Funny ideas like killing Rennick, you mean?" Mancini said as he picked the weapon up. "Nah. I'll gladly take him to Colorado. Craven will just *love* him."

Dan barked a sour laugh, and coughed violently.

More blood.

"Everyone got their dicks in a row?" Conny said abruptly from the window.

Nobody had an answer, other than her son's almost-stifled chuckle.

"Good," she continued, turning to face the room, "then maybe we can focus on getting out of here?"

"Without power? Without elevators?" Mancini said. "Good luck with that. You geniuses brought a vampire in with you, remember? And more on the way. There are probably half a dozen in here already, going floor by floor. Want to tell me how we're going to find our way out of here without stumbling into *that*?"

"Sure," Conny said, and she pointed at the dog sitting by her side. "We follow him."

CHAPTER THIRTY-SEVEN

The fear was like hands pressing on her back, squeezing her ribs until it became difficult to breathe. In darkness, the huge, sleek skyscraper felt like it might conceal threats in every gloomy corner.

The hallways in the residential levels were wide and straight, the floors lined with plush carpet which made the noise of the group's movement almost inaudible as they began to descend through the building. Conny was grateful for that, but she couldn't shake the feeling that the carpet would muffle more than just human footsteps.

The clicking noise the creatures made was certainly hideous—a sound that she was sure she'd hear in her nightmares if she lived to be a hundred—but at least it offered some advance warning that one of the creatures was close by.

In the corridors of the Shard, there would be no such warning. The apartments which the group passed were locked, and the hallways themselves offered little in the way of hiding places. Too much glass and wide open space. If she turned a corner and ran straight into a vampire, there would be nowhere to hide. Their only hope *then* would be Herb's strange friend, Dan—and his presence spiked Conny's anxiety almost as much as a vampire's might.

She walked in a half-crouch at the front of the group, resting her left hand lightly on Remy's powerful shoulders, waiting nervously to feel his muscles tense. On each floor, she led Remy to a stairwell and waited, gauging by his reaction whether it was safe to proceed further.

For his part, Remy seemed content enough, sniffing curiously at the doorways they passed, but showing no indication that there was any threat in the immediate vicinity.

So far, they had descended only three floors; not yet even getting clear of the residential levels. The Shard had been touted as a vertical city upon opening: residences at the top, a luxury hotel and restaurants below them; all of it sitting atop levels upon levels of offices and retail areas. While it didn't *quite* manage the scale that *vertical city* implied, it came pretty close. With only a couple of flashlights between the whole group, and the cloudy night making the moonlight that streamed through the windows weak and intermittent, progress was already painfully slow.

With the elevators out of action, each floor offered a couple of ways down: the main stairway, and a smaller version designed as a fire escape. When they tried the first of those smaller stairways, they found it to be windowless and pitch black, and worse: there was no way to be certain that if they took the fire escape, they would actually be able to re-enter the main part of the building itself.

Herb had immediately ruled out using the fire escape,

arguing that there was every chance they would end up trapped in there with no way to flee.

Nobody seemed to want to debate it.

Conny thought it would take them the best part of an hour to reach the ground level on foot—and that was without taking into account the possibility that they might need to hide or fight for their lives at any moment. She gripped the pistol that she had taken from Burnley, running her thumb over the cool metal grip. This time, carrying a gun didn't give her any sense of power; not at all. It made her feel afraid.

Her mind wanted to run back to Robert Nelson's face; his sightless eyes fixed on the tunnel roof; grief and remorse tried to clutch at her throat.

She blinked firmly, trying to clear her thoughts, refocusing only on what she could see as she paused at a railing which overlooked another set of steps leading down, to yet another residential area. Each level contained less than a handful of vast apartments, much of their interiors half-visible through the gleaming glass walls.

Not for the first time, Conny was struck by the sheer decadence of the place. In Herb's apartment, she had peered into a small bathroom, and noticed that the entire wall alongside the toilet was a *window*. There was no curtain to draw across; no need for privacy. The Shard loomed so far above everything else in London that the residents could shit right in front of the people far below and not worry about being seen. The notion had struck her as both oddly comical, and strangely sad. A bizarre thing to aspire to, she had decided; accumulating enough wealth that you could wipe your arse while staring down at an entire city from a glass box in the sky.

She glanced at Logan.

He still refused to meet her eye, but his sulk had mostly evaporated; boiled away by the terror of seeing the monsters up close. It was funny how quickly the sight of a vampire reorganised one's priorities. Logan was confused and scared enough without throwing giant carnivorous insects into the mix as well.

"You see anything, Lo?"

Logan stood alongside her at the railing, surveying the level below. Two huge apartments took up almost the entire floor. As far as Conny could see, they were empty.

"No, nothing," Logan mumbled.

She glanced at him in surprise. She hadn't expected an actual response.

Logan kept his gaze firmly on the level below, and Conny nodded to herself. Best to let him have time. He'd come around eventually.

She gestured at the others, filing along behind her toward the viewing platform, to follow her lead, and moved on, quashing her desire to hurry.

There were around a dozen of the creatures in London, if Herb's theory had been correct. If he was right about the power stations, any others that were hunting Dan Bellamy would take a long time to get there from other parts of the country. There was little point worrying about them—not as long as Remy continued to make good time.

A dozen, Conny thought. Even if they were *all* inside the Shard, there was a good chance that they wouldn't run into the vampires. The building was large enough to get lost inside for days, and once they were beyond the residential levels, there would be a lot more places to hide.

She made her way down to the next level, allowing her confidence to rise, just a little.

———————

THEY WERE ON THE FIFTY-FIFTH FLOOR, ALMOST clear of the residential levels, when Remy growled softly for the first time.

Conny froze immediately, holding up a hand to halt the others behind her. She knelt next to Remy, listening to his breathing, feeling the thrumming of his heart against her palm. He seemed anxious about something, but not in the same fraught way he had been back in the tunnels of the Underground.

Conny frowned, scratching the back of his neck, and listened for the sound of movement.

Nothing.

Herb shuffled alongside her.

"What is it?" he whispered.

"I don't know," Conny shook her head. "When he ran into the vampires before, he was terrified. Now...I'm not sure. He seems more *intrigued*."

"Maybe he heard something else," Herb offered, "there could still be people here who refused to evacuate, hiding out in their apartments?"

Conny focused her eyes on the distant stairwell which led down to the next floor.

"Maybe," she agreed uncertainly. "Have the others wait here for a moment. I'll check it out. Remy, *stay*."

Remy took a seat alongside Herb as Conny crept forward.

At the stairs, she paused. The level below was almost pitch black as clouds raced across the moon outside the windows, but she thought she detected *something* in the distance, making its way toward her. A shadow, which seemed to move among the others with purpose.

She squinted.

What is it?

For several tense seconds, Conny's eyes did battle with the low light as she scanned the wide corridor below. When she had almost decided that it was simply her imagination playing tricks on her, her eyes finally won.

A glint of light from the centre of the corridor, as if the weak moonlight had briefly caught something reflective.

Whatever it was, it was only about fifty yards away, moving toward the stairs at a slow, steady pace.

She gritted her teeth, praying for a break in the clouds; for some moonlight.

And her prayers were answered. A shaft of pale light illuminated the level below for just a second, but it was long enough for Conny to see.

Not a vampire.

A man.

One man, alone; stumbling along the hallway as though in a daze.

She retreated as far as Remy and Herb. The others were lined up along the wall, but she didn't dare lift her voice enough to speak to them all. Instead, she pulled Herb close, breathing directly into his ear.

"There's a man down there. Heading this way. Walking like he's drunk, or drugged or something."

Herb fixed his gaze on the carpet, his eyes widening.

"It's one of *them*," he said breathlessly, "using a human to search for us. Hoping we'll give ourselves away."

"Herb," Conny said, "he's coming straight for us. We have to go back up—"

"We'd just be cornering ourselves," Herb muttered. "We have to get out of the residential levels. Get down to the hotel and restaurants. We're sitting ducks in these damn corridors."

Conny nodded.

"Sure, so what do you suggest?"

Herb grimaced.

"We have to kill him."

CHAPTER THIRTY-EIGHT

Herb gestured at the group to follow, and led them back to the next set of stairs which led back up toward his father's apartment. The guy approaching them was moving slowly, according to Conny, but Herb needed more time to think.

Killing the man outright would bring the vampire that had control of him; there was no doubt in Herb's mind about that. Worse, the creature had to be close, maybe only a handful of floors away.

He felt frustration rising inside him. The Infinity Pool was only a couple of levels below, and it served as the 'roof' of the *Shangri La* hotel, which occupied the next eighteen floors. If they could reach the hotel, he was sure they would have more options: more rooms, more stairways; *anything*.

He flashed a glance at a door marked *fire exit*, which stood around halfway down the corridor.

The group had ruled out using the fire stairs for fear that once they entered what was in effect a maintenance stairwell, they might not be able to get back into the central part of the building itself, but it was the only place they *could* hide. If they didn't use it, the man searching for them would simply herd them all the way back up the Shard, right back to the apartment.

In the distance, at the far end of the corridor, Herb saw movement, and ducked back into cover.

"We can't just *kill* the guy," Conny whispered.

Herb grimaced.

"Not sure we have any choice."

"We could take the fire exit."

"And if we get stuck in there? We'd be putting ourselves in a place with only one way in and one way out."

"Like right here," Conny said pointedly. "We *can't* kill him."

"It's not 'him' anymore," Herb said. "Whoever that guy was, he's gone now. Just an empty shell. If there's any part of him still in there, he'd probably thank us for putting him out of his misery. We'd be doing him a favour."

Conny pursed her lips.

"Some favour."

Mancini hustled forward.

"What's the problem?"

In the distance, Herb heard a strange, soft *clunk*, and risked a peek around the corner.

The vampire's puppet had made it halfway along the corridor, and was checking the fire door.

Shit.

In around a minute, the group would be forced to retreat back up to the next level. And then the next.

Trapped.

Waiting to be discovered; waiting to die.

Even if we do kill him, we'll just bring his master down on our heads. No way of knowing how far away the vampire is. Could only be a level or two.

"We need a distraction," Herb whispered, focusing on Mancini. "We can hide on the fire escape, but he's checking the doors on each level. We need to find a way to get him to move right past without checking. Something to draw him away."

"Something like a cellphone ringing?" Mancini said, slipping a small black phone from his pocket and holding it up.

Herb frowned. He knew exactly what Mancini was suggesting—that he could run up a level or two and set the alarm on his phone. Maybe, if it trilled at just the right moment, it would persuade the approaching man to hurry past the next fire door without checking it.

Another desperate plan, he thought. He didn't dare risk another look around the corner. He nodded at Mancini.

"Go," he said, "quickly. The further up the building you get, the more time we'll have to run. Once you drop the phone, take the fire exit back down to us. We'll keep the door open for you."

"*Run?*" Mancini repeated, his eyes wide with doubt.

"Yeah, *run*. I've tried fooling these things before, and they are far from gullible. If it takes the bait, we won't be safe for long. I'm betting it will know straightaway that we have slipped past it. We'll have to make a run for the hotel. It's only a couple of floors down from here. We'll be able to lose them in there. I hope."

"Running will be noisy."

Herb nodded.

"Yeah. But it's all we have. *Go*."

Mancini turned without a word, and jogged lightly up the stairs, his footsteps inaudible. He might have time, Herb thought, to carry the phone up a couple of levels at most. It would have to be enough. Once he dropped the phone, he could enter the fire escape and make his way back down to meet them.

Herb waved at the others to follow, and made his way back up the stairs, following Mancini slowly, and quietly.

On the next level, when he reached the fire door, Herb pressed on the bar and eased it open quietly. They would all fit into the fire escape, of course, but there would be nowhere to hide once they were in there. If the puppet opened the door, the game would be up.

He waved the others inside, and waited.

He figured Mancini had around thirty seconds. He closed the door, stopping just before the lock engaged, and left a crack through which to peer. Outside, the hallway was still empty, but only for a few moments. He saw movement in the darkness by the stairs, shuffling toward him slowly.

His heart began to pound loud enough that he felt sure it would give them away, and he winced when he heard a fire door opening above. It sounded like Mancini had made it up a couple of storeys.

The man outside approached the fire door, and a cold sweat broke out on Herb's brow. If Mancini's alarm didn't go off...

The figure in the hallway was barely five yards away. Herb was desperate to keep the door open a crack to see, but he didn't dare. He closed it until he felt the lock trying to engage, and stared at it furiously, waiting for the man outside to push it open.

He didn't have to wait long.

Pressure on the door.

Starting to push.

This is it, Herb thought, and felt energy begin to fizz through him. The plan had failed. Running blindly was going to be the only option.

The door opened a crack.

And somewhere above, a loud, cheerful tune rang out, splitting the silence.

The pressure on the door lifted abruptly, and Herb heard footsteps departing in a hurry.

He felt Conny at his back.

"Shouldn't we make a move?" she whispered.

Herb grimaced, and shook his head.

"Wait," he said.

After a moment, he heard it. Clicking on the main stairs. Coming up fast. When it reached the hallway, the carpet muffled its approach a little, but the vampire was moving quickly, oblivious to the noise it was making. It thundered past the fire door, and Herb waited until he heard it clicking up the next stairway to the floor above.

"Move," Herb whispered. "Quietly. When it comes— and it will—just *run*."

He pushed the fire door open, and burst out into the dark hallway, breaking into a near-silent trot.

He had made it as far as the steps leading down to the next level when he heard the screech a couple of floors above, and knew that the ruse had been discovered. The monsters weren't stupid—far from it—and he was certain that the creature would immediately realise that it needed to descend.

Before the screech had receded into silence, Herb growled *run* in a seething whisper, and began to sprint.

And somewhere above, the vampire followed.

CHAPTER THIRTY-NINE

The Infinity Pool represented the top floor of the eighteen-storey *Shangri-La* hotel. The pool itself was small, set alongside a fully equipped gym and fitness centre. At any other time, the sight of the pool, nestling alongside a huge window which offered an extraordinary view of the city below, might have taken Dan's breath away.

If he had any left.

The others were pulling away from him, and with each stride, he felt pain shooting across his abdomen as he tore more stitches out of his wounds. Another screech somewhere behind and above him told him that running was an option with a severely limited shelf-life. He was just too weak to keep going, and the vampire sounded like it was closing fast.

There was nothing else for it. He felt weak and sick; unsure even whether he could repeat the trick that he had pulled on the hospital roof, but knowing he had no option other than to try.

He came to a stop alongside the pool and turned around, waiting for the monster to appear.

"Dan!"

Herb's whispered call barely made an impression on Dan's mind. He was already looking inwards, searching for the river, wondering if this was to be the last time he ever saw it.

Some part of him hoped that was true.

He took in a deep breath, focusing on the entrance to the pool, and flinched in surprise when the doors burst open and a man charged through.

The man from the hallway, he thought bleakly. He focused his eyes on the approaching man—a middle-aged guy in a business suit with a loosened tie and an untucked shirt who looked like he had probably slept through the evacuation of the building. Most likely, the man had awoken to find a nightmare looming over him, and had known terror for an instant before his mind was plucked away.

Dan focused on the man's eyes.

Nothing.

His mind is already taken.

Dan stumbled backwards, making it only a few steps before the businessman tackled him heavily around the waist and slammed him down onto the tiled floor surrounding the pool. For a moment, his vision blurred as the pain in his abdomen became a howling agony. Breath exploded from his lungs, and before he could suck in more oxygen, the businessman drove a solid fist into his jaw.

Dan's head ricocheted off the floor, and for a moment the world went dark.

Can fight vampires.

Can't fight people.

Still a pathetic, feeble weakling.

He lifted a hand, trying vainly to block the next blow, and suddenly the weight of the businessman pinning him to the floor was lifted.

Dan's head rolled weakly to the side, and he saw Herb hauling the businessman off him and swinging a savage flurry of punches. The man in the suit collapsed backwards, falling into the pool with a loud splash.

And Herb dropped to his knees.

His mouth opening in a silent scream.

The vampire had arrived at last.

It stalked into the room almost warily, as though unsure of exactly what it might face.

A good job Herb doesn't still have the gun, Dan thought dimly, *or we'd all be dead already.*

Sickly despair washed over him as he watched Herb pivot at the waist and drive his forehead into the tiled floor with a loud *smack*. The big man lifted himself up, his forehead dark with blood, and drove himself down again.

And, finally, the river crashed through Dan's mind, the rushing torrent of rage and fear and disgust, and suddenly his injuries were forgotten; the pain wracking his body a distant, faded memory.

He rose to his feet, still aware. Still conscious.

Not blacking out this time.

"It's me you want," he screamed, unnerved by how unlike his voice the words sounded.

The vampire whipped around to face him, and the terrible red eyes fell upon Dan. Herb dropped to the floor, lying still, like some kid's toy which had its batteries removed abruptly.

The vampire's attempt to take his mind was weak; water breaking against a vast dam. He batted it aside and took a step toward the monster, drilling his gaze into it, ripping whatever it called a soul to shreds.

And suddenly, he was the vampire.

Staring back at himself, and the group of people cowering behind him.

Dan's face broke into a wicked grin.

"I think," he said, watching himself speak through the monster's eyes, "that I'm getting the hang of this."

HERB'S HEAD FELT LIKE IT WAS ABOUT TO EXPLODE. The pain was one thing, but the presence of the vampire in his mind, like the residue of some terrible toxin, was something else entirely. It had only been in his mind for a couple of seconds, but felt like the inside of his skull was bruised and bleeding.

Groaning, he twisted his neck, levering his eyes open through the thick blood which stuck the lids together like glue, and saw the vampire take off at a sprint, charging past Dan, heading for the window which ran alongside the pool.

"Dan! No!" Herb tried to yell. The words emerged as a weak croak.

Dan turned to face him, his expression curious, and the vampire skidded to a halt. It remained still, like a freeze frame, a few yards from the window which Dan had been about to make it jump through.

Herb struggled to his feet, shaking his head in a vain attempt to stop the world spinning.

"How long can you control it?" he gasped.

Dan looked dubious.

"I don't know. Not long. Why?"

"The others," Herb grunted. "They'll be coming." He focused his gaze on the vampire once more. "We can use this one."

———

THE WINDOW ON THE EAST SIDE OF THE FIFTY-second floor of the Shard exploded, and the monster hurtled out.

But not to its death.

It clung to the exterior of the building like a spider, racing up past the residential levels. At the sixty-fourth floor, it passed the public viewing gallery, and kept going. The top fifteen levels of the building were dedicated to utilities: a heat rejection system and power plants. It raced past them, making for the spire at the very top of London's tallest structure.

When it reached it, clinging to the narrow glass spike a thousand feet above the city, it bellowed out a screech.

Calling its kin.

CHAPTER FORTY

"Will they fall for it?"

Dan tried to focus on Herb, but it was getting more difficult with each passing second. He felt his grip on the vampire's mind weakening; his grip on reality beginning to break as he struggled to occupy two minds at once.

He was staring at Herb, and seeing a dark city spread out far below him simultaneously; screeching in a language he couldn't understand and trying to form words in one that he did.

He felt a warm wetness running down his cheek, and knew that he was crying blood again.

"I...think so," he mumbled. "I think they're heading up to the top. But I can't hold it much longer. When I lose it, the game's up, Herb. They'll all know exactly where we are."

He felt the same warm wetness spring from his ear, and in his mind, the tumbling river became a cascading waterfall, threatening to tear his mind to pieces.

"I..."

He grunted, bending at the waist as an avalanche of pain crashed over him.

"I'll hold it as long as I can...think I'll pass out—"

He began to wobble on his feet.

"Get away from the windows," Dan slurred, "they're coming up the outside of the buil—"

He collapsed, and felt strong arms catch him.

"Gotcha," Herb grunted, and turned to face the others. "You heard him. Get down, get away from the windows. When they pass, we start running, everybody got it?"

None of the others spoke, but they scattered at Herb's words, moving away from the Infinity Pool's huge window and ducking down behind exercise machines and a small drinks bar.

Herb dragged Dan to a huge cross-trainer, ducking down behind the machine, praying that he was out of sight.

Moments later, he saw the first of them, thundering up the exterior of the building. It was followed by another. Another. Herb counted eight in total. Judging by the speed they were moving at, it wouldn't take them long to reach the top of the Shard.

When he was sure that there were no more coming, Herb lurched to his feet, throwing Dan over his shoulder once more.

"Go," he roared at the others. "Run!"

He broke into a sprint, barely slowed at all by Dan's weight, making for the stairs. Taking them three at a time; almost falling down them. Almost immediately, Burnley hurtled past him, the American woman running like a seasoned sprinter. A few seconds later, Conny's son also overtook him, his speed born of youth and terror.

Herb glanced over his shoulder.

The others were following: Conny and Remy close behind, the dog clearly matching its pace to that of its master. Behind them, struggling to keep up, he saw Mancini, and Jeremy even further back.

Dan moaned; a low, sickly sound.

"Hold on, Dan," Herb yelled, "just hold it for as long as you can."

Dan coughed a mouthful of blood across Herb's bandaged arm, painting it red.

AT THE TOP OF THE BUILDING, THE FIRST OF THE vampires arrived, shrieking in confusion at the one which had called it. There was no sign of the humans; no sign of the Hermetic.

The others arrived, circling warily, staring at their kin with naked suspicion.

And the creature at the top of the spire hurled itself at the nearest of them, driving it clean off the side of the building, its momentum carrying them both out into the night. The two vampires plummeted toward their deaths and, half a building below, Dan Bellamy's mind, too, fell a thousand feet, and landed in darkness.

HERB FELT DAN'S BODY GO LIMP AS HE PASSED A SIGN which read 29th floor.

"They're coming," he roared. He could no longer see Mancini's partner or Logan in front of him; he figured at the speed they were travelling they might even be two or three levels below already. Conny and Remy had also passed Herb a couple of floors back. He hoped the police-woman, at least, could still hear him. "Find a vehicle," he yelled, "get the engine running!"

28th floor.

Herb felt dismay rising with each stride, and when he heard a muffled screech, he knew.

Not gonna make it.

There was a good chance that the two women and the teenager would reach the ground floor, he thought, and maybe if he hadn't been carrying Dan, he might have had a shot himself, but though the guy was light, carrying him down near-pitch black stairwells was slowing Herb down too much. As for Mancini and Jeremy, well, the two older men were both a little larger than Herb, both a little heavier and a lot slower. Neither of them would reach the ground floor.

Leave them.

Let them slow the vampires down for you.

Herb gritted his teeth, and even as the thought raced across his mind, he knew that he didn't have it in him, no matter that Mancini had been prepared to kill him barely half an hour earlier, or that Jeremy had lied to him and called in the Americans in the first place.

Soft, his father had called him, more than once. Too concerned with the wellbeing of others; too willing to let feelings stand in the way of his sacred duty.

His run began to slow even before he was aware that he had made the only decision he *could* make. For the men, outrunning the vampires on the stairs looked all-but impossible, but he could buy Conny some time to escape.

He stopped, listening intently, and heard footsteps approaching fast. Mancini.

The big American almost barrelled right into him in the dark.

"Why have you stopped?" Mancini gasped.

Another shriek somewhere above—somewhere far too damn close—provided a better answer than Herb ever could.

"We won't make it like this," Herb panted, "not fast enough."

"Where's Burnley? And the police officer?"

"I lost sight of them about ten floors back. They're fast. They might make it if we can draw the vampires away."

"Draw them away *how?*"

"We've got almost thirty floors of office and retail space to lose them in. We can't keep running in a straight line."

Mancini grimaced in the dark, but he nodded.

"What about Jeremy?"

Mancini sucked in a lungful of air. "I don't know. He fell behind," he shook his head. "He's too slow."

Herb hoisted Dan on his shoulders, redistributing the weight of his limp body.

"We need to wait for him," he said, but the words had barely spilled from his lips when he heard a man screaming just a couple of floors above. The sound was terrifyingly close.

"Too late," Mancini said, and he kicked open a door which led into a wide, open-plan office space.

With a stifled curse, Herb took off after the American,

leaving the main stairs behind, and leaving the door wide open for the vampires to follow.

He ran, pouring everything he had into the sprint.

Praying that when Conny and the others reached the ground floor, they would wait for him.

CHAPTER FORTY-ONE

Jeremy was a shower man; he hated taking baths.

He couldn't remember getting in this particular one—nor could he remember falling asleep—but he must have, because the water was *freezing*. He supposed it was time to get out.

But he was *so* tired. It would be so much easier to just lie in the cold water and snooze a little longer.

He shuddered at the temperature, and groaned.

Better get moving.

Strangely, he found that it was difficult to open his eyes. He must have been asleep for a long time, he thought distantly. His eyes were glued together by sleep. Even stranger, he found that when he tried to lift his hands to find the edge of the tub, they were almost impossible to move.

Come to think of it, he couldn't seem to move *any* part of his body.

And since when do I take baths?

His eyes flared open, and for a moment he saw only

darkness, and felt the freezing bathwater chilling him all over.

Got to get out, or I'll catch a cold.

He tried to lift his arms again. This time, there was a little movement, but also a strange pulling sensation, like the water didn't want to let him go.

What the hell?

With an effort, Jeremy lifted his head, peering down the tub toward his feet.

No tub.

No feet.

The darkness didn't quite reveal the full horror, but it revealed enough.

Jeremy's muscles were not cold because he was lying in a bath of freezing water. They were cold because the skin which normally kept them warm had been peeled away. His body had been opened up like a ripe orange, revealing the glistening pulp beneath.

He saw his own exposed ribs; pulsing organs beneath. It looked like a surgeon had expertly carved his torso from throat to groin.

Was I in an accident?

Why is the hospital so dark?

Where are my fucking legs?

Both of Jeremy's legs were sheared off at the knees, like he'd been in some terrible car accident. Once, he had seen a motorcycle plough head-on into a car coming around a blind bend: the bonnet of the car had popped even as the bike rider flew over his handlebars, and the thin sheet of metal had cut his body cleanly in two. The biker hadn't survived.

He tried to summon up a memory, anything that

might offer some indication as to what had happened, but his mind felt spongey and unresponsive.

Come to think of it, his *mind* felt cold, too. How the hell was that possible?

He rolled his eyes up in their sockets, hoping to spot a doctor, wanting to scream that the anaesthetic he had been given wasn't nearly powerful enough.

I'm awake, he tried to shout, but no words emerged from his mouth. In fact, he couldn't even feel his jaw moving. It was almost like he didn't *have* a jaw.

Maybe the doctors had wired it shut.

What kind of fucking hospital is this?

His head lolled back, the effort of keeping it lifted suddenly too much for him.

And he saw.

Not a doctor.

A nightmarish creature stood behind him, its fearsome red eyes narrowed in something that looked almost like concentration as it pulled back a long, sinewy arm. In its hand, a flash of something red and white; a terrifyingly enormous piece of bone, clutched between fingers that ended in long, curved blades.

That's my skull, Jeremy thought, and he had the strange, almost irresistible urge to *laugh*.

The vision in his left eye suddenly just...switched off. Like someone had pointed a remote control at it and put it on *standby*.

Jeremy's one remaining eye worked long enough for him to see those wicked talons reaching for the top of his head once more, pulling on something grey and soft.

Finally, as he saw the hideous monster's maw opening —rows and rows of wicked teeth, worse than any shark— the darkness claimed him.

WE'RE GOING TO MAKE IT!

Conny rocketed down the last set of stairs and onto the ground floor of the Shard, just in time to see Logan pushing on a revolving door which spat him out into the night. She wanted him to wait for her; wanted to scream at him that it might not be safe out there, but she caught herself in time. Whatever was outside the Shard couldn't possibly be any worse than what was inside.

At the sight of the outside world, Remy picked up pace, pulling away from her easily.

She barrelled into the revolving door a few seconds after the German Shepherd reached it, and together they pushed themselves out into the cold night air.

The American woman whose gun Conny had taken was already outside, her hands on her knees, drawing in a deep breath.

"Where are the others?" she panted.

Conny turned back to the revolving door, breathing equally heavily, and shook her head.

"I don't know. I thought they were right behind me."

She gestured at Logan to move closer, and took hold of his arm, unwilling to ever let it go again. Her boy was dying, but he wouldn't die *tonight*. Not if she had anything to say about it.

"I heard Herb shouting to find a vehicle," Logan said through rapid, shallow gasps for air. "They're slower than us, that's all."

Conny's heart almost burst with joy at hearing her son speak. It was the first time she had heard anything other than the odd grunted word from him in weeks.

And all it took was the end of the world.

She almost burst out laughing.

"Okay," Conny said, casting her gaze around the street until she spotted a large black SUV, "anybody know how to hotwire a car?"

"I do."

Conny's jaw dropped as Logan spoke, keeping his eyes pointed guiltily at the ground.

We're gonna have to have a little chat about that, she thought, but she was already pointing at the SUV. "Go," she said. "Get the engine running, bring the car over to the front entrance."

"Are you crazy?"

Conny turned to face Burnley.

"You want to *wait* for them?" Burnley snarled. "They're probably dead already. Do you have any idea how fast these things move? We have to get in the car and *go*."

In the distance, Conny heard glass breaking. Logan, her innocent little boy, stealing a car.

She shook her head.

"Feel free to leave," she said, "but if you want to ride with us, you're going to wait. I don't care how fast these things move. I'm damn sure they can't outrun a car. We'll wait until the last minute. If we see *them*, we go. Otherwise, we wait, understand?"

The American dropped her eyes to the gun which Conny still gripped in her right hand.

"Try it," Conny said, as the SUV's engine roared to life.

Burnley looked away, clenching her jaw in frustration.

Conny turned back to face the entrance to the Shard, peering through the glass into the gloom beyond as Logan brought the SUV over. When he pulled up, she gestured at him to move to the passenger seat, and took the wheel, her eyes never leaving the revolving door leading back into the building. Remy jumped onto Logan's lap, and the boy hugged him fiercely.

Inside the vehicle, the radio was on at a barely audible volume, repeating a looped message. It took a few moments for Conny's brain to pick up on one vital phrase.

"...twenty minute warning..."

Keeping her eyes firmly on the windows, scanning for any sign of movement on the street, she reached down and inched the volume up.

And felt her stomach drop.

The recorded message was warning that the military had pulled out of London, and that in twenty minutes, the air force was going to employ what it hoped was a last resort.

Dropping napalm onto the streets of London.

She fixed her gaze on the entrance to the Shard, willing the revolving door to spin.

Come on, Herb. Where the hell are you?

CHAPTER FORTY-TWO

Sweat dripped into Herb's eyes, making them sting, blurring his vision. The vampires had taken the bait, following the fleeing men into the office levels. Judging by the sound of the creatures tearing the rooms apart above, they were only a couple of floors behind, and were obliterating every possible hiding spot.

And still closing on the fleeing men.

Herb forced himself to creep along quietly, aware that if he made any noise that carried, his death would soon follow. He glanced at Mancini, and saw from the big American's expression that he, too, knew that the plan to try and lose the vampires in the maze of offices was failing. They were simply moving too slowly, and there were too many vampires. Even with the creatures tearing the building apart as they went, it sounded like they were gaining ground.

On each level, Herb searched in vain for something that might serve as a hiding spot, but so much of the Shard was glass that it seemed impossible. He passed numerous offices and meeting rooms—many of which offered furniture that they could hide behind, or even supply closets which they could lock themselves in—but it sounded like the vampires were leaving no stone unturned. The Shard suffered the curse of most modern architecture: flimsy walls, style over substance. Perhaps unsurprisingly, whoever had designed the building hadn't foreseen that there might come a time when people needed to use the skyscraper to hide from monsters which had crawled out of the lowest level of Hell.

"Maybe we could get back out onto the main stairs?" Mancini whispered.

Herb grimaced. That thought had occurred to him, too, but he had a nagging feeling that there would be one of *them* out there, blocking the main stairwell, just waiting for the humans to attempt to flee again.

"Too risky."

He hoisted Dan on his shoulders again, redistributing his weight. Despite how light the guy was, carrying him for an extended period of time was beginning to sap Herb's energy alarmingly.

Mancini scowled. "They're catching us, Rennick. We've still got more than twenty floors to go, and it doesn't sound like hiding is an option. Got any bright ideas?"

Herb shook his head grimly, and kept pushing forward, increasing his pace as much as he dared, wishing that the office levels were furnished with the same deep, soft carpet as the residential levels had been.

His mind ran back to the Oceanus; to carrying another man *up*, trying to flee the raging inferno spreading throughout the ship. He had carried that man until his muscles shrieked in agony, never realising that he was already dead. And now, here he was, trying to save someone else, and seeing failure looming before him.

He felt a scream of frustration gathering in his throat.

Didn't let it out.

They were moving through the offices of what looked like a finance company. Judging by some party hats and half-finished glasses of wine, the people working there had been busy celebrating something when the world began to fall apart.

He snatched up a glass of white wine with his free hand, draining it in a single gulp, never breaking stride, and placed the glass quietly on the edge of a desk, blinking at the warm sensation spreading through his chest.

That, he thought, *could well be my last drink.*

Above, the still air in the skyscraper erupted to the sound of screaming. *Human* screaming. It sounded like there had been somebody hiding somewhere in the offices, and Herb had led the vampires right to them. He flushed guiltily as it occurred to him that whoever was dying up there might just slow the vampires down a little.

The scream ended abruptly.

Or maybe not.

He hurried toward the next set of stairs, and a sign which read 2 3rd *floor.*

And stopped.

To the right of the stairs, there was a large glass-walled boardroom, home to an enormous table. That room looked to have been the central point of the party the workers at the finance company had been having. A huge tablecloth was draped across the table, topped with plates of sandwiches and canapés.

He grabbed Mancini's arm, halting the big man as he made for the stairs.

Mancini flinched, looking at him with wide eyes.

"The elevators," Herb whispered. "We won't make it on foot. We need to get down *fast*."

Mancini frowned, casting a glance back along the offices. By the sound of it, the vampires were a couple of minutes behind them, maybe less.

"The elevators? The elevators are out of order, Renni—"

"But the elevator *cables* aren't." Herb pointed at the huge tablecloth draped over the boardroom table. "You know how to improvise a harness?"

"A harness?" Mancini's eyes widened. "You can't be serious."

Herb just stared at him.

"It's more than twenty floors, Rennick. And you're carrying an unconscious man on your fucking back."

"Exactly why we need to take the direct route," Herb whispered, and made for the boardroom without waiting for a response. After a second, Mancini followed, as Herb knew he would. Herb's idea was beyond risky, and might well end up killing them all, but it was the only idea either of the men had.

At least it will be a quick death.

He shrugged Dan off his shoulders and placed him on the floor before quickly scooping up the plates of snacks from the table and whipping off the huge white cloth. The material was thin, but if he tore it into strips and platted it, he thought it would take his weight—even with Dan on his back.

He began to rip the cloth, wincing at the noise of the

fabric tearing, and nodded when he saw Mancini move to help him.

"We'll tie Dan's arms around my neck," Herb whispered, "I'm gonna need both hands for this."

Mancini shook his head.

"You really are crazy. Even if we can climb down the cable, we'll be leaving the elevator doors wide open. As soon as they reach this level, they'll know exactly where we went. I don't think they'll have *any* problems following us down."

"We're not going to climb," Herb replied with an easy grin, "we're going to *slide*."

It took around thirty seconds for Mancini to secure Dan on Herb's back, and probably another thirty for the two men to loop the improvised harnesses around their wrists. With each passing second, the noise of the vampires above increased in volume. They were almost certainly on the next floor now, Herb thought, tearing the offices apart.

He tied off the makeshift harness on his right wrist, leaving the other side loose.

"We'll have to jump for the cable. Once you get a hold of it, loop the harness around your other hand," Herb said. "Don't tie it. I don't think you'll have time to untie it when we reach the bottom."

"And pray," Mancini muttered bitterly.

"Sure, if it helps. Come on, we have to move."

Herb ran for the nearest elevator, keeping his steps as light as possible, choking a little as Dan's weight settled around his throat.

It was all *so* familiar.

Except that this time, I won't let him die.

He grabbed the left elevator door, and nodded as Mancini grabbed the right. The two men heaved, muscles straining, and the doors opened a crack.

"That will do," Herb whispered, almost screaming when he heard a crash that sounded almost loud enough to come from the same level that they were standing on. "If we're lucky, they won't fit."

"They'll just open the doors themselves," Mancini whispered softly. "All this will do is slow them down for a second or two."

Herb nodded.

"It might be enough."

He leaned into the elevator shaft, peering down, and immediately wished he hadn't. It was too dark—and probably too *far*—for him to see the bottom of the shaft, but he could see enough. Looking at the drop made him feel dizzy, but there was no time to dwell on it. The decision had been made. The vampires were almost certainly just a matter of seconds away from reaching the twenty-third floor.

The cable was thick steel, and it would require a long jump just to reach it.

It would be so *easy* to miss.

The image of his fingers grazing the cable but failing to find purchase popped into Herb's mind, and a wave of nausea rolled through him as he imagined the fall that would inevitably follow. He would have several seconds to contemplate the ground as it rushed up to meet him. Time enough to contemplate his death, and all the terrible decisions which had led to it.

He grimaced, and shook the thought away, taking a

few steps back to give himself a run-up, and checking that the bonds holding Dan on his back were secure.

Mancini watched him, a stunned expression on his face, as though he couldn't quite believe that matters had reached such a desperate climax.

"Geronimo," Herb whispered, and he ran, throwing himself into the shaft.

Fingers stretching.

Grasping.

Closing around thick, cool steel.

Herb gripped the cable tightly in both hands as gravity began to drag him down, burning the flesh of his palms until he felt like screaming. He fell a couple of floors before he managed to slow his descent enough to loop the tablecloth harness around the cable, and then around his left wrist.

The cable lurched as Mancini latched onto it above him.

Herb didn't look up.

He could only look down as he pulled the harness as tight as possible, desperately trying to slow the descent to a manageable speed.

It sort of worked.

When he saw the ground floor rushing up to meet him, he couldn't help but scream.

So fast.

He pulled on the harness with all his might, his muscles straining until it felt like they were tearing apart.

And the bottom of the elevator shaft gave him a brutal welcome, snapping his legs back, sending bright bursts of white light shooting across his vision. For a moment, the entire world was pain, and he thought he would surely pass out.

A fraction of a second after he reached the bottom, Mancini barrelled into him, knocking the air from his lungs before he had even had a chance to fully draw it in.

Far above, echoing against the metallic walls of the shaft, he heard screeching, and the sound of moving metal.

The vampires forcing open the elevator doors.

Clickclickclickclickclick—

The noise of their approach was thunderous. No need for *them* to worry about cables or harnesses. The monsters were sprinting down the metallic walls, eating up the distance.

Herb groaned, lifting himself up onto legs which felt like they were made of fire, and grabbed at the doors, hauling them open with a strength borne of sheer terror, and bursting out onto the ground floor of the Shard.

He heard Mancini crying out in pain behind him, but it sounded like the American had also survived the fall mostly intact. He crashed after Herb, running wildly.

Herb heard the first of the vampires erupting from the elevator as he reached the revolving doors and barrelled through them, out into the night air.

He almost screamed in joy when he saw the SUV waiting for them, its rear doors open. He threw himself into the vehicle with Dan still on his back, the pair of them landing heavily on Burnley's lap, and a moment later, he felt Mancini land on top of him once more.

Outside, the night filled with the sound of screeching.

Vampires.

All of them.

Coming fast.

The engine roared as Conny stamped on the accelerator.

The SUV lurched forward, the rear door still open, Mancini's legs still dangling in the night air. Herb reached out a hand, pulling the American inside, just as something heavy charged into the side of the car.

In the driver's seat, Conny let out a horrified shriek and spun the wheel as the vehicle lifted up onto two wheels, threatening to tip...

...before crashing back down onto the tarmac, tires squealing, rocketing forward.

"Don't look back," Conny screamed, swerving as Herb tried to haul himself upright, dumping him back onto Burnley's lap once more. He heard the car door shut behind him. Mancini had made it.

The engine howled as Conny kept the accelerator pressed to the floor, the heavy vehicle picking up speed slowly...*slowly*.

The rear window imploded, and suddenly Herb's face was covered in blood. He blinked it away, glancing up in shock. Burnley was still sitting in the back seat, but her head was gone, torn away by the vampire racing along right behind the car.

Herb ducked down, waiting to feel the talons rending his own flesh.

Waiting.

"We're clear," Conny yelled, "they're falling behind."

The car speared through streets lined with bodies, past burning buildings, swerving wildly.

"Take it easy!" Herb yelled, "they won't catch us now."

"No time!" Conny roared back. "They're bombing the city."

She continued to increase speed, until the SUV was comfortably topping a hundred miles per hour. Outside the windows, the narrow London streets rocketed by in a terrifying blur.

"When?" Herb gasped.

Conny didn't answer. There was no need. Somewhere far above, the night air was split by manmade thunder as aircraft speared across the sky, and a shattering explosion boomed on the north bank of the Thames.

And suddenly, the whole world was fire.

CHAPTER FORTY-THREE

I believe you can get through it. You know I do.

Dan smiled, reaching out for his beautiful wife, but his fingers closed only on a memory.

His eyes flared open, and he found that he was sitting on an aircraft, with his hands tied in front of him. Awakening in yet another unfamiliar place. It was becoming a habit.

He looked to his left.

Across the aisle, he saw the face he expected to see, split by a broad grin.

Dan smiled wearily.

"Hi, Herb. Why do my legs hurt?"

Herb flushed.

"You...uh...sorta fell twenty storeys."

Dan just laughed.

"And my hands?"

He lifted his hands, tied together with plastic cord. The bonds weren't tight or uncomfortable.

"Mancini," Herb explained. "He thinks Jennifer

Craven might be more amenable to...er...not killing us if it looks like we're his prisoners."

Herb lifted his own wrists. Identically tied.

Dan nodded.

"Where are we?"

"We took off a few minutes ago."

"The others?"

"Conny, Remy and Logan are a few rows ahead. Mancini tried to put a leash on Remy." Herb chuckled. "It's a shame you missed *that*."

"What else did I miss?"

"Take a look out the window."

Dan turned his head to the right, peering through the thick glass. Far below, the land was a dark ocean surrounding an island of fire.

He turned back to Herb, alarmed.

"The military dropped napalm on the city," Herb explained. "Last resort."

"But...I thought you said vampires don't burn."

"They don't. All they've done is hand London over to the vampires. Probably killing millions in the process."

"Doing the vampires' job for them," Dan said absently.

Herb nodded.

"Yeah," he said. "That's just how they like it."

He settled back into his seat with a sigh, closing his eyes. After a moment, he was snoring softly.

Dan stared out of the window for a long time, his face expressionless.

Watching the world burn.

EPILOGUE

The Gulfstream touched down on a wide, flat strip of dirt in the middle of nowhere, and when Herb stepped out of the plane, he walked into a wall of heat that almost knocked him backwards, making him feel suddenly dizzy. He blinked at the blinding sun washing over him. It was morning in America.

Another morning, he thought. He hadn't been sure he would ever see another dawn; certainly, he hadn't expected to see the sun rising over the United States.

In the distance, he saw a large group of people waiting, watching the passengers disembark. Standing at the front of the group, he noticed an attractive blonde woman, dressed like a high-powered business executive. Her features were statuesque, but the beauty the woman's face projected was cold; undone by her hard expression.

She made her way toward the dirt runway, apparently in no rush.

"Well, here goes," Herb muttered, nudging Dan with his elbow. "This was your call, Dan. I hope you know what you're doing."

Dan barked a bitter laugh.

"You wanted to fight the vampires, right? Well, that wasn't going so well in Britain. We'll see how it goes over here, I guess."

"Yeah," Herb replied. "Except that vampires aren't rising *over here*."

Dan just shrugged.

"More likely," Herb continued, "that woman is going to put you in some laboratory and test you until she understands who...or *what* you are."

Dan set his mouth in a firm line, and said nothing.

Conny, Logan and Remy were the last to disembark the plane, and the dog charged around the dusty ground, barking excitedly, sniffing at every unfamiliar stone. Even Logan's perma-scowl had been replaced by an intrigued expression.

"So, this is *safety*," Conny said quietly, catching Herb's attention, "though *they* don't exactly look friendly."

She nodded at the group of people approaching the runway. There looked to be more than twenty in total, and several of those marching behind the blonde woman were clearly carrying powerful firearms.

"Yeah, I'm not exactly expecting a warm welcome myself," Herb replied. Now that she was closer, he could see a cold, calculating look in Jennifer Craven's eyes and he wished, not for the first time, that Dan hadn't insisted that he give Mancini his weapon back.

Mancini marched past Herb, heading to the front of the group, waving a greeting at Craven. She didn't acknowledge the gesture.

"The rest of the team?" Craven asked evenly, when she finally came to a stop, just a few yards from the plane.

"It's just me," Mancini said grimly.

"Hmm. Well, at least you brought back what I sent you for. And not just that. Who are all these people?"

Mancini gestured around the group.

"Herbert Rennick," he said, and Craven's eyebrows arched in surprise. "This is Cornelia Stokes, her son Logan, and her dog."

Craven nodded, but her disinterest was obvious.

"Which must make you Dan Bellamy," she said, turning to the only person that Mancini hadn't introduced. "The Hermetic."

"I don't know what that is," Dan said quietly, and Craven laughed. A harsh, bitter sound.

"Nor, exactly, do I," she said with a chilling smile, "but I will, soon enough."

She returned her gaze to Mancini.

"You were only supposed to bring the Hermetic, Mr Mancini. I'm not sure what use you think I have for the rest of them, though I *suppose* the boy could be trained as an initiate. He is the right age."

"The *boy's* name is Logan," Conny said hotly, "and if you want to *train* him, you're going to have to go through me to do it."

She fixed Craven with a penetrating gaze.

The American woman laughed, nodding pointedly at Conny's bound wrists.

"I have two dozen armed men behind me, sweetheart. And fifteen hundred more back at the ranch, all of them devout servants of the Order. You? Well, you have a *dog*. Trust me: your threats are worse than useless here."

Conny stared at her mutinously, but made no effort to respond.

"Fifteen hundred," Dan said absently, and all eyes turned to him. "Sounds like an army."

"Yes, Mr Bellamy," Craven said. "An army is exactly what it is. Unlike the rest of the Order, I was able to recognise that a full-scale vampire rising was inevitable and that we needed to prepare. The world is too small now, you see. Too difficult to keep a secret these days. At least it happened in another country, and we were able to get you out."

Dan nodded.

"I've been building my *army* for more than fifteen years," Craven continued with a hint of pride. "And the ranch is damn-near impregnable. If it *should* come under threat, we have a place in the mountains, buried in a million tons of solid rock. No way for anybody—or any*thing*—to get in."

"A good job," Dan said. "The vampires will be rising at nightfall."

Craven blinked.

"I don't understand," she said.

"No," Dan replied evenly. "I don't suppose you do. I'm only just starting to understand, myself. But as soon as I do...what I can do, they'll know I'm here. They'll be coming."

Craven just stared at him, perplexed.

"What you...can do?"

"Hey, Mancini," Dan said.

The big man turned to look at him, meeting his gaze.

His eyes widening.

Jaw slackening.

Arms moving of their own accord.

Mancini hoisted the MP5, and unloaded the entire magazine into Jennifer Craven's face.

Dan watched without emotion as the top half of the woman's body became a fine red mist, painting the desert red across several yards. When her ruined body collapsed onto the dusty ground, Mancini kept the gun aimed at her, his finger still curled around the trigger.

Stunned silence fell across the group of people gathered around the plane. The troops who had served as Craven's personal escort gaped in astonishment at Mancini. Apparently, without their leader, they were as terrified and rudderless as Herb's own people had been.

"I'm nobody's science experiment," Dan said absently, staring down at Craven's body. "Nobody's fucking *prize*. And I'm done with running and hiding. Done with being afraid."

Herb stared at him, aghast.

"You planned to do this," he said weakly. "You wanted him to have the gun—"

"The river knows I'm here, now," Dan interrupted. "You wanted to fight them, Herb? Now you have your army. After all, these people do serve *the Order*. And now, that means *you*."

Herb shook his head.

"I'm no leader, Dan. I've demonstrated that plenty. And I'm not like you; I can't *fight* the vampires. What do you expect me to do?"

Dan glanced at the sun. It was still rising into the morning sky, but it would not be long before it began its steady descent to the western horizon. Sand trickling through an hourglass. A countdown to darkness and destruction.

To sundown.

He returned his gaze to Herb, who was staring at him,

still waiting for an answer. Dan gave him the only one he had.

"Kill them all."

Thanks for reading Sundown!
Go to www.krgriffiths.org and join my mailing list to be the first to discover new releases and launch discounts, and to receive free annual bonus content

The Adrift Series:

Turn the page for more...

The Wildfire Chronicles:

Panic

Shock

Psychosis

Mutation

Trauma

Reaction

Other Novels:

Last Resort

Survivor: A Horror Thriller

Join my mailing list at www.krgriffiths.org to be the first to discover new releases, launch-day discounts, and free annual subscriber bonus content.